MONDAY'S CHILD

Recent Titles by Rowena Summers from Severn House

The Caldwell Series

TAKING HEART
DAISY'S WAR
THE CALDWELL GIRLS
DREAMS OF PEACE

The Hotel Saga

SHELTER FROM THE STORM
MONDAY'S CHILD

MONDAY'S CHILD

Rowena Summers

severn
House

This first world edition published in Great Britain 2005 by
SEVERN HOUSE PUBLISHERS LTD of
9–15 High Street, Sutton, Surrey SM1 1DF.
This first world edition published in the USA 2006 by
SEVERN HOUSE PUBLISHERS INC of
595 Madison Avenue, New York, N.Y. 10022.

British Library Cataloguing in Publication Data

Summers, Rowena, 1932-
    Monday's child
    1.   Weddings - Planning - Fiction
    2.   Hotels - England - Somerset - Fiction
    3.   Domestic fiction
    I.   Title
    823.9'14 [F]

    ISBN-10 : 0-7278-6321-5

Typeset by Palimpsest Book Production Ltd.,
Polmont, Stirlingshire, Scotland.
Printed and bound in Great Britain by
MPG Books Ltd., Bodmin, Cornwall.

One

In the small Somerset coastal town of Braydon, the 1937 summer season was well under way. Visitors who had discovered the delights of the bracing Bristol Channel air weren't slow in arriving by bus and train, and the wealthier ones came by motor car. The new hotel in its prime position on the seafront had risen like a phoenix from the ashes after a violent storm and disastrous flood that had been near ruinous more than a year ago. In honour of its re-emergence, the newly named Phoenix Hotel now stood four-square on its solid foundation, and was promised good business.

Donald Elkins, its owner and manager, would be closing it for one week in the middle of June, though, and for the very good reason that his eldest daughter was getting married and they needed no seasonal guests during that time. He could easily afford to withdraw the hotel's amenities for that period, now that they were far more affluent than Donald could ever have imagined.

He often let his thoughts stray in the middle of a busy day, to thank God or fate or whatever . . . especially thanking his far-seeing father and his delightfully eccentric mother, Clover, for giving the family this second chance. If it hadn't been for Tommy Elkins' investments in a small South African diamond mine many years ago, and the legacy of those investments that had finally come their way, despite Clover's forgetfulness, they would now have been living in Bristol, in a smoky city miles away from the fresh salt air they all loved so much.

He still shivered whenever he remembered how near they had come to that event, even to his seeking out a modest house for them all to live in, which he knew his family would hate. But now they didn't have to, and the future looked rosy. The only thing Donald would have changed, if he had had

1

his way, was the man his daughter was going to marry. Melvin Philpott was a roguishly handsome blacksmith with an eye for a pretty girl, but he was Charlotte's choice, so that was that.

He caught sight of her now, walking along the seafront with her sisters, and a very comely trio they made, he thought with immense satisfaction: Charlotte so pretty and blonde like her mother, Josie with darker and more dramatic looks like himself, and young Milly, twelve years old now, and blossoming in all sorts of ways since she had started at the grammar school, though with her plaits still flying about her head every time she got excited.

'Still thinking what a fine job you did with your offspring, Donald?' he heard Ruth say teasingly behind him, and he turned away from the window with a smile.

'I'm thinking they're a credit to you, my love. After all we've been through, you were the one who held us all together.'

She squeezed his arm. 'We held one another together. It's like your mother used to say: as long as the foundations are strong, the rest will take care of itself.'

'They weren't, though, were they? Not as far as the Retreat was concerned,' he replied, lapsing briefly into the melancholy that sometimes caught him off guard when he recalled how near they had come to disaster.

'I'm talking about the family, and so was Clover,' Ruth told him crisply. 'Now, stop thinking about the past and cheer up before the girls come back. We've got new guests to prepare for, and they won't want to see gloomy faces.'

He reverted at once to being the jovial 'mine host' of the Phoenix Hotel. It wasn't hard to do, since everything was going his way from now on. But he still managed a surreptitious crossing of his fingers as he thought it.

Charlotte Elkins was becoming alternately elated and nervous as her wedding day approached. She had loved Melvin Philpott for such a long time that she had begun to wonder if he was ever going to ask her to marry him, or if he was taking her for granted. Her younger sister, Josie, nearly seventeen now, would have had far less patience than she'd had, but then Josie always did want everything at once.

Milly darted ahead of her sisters now, having seen her best friend Dorothy in the distance, and yelling that she'd be back at the hotel in time for tea.

'I sometimes wish I was still twelve years old,' Charlotte said without thinking, 'with nothing to think about but going horse-riding and playing with dolls and whatever else those two get up to.'

Josie stopped walking, nearly pulling Charlotte over in the process.

'Are you mad? I'd never want to be twelve again. It's so boring. And if you were twelve you wouldn't be getting married to Melvin, would you? Though I still think Steve Bailey would give him a run for his money if you gave him half a chance. And I wouldn't be looking forward to seeing Tony again when the fair comes to town.'

'I thought you'd have forgotten him long ago,' Charlotte said, ignoring Josie's reference to the good-looking reporter who had definitely had eyes for her, as she very well knew. She would dearly like to add that the swarthy fairground chap with the bold eyes would probably have forgotten Josie long ago too, but she knew her sister's temper would be up in a minute if she did so.

'Well, I haven't. You're not the only one who can fall in love, and I do know how it feels, Charlie. I'm not a baby any more.'

'I know that.' Tony whoever-he-was would know it too, she thought, eyeing Josie's rounded shape, so different from when he'd first seen her as a gawky kid.

'You don't exactly sound like the bride-to-be, anyway. What's wrong? Have you and Melvin had another falling-out?' Josie asked, startling her.

Charlotte shrugged. Falling out seemed to happen too often lately, but since everyone said it was pre-wedding nerves, she wasn't going to let anything put a damper on her forthcoming wedding. Not even the fact that they would be living in the blacksmith's house with his father after they were married. It was not a prospect that thrilled her, but after his mother had died from a second bout of pneumonia during the winter, the housing arrangement was expected. Some had thought they would put the wedding off, but Josie had said pithily that the

Philpott men were too keen on having another woman in the house to look after them to do anything so drastic. Charlotte didn't want to believe it was true, but she also had her doubtful moments, remembering how Melvin's mother had pampered the two men. But all of that was weighed against the fact that she loved Melvin and he loved her, and there was no better reason for two people to be married.

'Have you done it yet, Charlie?' Josie asked wickedly, seeing the dreamy look in her sister's eyes.

'Done what?' Charlotte said.

Josie laughed. 'Oh come on, you're not that innocent. You know what I mean, and Melvin's a pretty earthy sort of chap, isn't he?'

'You know what I think? I think you should have been the elder sister, because you know far more than is good for you. And what you don't know, you invent. You're as bad as Milly with her story-telling.'

'That either makes me think you've definitely done it or you're too scared.'

'Or I'm doing what every girl is expected to do and waiting until her wedding night,' Charlotte retorted, knowing very well what Josie was talking about.

'I sometimes wonder if Clover waited,' Josie said thoughtfully.

'Good Lord, you can't say such things about your grandmother!'

Josie felt her face flush. 'Well, why not? You always thought you were so much like her, but I think she was more like me. I've got far more adventure in my soul than you have, and Clover certainly had that, didn't she?'

'Yes, she did.' Involuntarily, they squeezed each other's arms now, their heads filled with memories of the eccentric and flamboyant grandmother they had all adored. And thankfully, as they neared the hotel Charlotte realized Josie had forgotten her teasing about whether or not she and Melvin Philpott had actually *done* it. She wasn't about to tell her either.

In her bedroom, with only a few more weeks to wait, Charlotte's wedding dress hung between layers of tissue paper on the outside of her wardrobe door. There were times during the night when thoughts of the wedding left her unable to sleep; the room was lit only by moonlight from her window and the dress appeared to be a filmy, almost ghostly creation. Sometimes she even wondered if the dress had been made too early . . . and if it was a sort of bad omen . . . and then she told herself not to be so ridiculous.

Instead she reminded herself of those other nights when her grandmother had been seen wandering just as ghost-like along the seafront, in her own special world, while she searched for her beloved Tommy, long since dead.

People had thought Clover was mad, but she wasn't mad. She was still totally entranced by a love that had been so passionate, so wonderful and exciting and colourful, and that had ended far too soon when Charlotte's own father had been a small child. It was the sort of love that Clover had always wished for her granddaughters.

Charlotte turned over restlessly in her bed. She had loved Melvin for so long now that she could never imagine loving anyone else, even though she knew all his faults. But that was a part of loving too, she thought loyally.

And being a good wife meant cooking and cleaning for the breadwinner and keeping a tidy house . . . but she wasn't so noble that she didn't regret that this was going to include his father too.

Josie had no such noble feelings. She was quite looking forward to Charlotte's wedding, even if was to that oaf, Melvin, if only because she knew she was going to look stunning in the long frock the dressmaker was making for her. A year ago, before their fortunes had changed, the prospect of this wedding would have been so different. Their mother would have made all the dresses, but now they could afford to hire a dressmaker to do it, and she and Milly were going to look like the bees' knees in the silky lilac-coloured fabric that felt so wonderful against her skin.

Josie felt a small shiver ripple through her. She wished Tony could see her in all her finery, but the fair would have come and gone before the wedding. She had never worn a long frock before, and it made her feel really grown-up, which she *was*, in her opinion, even though her parents still thought of her as a child. Milly was the only child in the family now, she thought breezily, and once Charlie was married, it would be her own turn next.

With her head full of possibilities, she was foolish enough to say as much to her mother while they were folding table linen in the family sitting room, and got the sharp end of her tongue in return.

('Where's that then?' Milly always wanted to know, ever the stickler for what she called 'proper English' now she was at her posh school.)

'There's plenty of time for you to be thinking about marriage, Josie,' Ruth said now. 'You're only sixteen, and you've got your whole life ahead of you.'

'I'm nearly seventeen,' she scowled, 'and Charlie's been courting Melvin for years, so why shouldn't I be thinking about having a young man of my own? Don't you want to see me happy?'

Ruth started to laugh, not seeing how important this was to her daughter. 'Of course I do. We want you all to be happy, but not to go rushing into something just to keep up with your sister! Besides, we don't know any suitable boys.'

Josie's eyes flashed. They were dark and beautiful, and her body was taut against the summer dress she wore. Ruth caught her breath, as if suddenly registering that it wasn't only one daughter capable of turning a young man's head.

'I never do anything just to keep up with my sister, and if that's all you're worrying about, then I'll have to look around for an *un*suitable boy, won't I?'

Her father came into the sitting room in time to hear the last retort, and caught hold of Josie's arm as she was flouncing out.

'Hold fire, young lady. What's this all about? We're not going to have trouble with you, are we?' The words were short, but the tone was jovial, he having just had a very satis-factory lunch with his accountant, and learned that their assets were very healthy indeed now.

'It depends what you mean by trouble,' Josie muttered, not prepared to be mollified in a condescending manner as if she was as infantile as Milly.

Donald frowned. 'I think you know very well what's meant by trouble, Josie, and we'll have no shame brought home to our doors.'

Her face was brilliant with embarrassment now, and her heart pounded. She truly hadn't meant what he seemed to be implying. She never would. Even if the image of Tony filled her mind at that moment, she willed it away, because she wasn't a bad girl. She wasn't.

'Can I go now?' she asked in a strangled voice. 'Mum wants me to set the dining-room tables.'

He looked at her steadily for a moment. 'You'd better do as you're asked then,' he said, before she could open her mouth to say anything more. She didn't know what she could have said anyway, without making things worse.

He had always been fair with his girls, but Josie knew how important the reputation of his blessed hotel was to him. There had been enough of a whiff of scandal when the foundations of the old one had collapsed and some old bones had been found there, even if they had turned out to be those of a dog, long-dead, and probably a stray. There had been enough gossip about Clover and her night-time activities too, ranging from her being a wild old woman to a witch. Of course she was no such thing, but rumours stuck, and the hotel had been in danger of getting a bad reputation. Donald had fought hard to hold his head up high through all of it, and Josie wasn't about to let him down now.

She folded the napkins for the dining tables almost savagely. Her mother was implying that she was jealous of Charlotte. As if she would be jealous of her marrying the blacksmith with the constant smell of smoke about him, and horses too. But presumably Charlotte wouldn't mind that, having worked in the stables on the farm adjacent to the smithy when their future as hotel owners had been so precarious. Why would anybody be jealous of marrying *him*?

She paused in her work for a moment, biting her lips. Because she *was* jealous of Charlie. Of course she was, even if it wasn't something she was proud of. She was jealous of Charlie having a boy of her own and seeing him all the time. She was jealous of being the middle sister and not having the status of the eldest, nor the indulgence her parents gave to the youngest. She was jealous of sometimes feeling she was over-looked, especially now, when they had got over the excitement and importance of sending Milly to the grammar school, and their attention was all concentrated on Charlotte's wedding. She was jealous of the fact that Charlie wouldn't have to work at the family business once she was married, but would be running her own home. For the moment she ignored the fact that Charlie would be as much of a skivvy as Josie sometimes felt here. It wasn't the same.

And it wasn't that she didn't love her sisters, because of course she did. She loved all her family, and for some reason she was missing her grandmother even more of late. Clover could always be relied on to give wise words of advice, despite her being thought so eccentric, and there was no doubt that sometimes Josie just felt neglected. It was happening more and more lately, which was why she longed so much for the annual fair to return, when she would see Tony again and be assured that there was someone who valued her. Her heart beat faster at the very thought of his bold, dark eyes and ready smile.

At the sound of her mother's quick footsteps she bent to her task again, aware that her face was probably still flushed, and that it was no longer solely on account of her father's reprimand.

'Aren't you done yet, Josie?' Ruth exclaimed at once. 'I don't think I ever knew a girl so slow at doing simple tasks.'

Josie slapped down the last of the napkins. 'I thought Dad said that, when we had the new hotel, we'd employ outside staff to do the work.'

Now that he can afford it! she added beneath her breath.

'So we will when Charlotte is married. We'll need someone to take her place then, and it's all in hand. Your father will interview several girls in due course.'

'What about me? Will he find a replacement for me too?'

'Well, love, you're not the one getting married, are you?' Ruth said, not following the way her daughter's thoughts were going.

'No, but I enjoyed working at Hallam's Food Stores when we were in such trouble before. I'm sure Mr Hallam would have me back if I asked him.'

'Why on earth would you want to do that? It's far better to be working in a family concern than for other people.'

Josie was tempted for the briefest moment to say that her mother was as big a snob as Milly if she thought it was so wonderful to wash the piles of dishes and cutlery for a dozen or more strangers every day, to launder their dirty sheets and pillowcases, and clear up the mess they made in their rooms, especially some of the revolting infants their parents brought to the seaside. If that wasn't slavery, she didn't know what was, and she shuddered for a moment, wondering why anyone would want babies. She certainly didn't, not for years and years, if ever.

'What's wrong, Josie?' Ruth said, at last aware of the troubled look in her daughter's eyes.

'I want to work somewhere else,' she burst out. 'I want to earn proper money and feel a bit independent. Charlie never minded working at the hotel the way I did. And I bet Milly will want something different too. She's still young enough for the guests to make a pet of her, but she'll have all sorts of wild ideas once she leaves that grammar school.'

'Do you have all sorts of wild ideas too?' Ruth said calmly.

Josie knew that voice. It said that whatever Josie said now, it was probably going to involve a parental discussion about the way Josie was turning out . . . and with more than a little reference to her grandmother's influence too. For a fleeting moment, Josie wondered what Clover would have said about a young girl joining the fairground people and travelling around the country in a caravan. She'd probably have approved, she thought fiercely.

'Well, what do you have to say?' Ruth said more firmly when there was no immediate reply.

Without warning, Josie wilted. It wasn't that she was yearning to live in a fairground caravan, for goodness' sake. It must be horribly cramped inside, and some of those families seemed to have an awful lot of children – that wasn't it at all. It was the adventurous spirit of the thing that appealed to her. That, and the added attraction of Tony, of course. She took a deep breath.

'I'd really like to have a proper job somewhere else, Mum. It's nothing against you and Dad, but it made me feel really good to have a wages envelope from Mr Hallam at the end of the week and know that I'd earned it.'

'I'm sure your father would put some money into an envelope for you, if that's all the problem,' Ruth said with a smile. 'But it's not, is it, darling?'

Josie shook her head, and Ruth put her arms around her for a moment, feeling the tension in the slim shoulders.

'Poor love, it's not easy to be the middle one, is it? Charlotte's getting married, and we all know Milly's off on another planet since she went to the grammar school, and then there's you, no longer a child and not yet grown-up.'

Josie swallowed. 'You do understand then?' she muttered, even though she considered herself grown up enough to be in love.

'Of course, and if it means so much to you, I'll talk to your father about it. I'm sure he'll agree, but you have to meet us halfway on this, Josie. We still have the summer visitors to care for, and there's plenty to do before the wedding and arranging for a replacement for Charlotte and getting her used to our ways. So if you could contain yourself for a while longer, it would be a great help to us all.'

Tact should have been her mother's middle name, Josie thought, but she felt her eyes prickle, knowing that Ruth always wanted to do the best for everyone, and for her husband most of all. They had the perfect marriage, and she doubted that Charlie's would be anything near as good, living with Melvin Philpott and his father. She still thought Charlie was merely exchanging one sort of servile job for another, but she wasn't going to say as much and antagonize everybody.

She gave Ruth a hug and extricated herself just as quickly. 'I'm sure I can wait if I know I can have my chance at the end of it.'

And before then, the fair would have filled the usual field with its music and excitement and she would be seeing Tony again. Her earlier black mood was lifting at last, and when her mother asked her to go to Hallam's Stores to hand in the weekly grocery order she agreed with alacrity. It was a lovely sunny day and it was good to get away from the hotel, even for an hour, and to chat to people she met on the main road into the small town centre. The Elkins family was as popular as it had ever been after the dark days following the terrible storm, and the townsfolk were full of admiration for the way Donald Elkins had recovered himself. Even if it was mostly to do with the unexpected legacy Clover had left him, he had still stayed in Braydon. He hadn't got above himself, or chosen to move away and become more grand, and Braydon folk approved of that.

A large dog came ambling towards Josie when she had got halfway to the town centre, and she patted his nose cheerfully.

'Morning, Rex,' she said gaily. 'And how are you and your owner today?'

The good-looking young man caught up with the dog and grabbed his lead as he grinned at Josie. 'I see you're on fine form, Miss Elkins,' he said.

Josie wrinkled her nose. 'Don't call me that. It makes me feel old.'

Steve Bailey laughed out loud now. 'You poor thing, and you all of seventeen, I daresay.'

Nearly, Josie amended, but he didn't need to know that.

'How are the wedding plans going?' he went on. 'I haven't seen anything of Charlotte lately, but I imagine she's busily preparing for it. I hear your father's going to close the hotel for a few days too, even in the middle of summer.'

She was surprised he knew so much, but somehow reporters always did, even without being personally involved. They had a nose for news, if that was what Charlie's wedding was. But since her parents were treating it as the wedding of the year, she supposed that it was. She was unaware that she was frowning until Steve commented on it.

'Haven't touched a nerve, have I, Josie? Feeling a bit left out, are you?'

She glared at him now. He was very good-looking and far more intelligent than Melvin Philpott, but he didn't need to sound so patronizing.

'Of course not. I'm going to be chief bridesmaid so why should I feel left out of anything! Perhaps *you're* the one feeling grouchy now that Charlie will be forever out of reach,' she added, teasing him, and remembering how she was quite sure he had taken a shine to her sister a year ago.

11

Steve shrugged, not wanting to let this smart kid know how near to the mark she was. 'I'm sure I'll live,' he said lightly.

'You liked her, though, didn't you?' Josie persisted.

'Of course. Nobody could help liking Charlotte.'

The dog was dragging him away now and he was glad to go. It was one thing finding the love of your life, and something very different to know she was already engaged to another man and on the brink of marriage.

Josie glanced back at him for a moment before continuing towards Hallam's shop. She had always thought there was more than a spark between Charlotte and Steve Bailey, even though the whole family had resented the reporter's interference when the disaster happened. But without him and his news item about the adventurous Clover and her Tommy, the solicitor in Bristol wouldn't have picked up on Clover's unusual name and delved into his vaults or whatever they had. The old will wouldn't have been discovered, and the Elkins family wouldn't have been the legatees of a fortune. They had a lot to thank Steve Bailey for, and in Josie's opinion it was a real pity that Charlie couldn't have been marrying him instead.

Two

Arnie Hallam greeted Josie in his usual expansive manner. He always enjoyed chatting with pretty girls, and when Josie had come to work for him she had been like a breath of fresh air. He always hoped she would come back, and he knew she was hoping to persuade her father to let her do so instead of working at the hotel.

'How's my favourite girl today?' he asked her.

Josie tried not to squirm. She wanted to work here, but she didn't really care for his smarminess. His wife didn't care for it either, she thought, though she was sure it didn't mean anything. If a girl took him seriously and put him to the test, he'd probably take fright and run a mile.

'I'm fine, thank you,' she replied, resisting another shudder at the very thought of gazing wide-eyed into those pudgy features the way the film stars did in the pictures. There was a name for those doddery old men with the young girls ogling them. Sugar daddies, that was it. It was quite apt as far as old Arnie was concerned, since he dealt in sugar and spice and all things nice . . .

'So what can I do for you, Josie? Or have you come to tell me you're coming back to work for me?' he added hopefully.

His wife Laura appeared from the back room, in time to hear his words.

'I'm sure she's got better things to do, haven't you, Josie?'

'Well, as a matter of fact I'm trying to persuade Dad to let me get a job outside the hotel, but he won't hear of it until after Charlie's wedding, and until the season slows down as well, I daresay. I might be able to do what I want then.'

'And you know there's always a job for you here, doesn't she, missus? The customers always enjoyed seeing a bright young thing behind the counter instead of just we two old 'uns.'

From the way his wife glared at him, Josie knew she wasn't best pleased by this description. She wasn't that old, certainly not as old as he was.

'Mrs Hallam always looks smart,' she said quickly, 'and she has lovely hair.'

'Why, thank you, Josie,' the woman said, a little taken aback. 'So let me see what I can do for you while Arnie sees to his other customers.'

She took Josie neatly to one side while Arnie served the two ladies who had come into the shop now. 'You don't want to take too much notice of his nonsense,' Laura said in a confidential voice. 'Some men like to pretend they're still in their salad days even when they're long past it.'

For a second, Josie wondered how far past it Arnie Hallam really was. He was overweight and puffed quite a bit when he had to bend down for some of the shop goods, and his face went red and blotchy until he had got his breath back. She wondered if it was the same in the bedroom, and if he and

Laura still got romantic ideas, or if he found it too much of an effort. She didn't want to think such things, but somehow the image wouldn't quite go away.

'I'm sorry, my dear, I didn't mean to say such personal things to you,' Laura said now, seeing how Josie's eyes had gone a bit glazed.

'Oh, that's all right. I've forgotten it already,' she lied. 'But I'd better do what I came for and give you Mum's grocery order, and she said can we please have delivery tomorrow morning as we've got new people coming in next week.'

'Of course you can. The hotel's doing well then?'

Josie was on safer ground now, informing Laura of the telephone they'd had installed now, even though many people were wary of it and still preferred to make their reservations by letter. But Donald had insisted that they had to keep up with the times, and that a telephone would always be useful in an emergency. Besides which, it put the Phoenix up a step or two from the other hotels in the town that didn't yet have the facility. They always said that Milly was the snob in the family – the brainbox too, Josie admitted – always determined to pass the exams to go to her grammar school and achieving it without too much effort. Josie had decided by now that everybody was a snob in their own way, her father included, but that didn't make him a bad person.

She finally left Hallam's Stores with the assurance that she could come to work there any time she liked, and it was a good feeling, a kind of buffer in case she ever needed it. It may not be anything like Milly's vague aspirations of being a writer some day, but nor was it Charlie's humdrum future of being a wife and skivvy to Melvin Philpott and his father. As far as Josie was concerned, it wasn't an earth-shaking ambition to work for Arnie Hallam, but it was hers.

Milly Elkins had no intention of working in the hotel permanently, either. She was still young enough for the guests to make a fuss of her when she helped clear the dining tables at the weekend, and she liked to hear the tales the regulars told her. There were three of them: Captain Bellamy and the Misses Hester and Daphne Green. After the flood they had had to move out to another hotel in the town, but as soon as the

Phoenix was up and running, they had been welcomed back with open arms. They had been here for so long now, they were like an extended family.

Captain Bellamy, being an elderly military man, reminded Milly of the grandfather she had never known but whom Clover had thought so wonderful. Hearing the Captain's tales of army life made her feel, in a strange way, that she knew a bit more about Tommy too.

'You're a kind little girl to spend so much time with we three old codgers, me dear,' he would tell her, at which the Misses Green would twitter and protest at his cheek, and clack their knitting needles ever more loudly. She hoped none of them would ever die, Milly often thought fervently. It would be like that song the Captain sometimes regaled them with . . . *Ten green bottles hanging on the wall . . . And if one green bottle should accidentally fall, there'd be nine green bottles hanging on the wall.* And on and on, until there was nothing but the string hanging on the wall.

Hester and Daphne always joined in until they got short of breath, but Milly never liked it when they got to the last line, and it was a bit spooky too, since their name was Green. She wondered if they ever thought about that, or if it was only her.

But she wasn't going to think of that now. She and her best friend Dorothy were going for their horse-riding lessons today, and she was going to tell Dorothy about the dress they were going to put her in for Charlie's wedding. She scowled at the thought, although Dorothy had all sorts of sloppy ideas about weddings, far more than Milly did. She didn't really want to dress up and have to walk down the aisle of the church feeling stupid, but Dorothy told her it was good experience if she ever wanted to write about how it felt to be a bridesmaid. She could even do it for her next school essay if she was short of ideas – not that she ever was, she thought, preening.

The farm where they went for their horse-riding lessons was next to Philpott's smithy, where Charlotte had worked at the stables when the old hotel had been in the throes of collapse, and she still came to visit Mrs Miles, the farmer's wife, occasionally. Today, when the two young girls rode their bicycles to the farm, Milly could see her sister chatting to Melvin Philpott at the smithy, and waved to her as they passed.

'I wouldn't want to be marrying him,' Dorothy remarked, wrinkling her nose. 'He always stinks of smoke and horses.'

'He can't help it. It's because of the welding work he does,' Milly said, airing her knowledge. 'He sometimes smells of other stuff too, but you have to ignore it!'

'*I* can, but I'm not going to be marrying him, am I? I suppose you can forgive a chap anything when you're in love. It's so romantic.'

Milly snorted. 'You're too daft for your own good, Dorothy Yard. I can tell you it's not in the least romantic to be done up like a dog's dinner in that frilly dress Mum's having made for me.'

'A dog's dinner?' Dorothy hooted.

'That's what Clover used to call it. My gran, in case you've forgotten.'

'Nobody could forget your gran,' Dorothy said, grinning as they applied their brakes near the farmhouse and their bicycle wheels slewed on the gritty farmyard.

She almost said she couldn't forget how her mother had once forbidden her to see Milly any more, being the grand-daughter of that crazy woman, but she managed to bite the words back. It was all in the past now, but it always made a prickly moment between them, and once Mrs Miles had greeted them, they were both glad when the girl who gave them their lessons arrived to take them to the stables.

Charlotte had watched her sister go racing past, her blonde plaits flying in the wind as usual. She gave Melvin a rueful smile.

'That girl is always going to be a tomboy. She's still complaining abut wearing a frilly bridesmaid dress, so I just hope she'll remember to behave like a lady at the wedding.'

Melvin straightened up from the work he was doing, pushing the welding helmet back from his forehead with a sense of relief. Bridesmaid dresses and contrary little girls were the least important aspect of getting married, as far as he was concerned. In fact, he was more than thankful that the whole shebang could safely be left to the womenfolk and to Charlotte's family.

'Just as long as she turns up is the important thing,' he said, knowing how much store Charlotte set by her whole family being involved.

'She had better! Can you imagine the uproar there would be if she threw a tantrum at the last minute?' Charlotte said with a laugh, sure that no such thing could happen to mar her wedding day. Her mother would see to that little madam.

Melvin shrugged. Being an only son, and having worked at the smithy with his father all his life, he wasn't as family-minded as the Elkinses were. Since his mother died, they seemed to have lost the focal point of their existence too, and his father was no longer as alert as he once had been. He was often more distracted than interested in the work they did, and had lost much of his spark. It would be a good day when he and Charlotte were married and there was another woman in the house. A house needed a woman in it, quite apart from the lusty needs of a husband.

He put his arm around her and gave her waist a squeeze. 'Won't be too long to wait now, will it, sweetheart? Even though it seems like for ever, and I'll probably be bursting my breeches by our wedding night.'

Charlotte pushed him away with a small pout, wishing he wouldn't put things quite so coarsely. 'Is that all you can think about?'

'What else should a young chap think about when he's marrying the best looker in town? Especially one who's held me off for far too long. I thought once we were engaged you'd have stopped being so stand-offish,' he said, his voice suddenly sulky.

'I was never stand-offish, but one of us has to be sensible. We did agree about it, Melvin. And people would have thought it an insult to your mother's memory if we'd arranged our wedding any sooner,' she pointed out.

'I don't exactly remember agreeing to anything, but I had no choice, did I?'

Charlotte decided this conversation was getting too scratchy for comfort and told him why she was here – as well as seeing him, of course.

'I'm to invite you and your father to supper on Sunday, about eight o'clock because we have to see to the hotel guests first. Do you think he'll come?'

'Probably not. He never went anywhere much before Mum died, and he hardly leaves the house now. I've told him he'd better be at the wedding, mind, or there'll be trouble.'

'I hope you didn't speak to him like that, Melvin. You should respect your father, and he'll still be grieving and feeling a bit sensitive about us getting married less than a year since your mum died.'

'I don't know about that, but he's certainly looking forward to having another woman in the house to clean up after him.'

'Well, if that's all you think I'm good for!' Charlotte began indignantly.

The next moment he was laughing at her outraged face and pulled her into his arms. The welding helmet that was still fastened to his head made him resemble a kind of ancient gladiator, and despite her annoyance with him, she melted into his embrace, responding to his kisses even though they were outside in the smithy and anyone could have seen them.

She did love him, she told herself as she cycled back home, or why would she be marrying him? She had wanted him for so long and knew him so well, but there were still parts of his character that she didn't like. Milly had come home from her grammar school one day with a list of words the class had to learn, and had asked her what 'finesse' meant. At the time, the uneasy thought had flitted through Charlotte's mind that it was something Melvin Philpott certainly hadn't got!

She had felt disloyal then, and she felt disloyal now, remembering too how her father had always referred to him as a bit of a rough diamond. He had mellowed towards him since his daughter's marriage had become inevitable, and even more so after Melvin's mother had died so unexpectedly while still a comparatively young woman.

Melvin had always been the one she wanted, Charlotte thought determinedly, and any little problems they had could be ironed out in time. She ignored her acute disappointment at knowing that they wouldn't be starting out in a home that was totally their own, but Melvin's father had been more distraught after his wife's death than anyone had expected, and Charlotte certainly hadn't had the heart to suggest any other arrangements.

*   *   *

If Charlotte was determined about her own future, Josie's thoughts for the future were far more haphazard. All Josie wanted was love – and a bit of excitement thrown in, she admitted. She wished now she had paid more attention to Clover's stories of her life with Tommy, travelling the way they did, often into great danger, wherever his army career took him. They'd been kings of the road, in much the same way as Tony and his fairground people were – though she doubted that anyone else in her family would see it in the same way as she did, and she knew better than to say so. Milly, with her craze for learning new words, would probably think it was beneath her to *consort* with a fairground chap.

Josie felt the familiar sizzle inside her. *Consorting* wasn't exactly what she had in mind. She didn't even know what it meant and she certainly wasn't going to ask Milly. But it sounded far more wicked than the dull-sounding 'courting' did, and she absolutely couldn't wait for the next few weeks to pass until the fair arrived.

She had looked through her wardrobe a dozen times already, trying to decide what to wear to make Tony's eyes widen when he saw her. Since it was summer, she could wear a soft dress that would show off her newly-rounded shape, and with no coat to hide it. She was still sorting through her clothes when she became aware of a pair of eyes watching her from the doorway.

'What are you doing there, snooping as usual?' she snapped at Milly. 'I thought you were off horse-riding with your little friend – or was it fishing for tadpoles today? Dad won't let you keep them, you know. It's not hygienic in a hotel. Besides, they'll turn into frogs and frighten the regulars.'

She hid a smile as she said it, imagining the squirmy little tadpoles turning into horrible slimy things, and leaping and croaking at the Misses Green. No doubt Milly would love that, gleefully writing up the experience in one of her endless notebooks . . . she glared at her.

'What do you want, Milly? I'm busy.'

'I know what you're doing. You're thinking about what to wear to make that daft Tony fancy you,' Milly chanted.

'How do you know his name?' She tried never to say it when Milly was around, and she thought she would have forgotten it since last year when her father had insisted she took Milly to the fair on the first evening it was in Braydon.

'I just do.'

'Have you been looking in my diary again?' But she couldn't have done. It was well hidden and she always kept it locked away. The trouble was, it wasn't only Milly who had a vivid imagination, and Josie knew she had sometimes written far more in her diary than was sensible. If anyone else got hold of it they would see how strong her feelings still were for Tony, even after all this time.

Or perhaps that was *why* they were so strong. Absence was supposed to make the heart grow fonder, wasn't it? She only hoped it worked both ways and that Tony hadn't forgotten *her*.

It had been the proud ambition of Philpott's smithy to get a telephone installed some time ago, and when the phone rang at the Phoenix that evening, Donald answered it with his hotelier's voice as usual. His expression changed as soon as he heard the broad country accent at the other end, made more pronounced than usual by being disembodied.

'Evening, Mr Elkins. Can I speak to my intended, please?'

'You mean Charlotte, I presume,' Donald said unnecessarily, wondering why the fellow always managed to annoy him without even trying.

'Well, unless you're thinking of offering either Josie or Milly in exchange, I reckon I do,' Melvin joked.

Donald put down the receiver without replying and called out to Charlotte. She came running downstairs and picked up the phone.

'This is Charlotte,' she said, still unused to dealing with callers.

'And this is lover-boy,' Melvin chuckled. 'I've probably managed to annoy your father, but in any case it's you I wanted, and you know that, don't you?'

'Melvin, I can't talk for very long.' And didn't he know the woman at the telephone exchange might very well be listening in to every word he said!

'All right, well this is just to say that Dad's agreed to come to tea at your place on Sunday, so we'll see you then. Best bib and tucker, is it?'

'Oh. I don't think you need to dig out your top hat and tails; just be tidy,' Charlotte said with a grin. She would dearly have liked to add, *And get rid of the welding and animal smells*, but that would have been churlish, and he was always scrubbed up whenever he went out with her.

She replaced the receiver, still smiling, when she saw Milly scowling at her.

'Is your chap coming here for supper on Sunday with his father then?'

'That's right, little eavesdropper.'

'I'm probably having tea at Dorothy's,' Milly invented. 'She was going to ask her mother if I could go for the afternoon. That'll be all right, won't it?'

'No, it probably won't be all right. It's a family occasion, and Milly, I shall expect you to be pleasant to Melvin and his father on my wedding day too,' she warned. 'I know you don't want to get dressed up, but it's a very important day for me and I don't want anything to go wrong.'

'Oh, I daresay I can be good for one day,' she answered airily.

And that'll be just about her limit, Charlotte thought, hiding a grin. It was only for one day for everyone else, but it was for a lifetime for her and Melvin. The thought sent shivers through her. A marriage had to be right, and she was sure – most of the time – that theirs was. It was only very occasionally that the slightest doubt crept in, and she didn't even know why. Which just proved the old theory that pre-wedding nerves could play strange tricks on a person.

'How are the horse-riding lessons going?' she asked Milly, to divert her attention. 'Have you and Dorothy fallen off yet?'

'Of course not! Farmer Miles is going to have a gymkhana at his farm in September, and me and Dorothy will probably be taking part.'

'That'll be nice for you,' Charlotte said absently, and not taking any real notice of what her sister said. She had far more important things on her mind.

'I bet your other young man will be there writing down details of all the events for the newspaper. I might ask him if I can write some of it myself, as practice for my future career.'

This time Milly's words sank into Charlotte's brain.

'What other young man?' she snapped.

'You know. The one with the big dog – Steve somebody.'

'Steve Bailey is not my other young man, Milly. I've only got one young man, and I'm getting married to him in a few weeks' time, so you're not to go making remarks like that. It's embarrassing and it's nonsense.'

'You remembered his name though, didn't you?' Milly said slyly.

'She was only being *Milly*,' Josie commented later. 'You should know better than to take any notice of the things she says to try to stir you up.'

They were clearing away the supper things from the guests' dining room, ready to reset the tables for the following morning's breakfast.

'I know that. It's just – oh, I'm being silly. Forget I said anything.'

Josie slapped down the handful of knives and forks she was holding and looked at her sister through narrowed eyes.

'She didn't really annoy you, did she, Charlie? I always thought the reporter chap was more interested in you than you were in him, anyway. Did I tell you I ran into him when I went to Hallam's today? He asked after you and I reckon he wouldn't mind at all if you ditched Melvin and married him instead.'

Charlotte ignored the uneasy little flip of her heart at her teasing.

'You're as mad as Clover sometimes, Josie. It would take an earthquake to make me change my mind about Melvin. Besides, we've been making plans for far too long to disrupt everything now. Can you imagine how Mum and Dad would feel, and how upset the regulars would be when they're looking forward to the day so much? Even a couple of the Exmoor relatives are turning up – though they couldn't be bothered to do so for Clover's funeral,' she added in annoyance, remembering how her father had smarted at the time. 'Then there are our friends – and Milly – not that I think she'd mind not dressing up, but you would, wouldn't you?'

When she paused for breath, Josie had her say: 'Well, apart from all those other people who would have their day ruined,

22

you seem to have forgotten to mention the two most important people of all. I'd say that was pretty significant, Charlie, and perhaps you ought to think about it some more. It doesn't really matter what anybody else thinks, and it's never too late to change your mind, because once you and Melvin have tied the knot, it's for the rest of your life.'

It was so rare for Josie to be so serious, and to be acting almost like the older sister, that Charlotte was startled more than anything else. It was rare for her to look so troubled, as if she really was wondering if Charlotte was doing the right thing. Which of course she was! Impulsively, she gave Josie a quick hug.

'I know you mean it for the best – unless you're worrying that I really would ever think of calling it off, and then you won't get to be the glamorous bridesmaid,' she said, to lighten the suddenly strained atmosphere between them.

'All right, so you've seen through me,' Josie said, wriggling away in embarrassment as their mother came into the dining room, astonished by the unusual sight of her two elder daughters hugging one another.

'It's just sister-talk, Mum,' Charlotte told her.

'Good. For a minute I thought something was wrong. It's not, is it?' Ruth asked, more perceptive than usual.

Josie laughed and spoke breezily. 'What could be wrong? My sister's getting married soon and I'm going to wear a long dress and look absolutely *beautiful*! I shall probably outshine the bride.'

'You'd better not,' Charlotte said with a grin. 'Your main job on the day is to keep Milly in order, and don't let her scowl at the congregation or start pulling faces at that friend of hers. The last thing we want is for two giggling school-girls to disrupt the service.'

Three

It was a foregone conclusion that Sunday supper with the two families wasn't going to be a comfortable affair. Charlotte almost wished her mother hadn't insisted on this little pre-wedding ritual between people who hardly knew one another. She knew that Melvin's father was a changed man since his wife had died. He used to be almost as jovial as Arnie Hallam, with a twinkle in his eye and a ready line in chatter, but he was more often withdrawn these days, gazing into space and muttering to himself. In Milly's words, he was spooky.

Charlotte tried to reassure herself things would be different once she and Melvin were married and there was a proper family living in the smithy house again to brighten the atmosphere. But the thought didn't sit easily in her, and it seemed a heavy responsibility for a young girl who was not yet twenty.

However, Ruth was determined that this evening get together was the right way to go about things, and instructed her youngest daughter to be on her best behaviour when they had their supper guests.

Milly pulled a face. 'We've always got guests. The place is bursting at the seams with them right now, so we know how to behave, Mum.'

'Don't answer back, Milly,' Donald said sharply. 'These are special family guests, as you know very well.'

'I won't have to call him anything different when Melvin and Charlie are married, will I?' she asked. 'His father, I mean. He won't be a sort of uncle, will he? One of the girls at school hasn't got a dad any more, but she's got a couple of uncles who aren't really related to her. She says they come to stay at her house sometimes and they always buy her sweets and things. Do you think Mr Philpott will do that?'

Ruth frowned at Josie, who was trying hard to stifle her laughter at this innocent revelation. 'Mr Philpott won't be any kind of uncle, and you'll continue to call him Mr Philpott, you silly girl. Now, let me inspect your hands, Milly, before they arrive. I won't have you showing us up by having dirty fingernails at the table.'

That was ironic, thought Josie, considering the two Philpott men would probably have far blacker fingernails than anybody. She shuddered, making a mental note to try not to look at them too closely, while wondering how Charlotte could bear to have Melvin near her sometimes when he'd been dealing with horses all day. She caught her sister's glance and guessed Charlotte was thinking more about the various uncles who visited Milly's school friend's house and brought her sweets. They weren't all little angels at the grammar school then – at least, not their relatives!

But she stopped speculating when the men arrived, decently turned out, well shaved, hair greased down, and wearing tidy clothes. Melvin's father was never going to be the most fashionable of men, but he was spruce enough in a sports coat over grey flannel trousers and a knitted pullover that no doubt his dead wife had made for him. Melvin looked a deal tidier than in his usual working clothes, and he was undoubtedly handsome in an earthy way, Josie thought.

'Come and sit down at the table, both of you,' Ruth said, once all the greetings had been made. 'I've cooked a nice piece of ham for our supper, with baked potatoes and my tomato chutney to go with it, and I'm sure you'll have some of my special pickled walnuts too, won't you, Mr Philpott? They're always a favourite of Donald's.'

Charlotte realized her mother was nervous. This supper had been her idea, but despite her aplomb at dealing with the hotel guests, she didn't know Melvin's father, and he certainly wasn't the most articulate of men. But this evening was for the families to get to know one another, and she smiled brightly at the two visitors.

Melvin winked back and his father grunted slightly. Charlotte avoided looking at Josie, and her father cleared his throat as they all took their places at the table.

'So how's the smithy business these days?' he asked Mr

25

Philpott sociably. 'Always plenty of work about for you chaps, I suppose?'

Charlotte groaned, hoping it didn't sound patronizing. Everybody knew a hotelier was a cut above many other businesses in the town, but Donald didn't have to make it sound so obvious. Thankfully, Melvin's father either didn't notice or chose to ignore the fact.

'Oh well, I don't do so much nowadays. I leave it all to young Melvin now. He runs the smithy and it keeps him busy enough.'

'You're still the boss, though. A man doesn't choose to lose that status until he's forced to by circumstances, does he?'

The man shrugged. 'As I said, I leave it all to my boy now.'

Good Lord, thought Charlotte, it was like trying to extract teeth to make him join in a conversation. For the life of her she knew she was never going to warm to him. Never going to call him anything but Mr Philpott either . . . and the thought of sharing his home was either going to be a gigantic challenge to which she would rise magnificently, or a total disaster . . .

She wished such thoughts hadn't entered her head, especially as Melvin seemed to be making up for his father's lack of social skills, and had launched into a long tale about the work he was currently doing for the local manor house. Creating the ornamental gates with a special crest on them was clearly his pride and joy at the moment; the fat fee he was going to be paid for them was prominent in his mind, and he wasn't shy at boasting about it.

Donald considered it bad form ever to discuss money in public, especially at the dining table and in front of ladies and children, and he cleared his throat even more noisily, almost snapping at his future son-in-law. 'I presume all your own preparations for the wedding are going ahead?'

From his tone, Charlotte knew he would give a great deal to be addressing anyone else with the question, and she broke in hastily with a nervous laugh since Melvin still had his mouth full of food, and any moment now he would be waving his fork about to make a point, starting to speak without bothering to swallow first.

'Oh, Dad, you know the bridegroom's family don't have

much to do to get ready! We're the ones who are doing all the fussing – and enjoying it,' she added, unable to think of a more suitable word than fussing.

And paying for it too, Donald said beneath his breath. But it was a bride's right, to have her father give her away and pay for the privilege. He felt a momentary stab of emotion, having to give his beloved daughter's hand in marriage to the oaf sitting opposite him now. Charlotte had always been so fastidious, the way her mother was, and Melvin Philpott was anything but that.

'I still think 'tis too soon. A marryin' shouldn't come so soon after a buryin'.'

The unexpected sound of Mr Philpott's voice took them all by surprise. Milly giggled and was quickly shushed by her mother. Ruth turned to Melvin's father and spoke as delicately as she could.

'I'm sure we've all considered the loss of your dear wife in these past months, Mr Philpott. I know Charlotte and Melvin have had serious discussions about their plans to marry, but if I remember correctly, I believe your wife wanted them to continue, no matter what happened to her.'

'It still ain't right,' the man almost growled. 'But I've had my day, so I s'pose I can't begrudge the young 'uns theirs.'

'Who are you having as your best man, Melvin?' Josie asked brightly, hoping to change the general gloom of the last few minutes.

'My cousin Idris from over Newport way.' He gave her one of his broad winks that was sure to annoy Donald still more. 'He's a miner, works down the pits, and comes out as black as the ace of spades at the end of his shift. He cleans up all right, though, and I reckon he'll take a fancy to you, Josie, being such a comely girl now. You could do a lot worse than old Idris – and we'd be keeping it all in the family then, wouldn't we?' he added with a chuckle.

By now Josie's face had turned a brilliant red, and Charlotte was sure she was going to explode at any minute. She saw her mother put a hand on Josie's arm and squeeze it tight.

'Josie's far too young to be thinking about courting, Melvin,' she said pleasantly, even though they all knew that Charlotte had been walking out with him when she was little older than

Josie was now. Charlotte prayed he wouldn't say any more, but he could never resist a passing shot.

'Oh, I reckon she's old enough for anything, Mrs Elkins. You'll have to keep your eye on her, if you know what I mean.'

'I think we all know what you mean,' Donald said stiffly, and turned to his wife. 'I think we're about finished here, my dear. Perhaps the girls can clear the plates away and then you can bring in the apple pie for pudding. The men won't want to stay too late, I'm sure.'

Charlotte and Josie stood up at once, thankful to get away from the awkward scene at the table before they were joined by their mother in the kitchen.

'How can you even *think* of being part of that family?' Josie hissed at her sister. 'Melvin's as uncouth as ever and his father is just awful. You'll turn into one of them if you live with them long enough.'

'Don't say such mean things,' Charlotte said angrily. 'Melvin's on edge, which is why he comes out with those stupid remarks; and his father's still grieving. It probably brings it home to him even more by seeing how close we all are.'

'It's a pity Clover's not still here, then. She'd be giving Melvin a piece of her mind, talking in that coarse way in company,' Josie went on relentlessly. 'Honestly, Charlie, I wonder if you really know what you're getting yourself into.'

'I'm getting married to the man I love, that's what I'm doing, and I wish you'd stop trying to put doubts in my mind. And when did you set your sights so darned high, with all your soppy talk about a fairground chap?'

'What's this?' Ruth said, coming into the kitchen in time to hear the last words. 'What fairground chap is this?'

Josie turned the cold water on to the pile of dirty supper plates in the sink to rinse them, and chewed her lips.

'It's just a boy I talked to once before, Mum. He works on the dodgem cars. His father owns it, I think,' she added, as if to give Tony a bit more of the status her parents set so much store by.

'Your father wouldn't like you hanging around with those sort of people,' Ruth told her predictably. 'We have a position to keep up in this town, Josie, and you should remember it.'

28

She took the apple pie out of the oven, and the kitchen was immediately filled with the gloriously sweet smell of apples and cloves and shortcrust pastry. And Josie's eyes smarted, wondering why she was suddenly turning into the bad girl here, when it was the Philpott men and their crude manners who were the cause of it all.

'I'll wait for you outside, lad, so don't be too long,' Melvin's father said to him when they could all finally take their leave of one another.

Josie had gone to help her mother with the washing-up; her father had gone to his den; Milly had been sent upstairs to bed. Charlotte and Melvin stood awkwardly in the hallway, knowing this evening had been anything but the happy time it should have been.

'That didn't go so badly then, did it?' Melvin said, pulling her into him.

'Melvin, we can't—'

He nuzzled his chin against her face. 'Course we can, sweetheart. What do you think Dad left us alone for? And yours have made themselves scarce, so we can at least have a goodnight kiss to keep us going. Roll on the time when we don't have to be satisfied with just that, eh?'

She let him kiss her and then she was kissing him back, fervently, almost desperately, as if to convince herself that everything was still all right, and that she truly did love him and wanted to be with him for the rest of her life. That was the reason for marrying someone, wasn't it? To love and to cherish and to have children . . . She shivered suddenly, as a swift image of Melvin's future children filled her head. Hers and Melvin's, she amended, but with him for a father, his personality would almost certainly be dominant in them. They would be little hooligans, the thought raced through her mind . . . uncouth, slovenly little hooligans . . .

'You're in a funny mood tonight, Charlie,' he murmured against her cheek. 'You hardly said a thing at supper. I know my old man can be a bit of an old bore, but at least that's one ordeal over now.'

'Was it such an ordeal to be civilized and pleasant towards my family then?' she said before she could stop herself.

He laughed, not seeing how annoyed she was becoming. 'I

was pleasant enough to Josie, wasn't I? I reckon her and our Idris would make a fine pair.'

Charlotte tried to twist out of his arms but he still held her fast. 'That's all you know then. Josie won't have the slightest interest in your Welsh cousin.'

'Why not? Has she got somebody else sniffing around?'

'No. And hadn't you better go now? Your father will be getting impatient.'

He finally sensed how tense she had become and gave a shrug before pulling her towards him and kissing her hard.

'All right, sweetheart. I don't know what's got into you tonight, but as long as you're not so stand-offish once we're married, I guess I can wait. Once you've promised to love, honour and obey, you won't have much choice, will you?'

He spoke with a smile in his voice as if it was one huge joke, but Charlotte wasn't smiling once she had closed the door behind him. She leaned against it for a few moments, her eyes closed, finally wondering for the first time if she was making a huge mistake. She had loved him for a long time, but there was no longer the same intensity of blistering excitement she felt whenever he came near her. All the romantic notions she had once had about them starting a home together in a little house of their own had also faded now. She wasn't sure she could live with him and his father – but that was exactly what she had committed herself to do.

'Are you all right, Charlotte?' she heard her mother's voice ask, and she blinked her eyes open to smile as normally as possible. 'I'm afraid that wasn't quite the success I had hoped it would be.'

'I'm fine, Mum, just needing a little time on my own. In fact, I think I'll go for a walk along the seafront to blow the cobwebs away.'

It was what Clover used to do whenever she needed to think, or dream, or reminisce, reviving the treasured memories that were all in her head, so that she could be with her beloved Tommy again. But Charlotte had no such memories of a lifetime of love to dream about, only a future that was more uncertain than she had ever expected it to be. Almost on the eve of her wedding, it was a terrible time to be having such doubts, and she wasn't sure now just who had put them there: Josie; or Melvin himself; or his morose father; or the marked difference she had observed tonight between her own happy family and the one she would be joining so soon.

It could even have been her mother, insisting on this supper in order to bring the differences to Charlotte's attention before it was too late. But she didn't think so. Ruth wasn't that devious, nor would she want anything to prevent the wedding taking place when so much had gone into preparing for it.

It was a mellow summer evening, and the sun was low on the horizon, throwing a pearly pink sheen across the waters of the Bristol Channel. In the distance the smudgy outline of the Welsh coast could be seen, house lights not yet starting to glimmer from buildings. Plenty of others were taking advantage of the balmy weather and if Charlotte thought it was going to be a time for thinking she was wrong, as friends and acquaintances stopped to ask about the coming wedding, or just to stop and chat, glad about the revived fortunes of the Elkins family.

In the end she felt almost obliged to escape from their interest and well-wishes, and found herself walking down the rough-hewn stone steps, fashioned over the years by many feet, into one of the coves where Clover used to sit and dream.

Charlotte sat on a rock, still warmed by the sun, her arms around her knees, and asked herself what was wrong with her. This should have been an idyllic time of her life, and somehow it wasn't. She and Melvin were about to start on the biggest adventure of their lives, and it lacked all the lustre it should have. Her mother was more enthusiastic than Charlotte herself, and the thought was beginning to alarm her. It shouldn't be like this. All these years she had loved Melvin; all these months since his mother died they had been planning for their wedding and to be together for always; and somehow it had all gone flat. The worst of it was, she didn't know why.

The noise of several dogs barking on the promenade above made her turn her head. It was the usual thing for people to walk their dogs on the promenade in the evening and it had become such a social event it was a wonder the owners didn't form a club. And then she saw one of those owners leaning over the railing and her heart gave an unexpected leap as she recognized him.

31

'Are you practising the art of solitude or do you want some company?' Steve Bailey called out.

He didn't wait for an answer, and the next minute Rex came bounding down the stone steps, slipping and sliding until he reached the pebbles, and raced over to her. The next moment Charlotte was assaulted by a large canine body hurling himself at her enthusiastically, and a wet nose was being thrust in her face, and she was spluttering and laughing at the same time as she tried to ward him off.

'Can't you control this animal?' she said as Steve reached her.

'He only wants to show you he loves you. Dogs have got more sense than humans in that respect. They never hold back on their affections. It's one of their more endearing facets.'

He sounded so serious that she blinked, wondering if she was supposed to be taking this information as a kind of mini-lecture on the canine species, or if there was something more personal in his words. If there was, she didn't want to hear it.

'So what are you doing here, all alone?' he went on before she could think how to answer him. 'I thought you'd be poring over fashion books or gazing in jewellers' windows or planning the flowers, or all those other essential things young ladies have to do before their wedding day.'

'You sound very knowledgeable about such things! You have experience of it all, do you?'

For all she knew he might be married by now, or walking out with someone, or even been jilted. She didn't really know him at all, except as an acquaintance who had been sympathetic over her grandmother's death and the situation in which the family had found themselves after the flood. He wasn't even a friend in the usual sense of the word. He was an acquaintance, no more, and she didn't really know why she was trying to convince herself on that score when there was no need. No need at all.

'You forget that I'm a reporter, Charlotte. I've seen enough weddings in my time to be pretty jaded by the whole ritual.'

She looked at him in surprise. 'That's a very odd thing to say, and a pretty miserable outlook too. If your job involves you in attending weddings, even on the sidelines, you must see how happy people are on such occasions.'

'I don't deny that. I also see them a few years later, even less sometimes, when the gloss has faded and there's only unhappiness between two people who once thought they were made for each other. Marriage can be the biggest mistake of anyone's life if they're marrying the wrong person. The hell of it is that once it's discovered, it's too late and they're trapped.'

Charlotte scrambled off the rock, feeling her heart pound.

'I never heard such a cynical view of marriage in all my life, and I'm not going to stay here and listen to you a moment longer. And one more thing – I'd be obliged if you didn't turn up at *my* wedding like the spectre at the feast. I know my father will want a report of the day in the newspaper, so please see to it that your editor sends someone else.'

She tried to make as dignified an exit as she could, but it was difficult to hold her head up high and stalk away over the rough rocky cove, and it didn't help to hear Rex whining after her as if he was sorry to see her go. But how *dare* Steve Bailey say such things to her, almost on the eve of her wedding, as if to undermine her confidence in marrying the man she loved.

By the time she had climbed the stone steps to the promenade again she had become so tense that she had an uncomfortable stitch in her side and she had to pause for a moment to let it subside. The sun had dropped below the horizon and the daylight had nearly gone. The change had come so swiftly and subtly that the Channel looked dark and forbidding, and the man sitting on her rock now looked as alone as she must have done earlier. Well, serve him right. She couldn't imagine any girl wanting to marry a man with such cynical views.

At that moment he turned around and her heart began to beat faster. She still couldn't be sure whether or not he had been speaking in general terms, or his meaning had been specifically for her. Josie had always said he fancied her, and there had been that one unexpected kiss a year ago when the joyful news of Clover's legacy to them had turned the Elkins' fortunes around. Steve's newspaper article about the flamboyant Clover and her life had been the catalyst to arouse a Bristol solicitor's interest in the family and that kiss had been a spontaneous and joyful gesture. And she hadn't forgotten it, no matter how deep she tried to bury it in her memory.

He waved to her now and, crazy though it was, she felt as if he could see right into her soul and know that, despite all her instincts, she was questioning herself. Had her love for Melvin already wavered to such a degree that she would be making the most appalling mistake of her life to marry him? And even if that were so, how could she possibly go back on her promise now? It would be unforgivable, and so many people would be upset . . . she remembered Josie's words again, asking her who were the most important people in this marriage . . .

She wrapped her arms around herself, feeling suddenly chilled in her light cotton dress as the heat of the summer day faded. She didn't wave back to Steve Bailey. Instead, she hurried back to the hotel, more unsettled than when she had left it.

Four

The fairground wagons trundled through the streets of Braydon early one Saturday morning and into the field near the seafront leased to them every year. By late afternoon the entire field was full of light and music, the stalls and rides having been erected with local children racing around in a fever of excitement, trying to help and more often hindering.

'It's here! It's here!' Milly Elkins came thundering into the hotel kitchen with her friend Dorothy panting alongside her. 'Can I go tonight, Mum? Can I? Dorothy's mum says she can go, so you will let me, won't you?'

Ruth turned from the stove to see her daughter's eyes blazing with expectation. She hated to put a damper on anything her daughters wanted, but she knew Donald had to have his say in this.

'You'll have to see what your father says, love.'

'Where is he?' Milly said at once, not wanting to waste a minute before finding out that there would be no objections. The first night of the fair was always the most exciting, and sometimes the fairground people gave free rides to the first people to turn up.

'He's outside in the work-shed,' Ruth began, but by then the two children had disappeared, too eager to consult Donald to wait any longer.

'What was all that about?' Josie said, coming downstairs from showing the new visitors their rooms and giving them some information about the town and their new surroundings.

'Just Milly, wanting to go to the fair this evening, and probably going about it all the wrong way with your father,' Ruth sad with a rueful smile.

'Well, just as long as he doesn't expect me to take her, as he did last year,' Josie said. 'She's old enough not to need baby-sitting any longer.'

And she was old enough not to want a mischievous younger sister hanging around when she wanted to see Tony, she thought. She had plans of her own for going to the fair that night, and she didn't need anyone's permission, she thought defiantly, though she knew only too well that Donald could put his foot down if he chose to, and forbid her to go.

But Josie prided herself on the ability to be more subtle than Milly when it came to getting round her father. Nor did she intend to say where she was going, just that she was meeting the new friend she had invented especially for this occasion. By now the family had heard the name of Barbara Venn enough times not to think anything of it when Josie said she was going to see her. The fact that Barbara Venn was supposed to be slightly lame and didn't leave her house very often was enough to prevent Ruth and Donald expecting to meet her.

They were only little white lies, Josie told herself whenever she felt guilty over what she was doing. It was all for the sake of the freedom she needed to see Tony as often as she could during the five days the fair was in Braydon. It made her feel somewhat ashamed of the deceit, knowing that her family also thought she was being a good friend to visit

Barbara now and then, but it didn't stop her going on with it. That was the trouble with lies, she thought uneasily, because once started, it was impossible to stop. The only person she had confided in was Charlotte, and that was only because Charlotte had caught her out one evening when she was supposed to be seeing Barbara, and had seen her going into the cinema by herself.

'Josie, you're such an idiot,' Charlotte had said. 'You're bound to be found out, and Mum and Dad will never trust you again.'

'They won't find out as long as you don't tell them!'

'So how long is Barbara Venn going to exist and what are you going to do with her once the fair's gone again? Is she going to die from some mysterious illness or leave town with her parents?'

'I don't know. Something like that,' Josie said feebly.

'In other words, you haven't thought this through at all, have you? Josie, you're being more stupid than I ever thought you could be.'

'All *right*! If it pleases you, after the fair's gone I'll say I had a gigantic falling-out with Barbara and we decided not to see one another for a while. When I stop mentioning her name, it will seem as if it's permanent. Does that suit you?'

Charlotte shook her head slowly. 'I thought Milly was destined to be the storyteller in this family. I just hope you think this boy is worth it, Josie. Having a crush on him is one thing, but telling lies to your family is something else.'

Josie felt her face flush. 'Well, I'm sorry I can't be the saint you always seem to be, Charlie, but there's not much I can do about it now, is there, apart from telling Mum and Dad that Barbara's died, like you suggested.'

'Don't go putting words into my mouth! But if you must continue with this charade I guess the gigantic row is the best option. Not that I approve of any of it.'

Josie had flounced off, seething and wishing she had never said anything at all. Being in love herself, she thought Charlie would have understood. But now the fair was here, and providing her father didn't make any conditions about her taking charge of Milly, she was going there on her own, although as far as the family was concerned she'd be hoping Barbara was well enough to meet her there too.

She felt unexpectedly depressed. She had never lied to her family like this before, and she knew it wasn't right. Clover would have disapproved completely, and probably disowned her. It was worse than the way little kids invented imaginary friends to take the blame for any of their wrongdoings. They were understandable because it was part of growing up. Josie was supposedly grown up already and it shamed her to be keeping up the myth that Barbara Venn really existed.

Her father came in from the work-shed with Milly and Dorothy trailing anxiously behind him. 'These two little tykes are pestering me to let them go to the fair tonight, and I've no doubt you'll be wanting to go too. I'm not asking you to take them, Josie, but you should also keep a watchful eye out for them.'

'Of course I will, Dad,' Josie said, hardly able to believe her luck, and knowing that as soon as Milly and Dorothy reached the fairground, the last thing they would want was to have her hovering around. So they would all be suited.

She began to feel almost angelic now, as if her going to the fair was meant to be, after all. Providing she caught sight of Milly and Dorothy now and then – and, more importantly, providing they caught sight of her too – they could all enjoy themselves in their own way.

Her nerves began to tingle, picturing the moment when Tony would see her again for the first time in a year. His image was imprinted so indelibly in her mind that she could only pray that he remembered her as vividly. Everything else was forgotten as she tried on one dress after another, deciding which one would impress him. She finally chose a soft blue daisy print that showed up her dramatic dark looks, and as she said goodbye to her family after her hotel duties were done that evening, she had the feeling that tonight she was moving closer to her destiny.

Antonio Argetti was generally thought of as quite a jack-the-lad. Known to everyone as Tony, except when his father had been displeased with him over something, he also thought of himself as king of the fair, since he was the young chap the girls always flocked to see, and he had an easy and flirtatious manner with them all. He was the best-looking male on any of the rides, and could have his pick of the girls wherever he went. He had definitely become king of the dodgem ride since his father had passed away, he thought. He was its sole owner now, aided by any of the other young lads in the company when necessary. They all followed the travellers' code of helping one another when the need arose.

He turned his thoughts away from those dark days after the Argetti patriarch's sudden death and thought of more cheerful things. For Tony that inevitably meant the fair sex. So far he'd managed to steer clear of any serious entanglements, since the transitory life of the fairground people was only suited to those who had been born into it. Eventually, when he had to think about settling down, he knew it would be to one of the daughters of his contemporaries. It had been drummed into him since childhood that those who married folk from outside their environment always came a cropper, and it usually ended in disaster. It didn't stop him flirting, though; that was part and parcel of his trade.

Tony liked the annual visits to Braydon. Some of their venues were in far less salubrious locations than virtually on the seafront of a small country town. The sea air was bracing, diffusing much of the cloying oil and petrol and various hot mechanical smells that were involved in keeping the rides going.

There was a girl here, he remembered . . . there was always a girl . . . but he seemed to remember this one more than most. He'd kissed her hand and she'd blushed from her chin to her hair. She was a pretty, dark-haired girl with flirty eyes to match his own. A bit young for his tastes, as he recalled, but that had been a year ago, and time changed people. He wondered if he would see her this year, or if she would even come back to the fair.

Once the raucous fairground music began, it could be heard over a wide radius, which was what it was designed to do. The music reached into the town, the surrounding country-side and along the seafront. It stretched as far as the Phoenix Hotel, where the guests were having their evening meal and where Josie Elkins was impatient for them to finish so that she could change into her blue daisy dress and go to the fair.

'Do you have somewhere to go tonight, dear?' one of the lady guests with a strong Birmingham accent asked her smilingly, and Josie hoped she wasn't hovering too obviously to whisk the plates of the family group away.

'I'm going to the fair,' she said. 'It only comes once a year and most of the young people in the town go there.'

'How nice. We might take our children along there ourselves,' the lady said, and Josie groaned, wondering why she had said so much. The last thing she wanted was for the hotel guests to see her hanging around Tony Argetti's dodgem cars. Her mother wouldn't like that at all.

'I think we'll leave it until another evening,' the father said, to her relief. 'The boys are tired after travelling, and we could all do with an early night.'

The young boys protested at once, but the father was adamant, and for once Josie blessed the strictness of a family's routine.

At last she was allowed to leave, with her mother still warning her to keep an eye out for Milly and Dorothy and not to stay out too late.

'Keep an eye out for yourself too,' Charlotte murmured beneath her breath. 'Don't get carried away by excitement and charm, Josie.'

'I won't. Anyway, you'll have no need to worry about that, will you?' she retorted. 'Are you seeing Melvin tonight?'

'We're going to the pictures,' Charlotte said, ignoring the barb. 'If we look in at the fair later, we'll probably see you there.'

Not if I see you first, thought Josie. But she smiled sweetly and said how nice if it turned out to be a family affair. At which Ruth put in sharply that Milly and Dorothy would be home long before that and safely tucked up in bed.

For no reason at all, Josie's heart gave a small surge. In a week's time, Charlie would be married, and she and Melvin would be safely tucked up in bed together, that night, and every night for the rest of their lives. For all that she was eager to know every little detail of grown-up life, Josie imagined it would be very strange to go to bed with a man. She had slept in the same bed as her sisters on occasion when it was necessary, but sleeping with a man would be very different.

There were all those man bits pressing against your body that you had never felt before. There was your own body that you had always kept private that you were now obliged to share, since you promised in the wedding service that with your body you would worship him . . . Josie shivered, wondering exactly how worshipful that actually meant, and just how embarrassing it would be, and if it would hurt when things – *it* – first happened. Did a man want to look at her naked, since she had promised to worship him with her body? And would he expect her to look at him naked too?

She felt a sudden resentment against Charlie, who she was darned sure knew more about it than she was letting on. Charlie could have been more open with her sister and explained things that Ruth never would, or could. And in a week's time, what she didn't know now Charlie would know everything about anyway, and Josie was sure she would get nothing more out of her sister then. Josie simply didn't see why something that was so fundamental to men and women should be kept such a secret between those who knew all about it, shutting everyone else out. But now wasn't the time to pester Charlie some more. It was time to leave the hotel and put everything else out of her mind.

The fairground music grew louder the nearer she got to it, and she couldn't deny the excitement in her veins now. But as if to put off the moment a while longer, while she simply revelled in the anticipation, she wandered all around the various stalls and rides before reaching the dodgems, where the cars were swinging around the track, the smell of rubber was strong and pungent in her nostrils, showers of sparks flying from the ceiling. And there was Tony, just as black-haired and handsome as she remembered, the lines of his body taut against his checked shirt, lean and athletic and leaping from car to car as he kept the customers happy with his cheeky remarks.

She drew near, feeling her mouth go dry as he leapt back from helping two of the shrieking car passengers to untangle their cars from each other, and reached the side of the ride near Josie. She vaguely registered that there was another young chap helping him, but he might as well have been invisible as far as Josie was concerned.

'Hello again!' Tony said at once, his smile widening. 'I was wondering if you'd be here tonight!'

'Were you?' she said inanely. 'I didn't think you'd remember me.'

He laughed, his eyes flicking over her shape; her newly-rounded shape since the last time he had seen her. 'I never forget a pretty face, especially one like yours, darling. It's Josie, isn't it? Do you want a ride? Once this lot's finished, you can have one for free.'

'Can you do that? Won't you get into trouble?' she said, knowing she was sounding like an idiot, but seemingly unable to stop herself. And secretly thrilled that he remembered her name.

'Oh, I can do anything I like,' Tony boasted. 'The ride belongs to me now, so if I want to give free rides to all my girls, I can. Not that I've got dozens of them, mind,' he added, seeing the small frown on Josie's face. 'It was just a figure of speech, and I only give my favours to somebody special.'

Josie felt herself blush. It may be just a line of patter, and he probably used it on plenty of other girls in plenty of other towns, but right now he was saying it to her, and there was a look in his dark eyes that she couldn't fathom but which was making her go weak at the knees.

'Josie!' she heard someone shriek, and she turned with a groan to see Milly and Dorothy rushing her way. 'Are you going on the dodgems? We're not allowed unless we've got a grown-up with us. Will you take us?'

'Don't be silly. We can't all cram into one of those cars,' she snapped.

'Course you can,' Tony said easily. The ride had stopped now, and the other young chap was helping the customers out of the cars. 'You can all squeeze up together for one ride, and then I'm giving Josie a ride on her own. Is it a deal?'

'Is she your girlfriend then?' Milly asked him directly. 'Mum says she's not old enough to go out with boys.'

'I'd say she's old enough for anything,' Tony said, so softly that only Josie could hear. He said to Milly: 'Josie's just a

41

friend, and everyone who has a ride in one of my cars is my friend too.'

Josie saw Milly squirm. Any minute now and she'd be saying something about boys being daft, and she didn't want anything to spoil the moment when Tony had said he thought she was old enough for anything. It sounded daring and wicked, and far beyond the comprehension of these two little idiots squabbling now over who was going to sit on the outside of the dodgem car.

'Look, if you can't make up your minds, you can both sit on the outsides,' she said impatiently. 'I'll sit in the middle, and when you've had the ride you can clear off, all right?'

It was a horrible squash, but it was worth it to be rid of them, and since they were all hopeless at steering Tony stood on the back of the car with them, and she could breathe the healthy maleness of him, a mixture of body warmth and sweat and hot cloth. In that instant she knew why her sister was never repulsed by the aura often surrounding Melvin Philpott. If you were attracted to someone it was all a part of them.

She allowed herself to enjoy the ride and to shriek and yell with the girls and the rest of Tony's customers, knowing that soon she would have him all to herself. Or at least for the duration of the ride he had promised which would be hers alone. And to her amazement and delight, once Milly and Dorothy had gone on their way, he slid beside her in the dodgem car and she felt as though he was steering them to a private heaven of their own while his assistant took charge of the ride.

'How is it that you're in charge now?' she asked, trying to act as normally as possible, considering her heart was thudding so fast, and having to shout above the noise of the machinery and the sparks flying down.

'My dad died last year, so the ride and the caravan belong to me now.'

'Oh! I'm sorry,' Josie said, embarrassed at having asked such a question. She could feel the warmth of his thigh close against hers and she wished she dared put her hand on his leg as she sensed the brief sadness in his voice, and that she knew how to offer sympathy that didn't sound stupid and banal.

'It was a long time ago now, and the work has to go on or we'd never bring pleasure to folk like you, would we?'

He suddenly rammed the car into another one, bringing yells of delight from the two people inside it, and Josie didn't know if it was deliberate to change the conversation or one of his usual tricks. She was sorry when the ride ended, but thankful that by then the atmosphere between them had returned to its usual lightness. She clambered out with Tony's help, and felt his hand squeeze hers.

'Hang on there a minute while I have a word with Harry,' he said.

He came back after a brief chat with the chap on the ride and tucked her arm in his. She immediately felt grown-up and conspicuous and important all at the same time, and she also found herself hoping that Milly and Dorothy had gone off somewhere on their own, and that Charlotte was still at the pictures . . .

'It's thirsty work on the cars, Josie, so do you fancy something to drink?' Tony asked.

'Some lemonade would be nice,' she said, knowing there were snacks and drinks to be had at one of the stalls. In fact, the tang of hot dogs and onions was wafting towards them now and making her mouth water.

He laughed, squeezing her arm tighter against him.

'I was thinking of something a little stronger. Nothing alarming, mind,' he added, seeing the wary look in her eyes. 'I've got some cider in my caravan, and I bet you'd like to take a look over it, wouldn't you? Have you ever seen the inside of a caravan? You can tell me if it's anything like you imagined.'

He carried on talking while they were walking through the fairground, aware that if he didn't, she might just as easily take fright. And he didn't want her to do that. She was a lovely-looking girl, almost as foreign-looking as himself, and different from most of the country folk around here. Not that Tony despised any of them. He made his living from them, after all, but he could almost predict the kind of customers he got on his ride: giggling schoolgirls; brawny lads who thought they were going to wreck his cars by bashing them into each other; middle-aged matrons having a bit of a dare

43

to go on the dodgems; dads with children . . . Josie was different. He'd known that from the first moment he saw her, even though she'd still been a kid then. She was anything but that now.

'I've only drunk cider once, and that was when my dad let me have a drop when our hotel was rebuilt after the storm,' she said dubiously.

'I heard something about that,' Tony said, although his information was so sketchy as to be practically non-existent. It didn't hurt to show concern and interest, though. 'How did your gran take it?' he added, remembering the gaudily-dressed elderly woman who was well known in Braydon.

Josie looked at him dumbly. If there was anything to remind her that they hadn't met in a year, that was it. He knew nothing of the fact that Clover had died and that her death and the storm had somehow been the unlikely catalyst to restore the Elkins fortunes.

'She died,' Josie said starkly.

'Oh Jesus, I've put my foot in it now, haven't I? Makes us kind of soulmates, though, doesn't it? Your gran and my dad, dying in the same year.'

'Does it?'

She realized they had skirted all around the fair now, and they were in sight of the business end of it all: the generators; the heavy trucks that pulled the dismantled rides and other equipment through the streets of so many towns; the caravans where the fair people lived. They looked clean enough, despite the raggle-taggle of children running in and out of them, Josie thought, and was immediately annoyed with herself for being so patronizing.

'Look, if you'd rather have a cup of tea or cocoa, I can rustle that up as well,' Tony said coaxingly. 'I'm a dab hand at fending for myself now that my dad's gone. And before you ask, my mother died years ago and I can barely remember her. For years it was only my dad and me, and now it's only me.'

Josie felt a wave of sympathy, knowing how bereft she and her sisters and the whole family had felt when Clover had died. But they still had each other. It must have been worse for Tony, being left completely alone.

'Just a cup of tea then,' she said at last. 'And I can't stay long, Tony.'

'Of course not. I've got to get back to the ride anyway,' he said easily, already planning his strategy. *Come into my parlour, said the spider to the fly*, and a very delectable fly she was. But not to be rushed. Definitely not to be rushed.

Five

Josie was surprised to find how spick and span it was inside the caravan. She had never been inside one before and she was intrigued by the way everything was stored away neatly, plus the tiny cooking stove and the tidily arranged pots and pans. She couldn't see any evidence of a bed, just two long settees, although there was a curtained-off area at the far end of the caravan which was presumably a bedroom. Tony busied himself putting the kettle on the gas stove, and then turned to her with folded arms as she continued to gaze about.

'Well? What do you think? Is it a palace fit for a king? Providing he's a very small king, of course.'

She laughed, made more comfortable by the homeliness of the place and the way the kettle added to that feeling as it started to sing.

'It's nothing like I expected,' she admitted. 'I thought . . .'

'What? That we would all live like gypsies, even if some of us are not?' Tony said, with a slight edge to his voice. 'People always get the wrong idea about them too, since most of them take a pride in their caravans.'

'I didn't mean anything of the sort,' Josie said, sitting down abruptly. 'I just never imagined how neatly everything fitted in, that's all, and people living in muddles in big houses could take a tip from you.'

She didn't know if she was making it better or worse, but at least Tony was smiling again now.

'When you've been brought up in a confined space, you learn how to make the most of it, and to throw out the rubbish. There's no sense in hanging on to things that have passed their usefulness.'

'You're a bit of a philosopher, aren't you?' she said, pleased that she remembered the word.

'No, just tidy. Now, how about that tea? I have to get back to the ride soon, but we'll have more time tomorrow.'

'Who says I'm coming back tomorrow? Anyway, the fair doesn't open on Sundays, does it?'

'That's why we'll have more time to get to know one another. We can go for a walk in the evening, if you like. You're not religious, are you?'

Josie spluttered as she sipped the hot mug of tea too fast and put it down on the small table. 'Not so as you'd notice. We were all sent to Sunday school when we were younger, of course, but we weren't regular church-goers, and I'm not even sure if my gran believed in anything. She must have done, I suppose, as she was quite sure she was going to meet her Tommy in the afterlife.'

She blushed, knowing she was gabbling too fast because she was nervous at being alone here with him. He hadn't touched her, and she felt safe enough in that respect. If he did anything to alarm her, she had no doubt she could shout and scream and attract someone's attention. But she didn't want to do that. Her nerves settled, because this was a kind of adventure after all, even if a very small one compared with Clover and Tommy's wanderings. She began to wonder how it felt when the time at each fairground venue ended, and the whole company travelled off together, their caravans trailing behind the big wagons to the next site. That seemed like a continuous adventure to Josie, and it must be wonderful to be so free.

'You're a funny kid,' Tony said softly.

She spoke quickly. 'I'm not a kid. My sister's getting married next week and I'll be next in line when I meet the right chap.'

'You haven't met him yet then?' Tony said lazily. She realized his arm had slid around her shoulders as he sat beside her on the settee now, their mugs of tea forgotten.

'I may have done,' she said, hoping she sounded mysterious and interesting.

Tony laughed. 'Well, whether you have or not, you don't want to think of marriage and settling down yet. You need to have some fun first.'

'Do I? Don't any of the fair folk get married and settle down then? There are enough children running around – and you and your dad must have had a sort of family life. And oh Lord, I suppose I'm being very rude, aren't I?'

His laugh was louder now, and his arm squeezed hers. 'No, you're not. You're a sweetie. But to answer your question, some of the folk here are married and some aren't. As long as we all do our jobs it makes no difference to us whether they're living over the brush or have got a piece of paper said over them by a vicar.'

Josie felt her eyes widen. She had never heard anything like this before. It sounded reckless and daring and scary, yet wickedly romantic too. She knew at once that her parents would never approve of such ideas, but nor did she intend telling them, or anyone else, about the things Tony said.

'I think I'd better go now,' she said, realizing that the conversation had momentarily dried up.

'And I must get back to the ride too. But we'll meet tomorrow, won't we?'

'Well, I don't know. I have to help my family at the hotel.'

'You came today, so I'm sure you can get away at the same time. I'll meet you at the bandstand tomorrow evening, all right?'

'Perhaps,' Josie said nervously, not quite sure why she was resisting.

He leaned forwards and kissed her on the lips, a sweet touch that was more a kiss of warmth and friendship than filled with passion. It made her tingle. It made her want more. But as she leaned slightly towards him, he pulled back and put his fingers to her lips.

'Until tomorrow,' he whispered.

He stood up and held out his hand, the perfect gentleman, and as she left the caravan, her ears were assaulted at once by the raucous fairground music, muted while they had been inside. Tony led her back through the maze of vans and machinery until they reached the dodgem cars again, and they parted company.

She stayed at the fair a while longer, wandering around and taking stock of the people in charge of the rides and the stalls, subconsciously trying to assess who was married and who was living 'over the brush', as Tony put it. She couldn't see any difference at all. The only difference would be to have a ring on your finger, which her sister Charlotte was soon to do.

She knew then that even if she didn't tell Charlotte everything, she couldn't bear to keep to herself the fact that Tony had remembered her, had invited her into his caravan and behaved himself perfectly, and that she was walking out with him on Sunday night. It was too important an event to keep completely to herself.

While Josie was learning a bit more about a very different way of life, Charlotte had spent almost the entire evening arguing with Melvin over some of the household arrangements after the marriage. It was hardly unreasonable for her to expect to have the biggest bedroom for herself and her new husband, but although she had mentioned this enough times to Melvin already, she was told that his father was finally adamant that he wouldn't move out of it.

'It's where he and my mother slept for forty years, so you can't expect him to give it up now.'

'But I do expect it. We'll be the married couple in the house, Melvin, and your room is hardly big enough to swing a cat. I think your father is being totally unreasonable. You want me to do all the cooking and cleaning and washing your clothes, and yet you won't try to persuade him to give way in this one thing. And don't tell me it's just your father, either. It seems to me you're too lazy to want anything to change. You just want me to move in and for everything to be exactly the same as it was when your mother was alive.'

When she paused for breath she saw that he was furious.

'Nothing will be the same as when my mother was alive. She was the best cook and housekeeper in the town, and she kept things the way me and Dad liked it. You'll have to get used to our ways, my girl, because we're not planning on changing them.'

48

Charlotte was outraged by his words, and by the way he was almost snarling at her now. He was far from being the boy she had always loved, and more the selfish oaf that her father had always thought him to be.

'Well, if you're planning on keeping me chained to the stove making those awful stodgy puddings your mother was so fond of cooking, you can think again,' she snapped. 'I'm used to the good, wholesome food my mother provides at the hotel, and that's what you'll get used to as well.'

'We don't want none of your fancy ways around here, madam,' Melvin shouted at her. 'And if that's your opinion of my mother, I'm beginning to think it's a mistake I ever wanted to wed you.'

'Perhaps I'm thinking it's a mistake too,' Charlotte said, her voice shaking.

The silence between them seemed to stretch. They were walking back to the hotel from Lovers' Walk, an ironic name, since they were behaving more like enemies than lovers. Charlotte stopped walking and folded her arms, trying to stop herself shaking. She had said the words she had never expected to say. Now, on the brink of their wedding, it was hardly the right time to be even thinking them.

'Do you want to call it off then?' Melvin demanded, as aggressive as ever. 'You say the word, and we'll forget it, cancel everything.'

'Is that what *you* want? Is it as easy as that for you, Melvin? Is that all I mean to you then?'

Oh God, how perverse she was being, and didn't she know it too! But right at that moment, when they both seemed to be facing something they had never believed possible, the shame and embarrassment of it all swept over her, together with the humiliation of wondering if he had ever really loved her at all.

'Of course I don't bloody well *want* to call it off, and you know damn well what you mean to me. I've told you so a thousand times, haven't I? I've tried to show you often enough as well, but you'll never bloody well let me until you've got the bloody ring on your finger, and I've bloody well gone along with that too.'

Charlotte didn't want to smile as he almost growled out his

49

frustration. The moment was too serious and too important, but she found her lips twitching at his language, and her voice came out in a sort of strangled gasp.

'I hope you're not going to swear like that in front of the vicar, Melvin.'

He looked at her suspiciously, and then he grabbed her to him, knocking the breath from her body and pressing his cheek to hers. And not only that.

'Christ Almighty, Charlie, look what you've done to me now. I swear if I had to wait more than one more week, I'd explode clean out of my breeches.'

She felt the laughter bubbling up inside her. He could usually manage to deflate the worst moments, although deflating was hardly the word she would use now for the hardness of his nether regions pressing into her. His was such a raw passion, and for now, at least, the anger of the last few moments had gone.

'Well, I'm sure it won't kill you to wait that long, so you'll just have to be patient, won't you?'

'So you are going to marry me then?' he demanded again.

'I reckon I am,' she said coolly, and then she was prevented from saying anything else as he kissed her hard, regardless of a few passers-by who tut-tutted at such a public display in broad daylight.

By the time the two older Elkins girls met later that evening, Josie was bursting to tell her sister about Tony's caravan, and what a bohemian sort of life the fairground people really lived. The more she thought about it the more fascinating she thought it was. The fact that people could live over the brush – a phrase that was intriguing her more by the minute – and yet live as if they were normal, married people, the more sophisticated she thought it must be.

'Are you completely mad?' Charlotte was horrified at listening to Josie's dreamy comments. 'I don't know what sort of nonsense that Tony fellow has been putting into your head, but I can tell you Mum and Dad wouldn't be at all pleased to know about the things he's been saying. And those people aren't living some kind of romantic existence, whatever they call it. If you paid any attention at all to the Bible, you'd know they're living in sin.'

Josie stared at her. 'Good Lord, you're in a bad mood tonight, but you don't have to snap my head off! You're either getting all religious or having second thoughts about marriage yourself.'

Charlotte glared at her. It was too near the truth for comfort. Oh, she and Melvin had ended the evening with everything sweetness and light between them, but the underlying problem wouldn't go away so easily. The fact that she was only now admitting that there *was* a problem was even more disturbing.

'Anyway,' Josie went on, 'Tony says there's nothing wrong with people living together as long as they're faithful to one another. It's no different from the way married people live their lives.'

He hadn't said those exact words; but if she'd thought it would put it all in a more acceptable light as far as Charlotte was concerned, she couldn't have been more mistaken.

'It's *completely* different, you silly girl. You know very well it's living in sin, however romantic this chap makes it sound. And what about the children of couples who haven't been blessed by the Church? Society has a name for them, and it's not very nice, even though it's not their fault.'

Josie snapped back. 'Crikey, Charlie, you've really missed your vocation. You should be a nun or turn into a lady vicar, if women could do such a thing. Are you sure Melvin knows what a prig you really are?'

'Leave Melvin out of this. I'm more concerned with these wild ideas you seem to have got into your head now.'

'You're not going to tell Mum, are you?' Josie said in sudden alarm.

'I'm not a sneak, but I'm not sure I'm happy about having a chief bridesmaid who doesn't understand the vows Melvin and I are going to make next week.'

'I do understand them. All I'm saying is that different people live different kinds of lives – and I wish I'd never mentioned it at all now.'

'Well, at least that's something we agree on. I don't want to argue with you, Josie. I'm supposed to stay calm and serene before my wedding, remember?' Charlotte said, trying to make a joke of it.

'You didn't look calm when you came in. You were all flushed. Have you and Melvin been having a row?'

Charlotte sighed. 'I'm sure all couples go through a few problems the nearer the time comes to the wedding. It's only nerves at taking such a big step.'

'It's a blessed final one too! Once next Saturday is over, things won't ever be the same again, Charlie. You'll be somebody else.'

Charlotte laughed at her gloomy face. 'What nonsense you talk. I might have Melvin's name then, but I'll still be me.'

Josie shook her head. 'No, you won't. He won't let you. He'll turn you into his mother. It's not too late to change your mind, Charlie.'

'Now you're really being stupid and I'm not going to listen to any more of this. I'm going to bed, and I suggest you do the same and get those other thoughts out of your mind.'

It was easier said than done. There were far too many thoughts spinning around in Josie's mind to let her sleep easily that night. She knew her parents wouldn't approve of her walking out with Tony Argetti tomorrow evening, so the fiction of Barbara Venn would need to be revived. Barbara wasn't well, and Josie was going to sit with her and tell her all about the fair. In Josie's mind it was a fiction well worth continuing, if only to save her mother any anxiety she might feel about her daughter's temporary companion.

She felt a twist of sadness, knowing it *was* only going to be temporary. Thursday was the last evening of the fair. They only opened for five days, with Sunday in between the openings, although people were free to walk around the field any time they liked, which Melvin Philpott always said cynically was to make the townsfolk all the more eager for it to open again on Monday.

Thoughts of Tony and Melvin became entwined in Josie's mind as she finally drifted off to sleep. Fantasies of herself and Tony enjoying a fantastic life on the road were interwoven with Charlotte and Melvin's little love nest at the smithy house. Except that it wasn't so much a love nest as a place of drudgery for her sister, with the dreaming face of Charlie being ever more unhappy. Occasionally in these dreams Josie would see another face that she couldn't identify at first. She struggled to see the face, and when it became clearer, she realized it was Steve Bailey, looking just as unhappy and miserable as Charlie.

Josie awoke with a start, wondering if it had really been a dream, or more of an omen of what the future was going to be for Charlie. And for herself, perhaps, she thought, with a burst of excitement that took away all else for a moment. Perhaps it had even been something of Clover's doing, reaching out from beyond the grave like the ghost of Christmas Future in *A Christmas Carol*, to show what lay ahead for those foolish enough not to heed the warnings.

Josie shivered, not wanting to think of anything as macabre as Clover reaching out from beyond the grave. Not that her own dream had been anything but exciting . . . but if she believed any of it, then for Charlie there seemed little more than heartache ahead. And for that nice Steve Bailey too . . .

By now her mouth was so dry that she had to get out of bed and tiptoe downstairs to get a glass of water. Her mind was still so full of the dream-that-might-have-been-more-than-a-dream that she stifled a small scream as she saw a figure in a long white gown in the softly-lit kitchen. Ruth turned around at once, and Josie's heartbeats slowed down their frantic rhythm.

'I thought you were a ghost,' she stuttered.

Ruth gave a half-smile. 'I could say the same about you, my love. What's the matter? Couldn't you sleep either?'

Josie shook her head. 'I've been asleep but I've been having so many dreams I woke up with my mouth all dry and I need some water.'

'I've just made some tea, so let's both have some, and you can tell me all about it. Clover always used to say it cleared the ghosts out of your dreams if you talked about them.'

Josie shivered again. 'I heard somewhere that it was dangerous to talk about your dreams, or they might come true.'

She wouldn't mind if hers came true, but not Charlie's. For all that they argued like mad sometimes, they were as close as sisters should be, and she loved Charlie too much to think of her condemned to a life of drudgery.

'That's nonsense, Josie,' Ruth said quietly, realizing that her daughter looked really troubled. 'Now, have some tea and tell me all about it. I promise you'll feel better afterwards.'

But would she? Josie knew her mother meant it honestly, but it was not a promise she was able to keep. Nothing was going to make Josie feel better about Charlie marrying Melvin Philpott; and the other dream – about herself and Tony living happily ever after – was just as crazy and unreal as it was possible to be.

'Mum, do you think two people are meant to be together, or that we all have choices?' she asked finally.

Ruth looked startled. 'Good heavens, Josie, when did you start to think so deeply?' Then, as she saw her daughter flush, she spoke hastily. 'I'm sorry, darling, that was insensitive of me. But you must admit, you don't often come out with such deep thoughts. Do you have any special reason for them?'

She knew she must tread delicately, seeing how tense Josie was. Perhaps none of them had noticed whether Josie had any problems of her own during all the frantic wedding preparations. But Ruth was noticing her now.

'What is it, darling?' she said gently. 'Whatever it is won't go beyond these four walls, and I'm sure everyone else is sleeping now.'

'Do you think Charlie and Melvin are really suited, Mum?' It came out in a rush, because otherwise Josie knew she would never dare to say it at all.

Ruth was taken aback. 'It's a bit late in the day to be asking such questions, isn't it? I also think it's up to them to know that, don't you?'

'*Do* they, though? Or is Charlie being carried away by the fact that it's been understood for so long that there's no getting out of it now?'

'Does Charlotte want to get out of it?' Ruth said in real alarm. 'Has she said something to you?'

'No. It's just a feeling I've got. I want to see her happy, Mum, and I'm not sure that Melvin is the right one to do that.'

'Josie, all brides have pre-wedding nerves, and all couples have their little squabbles just before the big day. It's perfectly natural when the plans have been made for so long. If there's anything amiss, I'm sure that's all it is.'

'But if a couple decided – even at the last minute – that it was all a mistake . . . would you think it wrong for them to change their minds?'

'I certainly would not,' Ruth said more briskly. 'I can think of nothing worse in all the world than marrying a man you didn't truly love – nor the other way around. But since none of that is going to happen to Charlotte, I think it's time you put these silly thoughts out of your mind and went back to bed. And you haven't even told me what your upsetting dreams were about.'

'They weren't important after all,' Josie murmured. 'Goodnight, Mum.'

Once Ruth also went back to bed she lay awake in the darkness for a long time, listening to Donald's rhythmic breathing beside her. On the verge of their eldest daughter's wedding, she was feeling more nostalgic than usual. She and Donald had been married for many years, and she couldn't imagine life without him. She firmly believed in the words she had said to Josie. There must be nothing worse than being married to someone you didn't truly love. And if she thought any of her girls was heading for that situation, she would do her utmost to stop her. Even at the last minute.

She wished Josie hadn't put such thoughts into her mind, and she wondered what had put them into Josie's mind too. Surely Charlotte hadn't said anything to make her think she wasn't entirely happy in her forthcoming marriage? She and Melvin had been together for so long now, it would surely break her heart not to be marrying him. But would it?

Ruth turned restlessly in the bed, and Donald grunted in his sleep and turned over. She tried to lie rigidly beside him, but she had never believed in putting something off that was nagging away at her. And this was something too important to be ignored. Finally, she slipped out of bed, went along the landing to Charlotte's room and opened the door quietly.

She stood motionless for a moment, wondering, even now, if she was doing the right thing in questioning Charlotte when her daughter had never intimated to her that she was unsure about her future. The only thing she had ever mentioned to Ruth was that she wished she and Melvin could have begun married life in a home of their own, not sharing it with his father. But in the circumstances, how could she have agreed to anything else?

In the light from Charlotte's window Ruth could see the wedding dress hanging beneath its folds of tissue paper on the wardrobe door. Inside, folded carefully in a box until it was pressed on the morning of the wedding, was Ruth's own veil that she had worn to her wedding to Donald. There was a small coronet of mock pearls to go with it; and a frivolous blue garter that Clover had once worn to a dance. Something old, something new, something borrowed, something blue . . .

'Mum? What are you doing?' came Charlotte's whispered voice. 'Is anything wrong?'

She half sat up in bed, still sleepy but alert to the small intake of breath her mother had made. Ruth moved swiftly to the bed.

'Nothing's wrong, darling. I wanted – well, I don't really know what I wanted. Just to watch you sleeping, perhaps, the way I used to when you were a child. And now you're on the verge of being a married woman.'

She felt the tightness in her throat. She hadn't meant to say such things at all. It was overly sentimental, and she wasn't a sentimental woman who expressed such things easily.

Charlotte sat up properly, stretching out her arms to her mother. 'Come and sit on the bed, Mum. You'll catch cold.'

'No, I won't. It's the middle of June, darling.'

It was also the middle of the night, and what a mundane thing to say to a daughter who knew very well what date it was. But she did as she was told, feeling more like the child than the mother at that moment as Charlotte squeezed her hands.

'If you don't want us both to get all sloppy about weddings and start weeping like idiots, you'd better tell me the real reason you're here, Mum.'

Ruth took a deep breath. 'I just want to be sure that you're happy, Charlie. That you really do want to spend the rest of your life with Melvin, because that's what marriage means – to spend the rest of your life with the man you love. And if there was the smallest doubt – even now – I want you to know that I wouldn't think badly of you if you changed your mind. I would only applaud your courage.'

There was an imperceptible pause before Charlotte answered.

'Good Lord, Mum, of course I'm not changing my mind. I suppose Josie's been putting this idea in your mind, and I'll have something to say to her in the morning.'

'Then everything really is all right?'

Charlotte leaned forward and kissed her. 'Of course it is, so stop worrying. Now can I please go back to sleep?'

Once her mother had left her, Charlotte lay down again, turning her face into her pillow, and trying not to think of the loophole her mother had offered her. Trying not to think of it as a loophole at all! Nor of the uproar and scandal it would cause if the wedding was called off. But it wasn't going to be. It wasn't. There was no possible reason for doing such a thing.

Six

Josie was all fingers and thumbs when she left the hotel the next evening and walked along to the bandstand. She felt that every eye was watching her. It hadn't been such a clever idea, arranging to meet him somewhere so public. There were plenty of people about on such a fine evening, and she imagined that every one of them was aware that Josie Elkins was meeting a young chap from the fair. Which was ridiculous, since no one knew about it but herself – and her diary, in which she hadn't been able to resist putting the words on paper, just to see how marvellous they looked: 'Meeting T at bandstand tonight.'

She hadn't written anything more than that, but just writing Tony's initial made the whole thing seem mysterious and exciting. Which it was, she thought, as her heartbeats lurched.

She was a little anxious when she couldn't see him at first, but when she did, lounging against the wooden construction and gazing out across the Channel, he looked so different from the way he usually was at the fair that she caught her breath. The thought swept through her mind that if her father could have seen him now, so dapper and tidy, his hair combed flat against his head, he would have thought him a very fine fellow indeed. He looked exactly the way a young man should look when he was meeting his girl. And even if it wasn't for very long, she definitely thought of herself as his girl, Josie thought, her heart swelling with pride now.

Tony turned and saw her, and his smile widened as she reached him.

'I thought you weren't here,' Josie said, her voice strangled since she was finding it hard to breathe normally.

'I never let down a lovely girl, and you look beautiful tonight,' he replied, making her blush. 'So where are the best courting places around here?'

She was struck dumb for a moment, wondering how she was supposed to know that, since she had never been courting before, let alone walking out with a boy in the evening!

She thought quickly about the places where Charlie and Melvin would go to be alone. Not Lovers' Lane, which would probably be full of couples by now. So would Priory Hill, but it would be the most romantic place to go, where they could look down on the town and imagine themselves kings of everything below.

Tony chuckled, and tucked her arm in his. 'I can see I've stumped you, so let's go walking along the promenade like Darby and Joan while we think about it; then we'll go and listen to some music.'

'Music?' Josie said, hoping she didn't sound like a parrot.

'I've got a phonograph and some records in my caravan. There's not much room to dance but we can always snuggle up close.'

Her heart jumped again, because she didn't know what she felt about that. It wasn't what she had imagined doing this evening, but she didn't really know what she had imagined, either. She was seventeen – nearly – and old enough to know how to behave with a boy, but the plain fact was that she didn't. Her hands felt clammy in her cotton gloves and she didn't know what her strait-laced mother would have said to the notion of her dancing to records on a phonograph in a fairground caravan.

From out of nowhere came a swift image in her mind of her grandmother, dancing along the promenade in her night-gown in the middle of the night. Clover would have dared. Clover had been anything but strait-laced. Clover had often told them how she used to adore dancing in her Tommy's arms . . . and it was funny how until that moment, Josie had never realized how similar their names were: Tommy and Tony. Clover had always believed in omens and signs, so this must mean something, even if Josie didn't know what.

'Come on then, what do you say?' Tony persisted. 'Most girls like to dance, don't they?'

'Yes. I think so,' Josie stuttered, even if she had never danced properly in her life. There had never been any opportunities to do such a thing, and her parents were too busy to think of teaching their daughters such social skills. Clearing tables and making beds was what they had been trained to do . . . But common sense told her they couldn't do proper dancing in a small caravan – not the kind you saw on the silver screen where a glamorous Hollywood film star floated around a ball-room in a handsome gentleman's arms . . . so if she didn't know the steps, it wouldn't matter. She would still be in Tony Argetti's arms.

She gulped, and then heard him speak softly.

'You're so graceful I bet you're a lovely dancer, Josie.'

'I don't know about that,' she murmured. 'My grandmother was, though. She used to tell us lots of tales about how she used to dance with the officers when she and my grandfather travelled everywhere together in his army days.'

She felt oddly as if she was on safer ground, as if mentioning Clover and her skills put Josie up a notch in the dancing stakes.

'You mean the weird old bird with the gaudy clothes?' Tony said, grinning.

Josie stopped dreaming and glared at him. 'Don't call her that. Clover was a darling, and she wasn't weird. She was just eccentric, that's all.'

'Whatever you say, darling.'

It didn't sound like an endearment, just something to placate her. But right then, Josie was more concerned at seeing Captain Bellamy, one of the regulars from the hotel, out for a walk on the promenade on this fine evening, than to take too much notice of Tony's tone of voice. And, too late, Josie remembered she had told her family that she was going to visit her 'friend' Barbara that evening, who wasn't well.

'Nice evening, Josie, though you'd better watch out for rain later,' the Captain boomed as they came towards one another.

'I will, Captain,' she answered, aware that Tony was still gripping her arm and that they looked far too friendly for comfort.

'Who's your friend?' he said, as they walked towards the fairground. 'A bit of a weatherman, is he?'

She gave a small laugh, trying to suppress any worry about the Captain telling her parents he had seen her out walking with a boy. He always said that discretion was part of a soldier's code, and she hoped he would remember it now. But she felt obliged to defend him to Tony.

'The Captain's one of our regular hotel guests, and he's a nice old chap. He was very loyal to us after our old hotel was wrecked. As soon as the Phoenix was ready to reopen, our regulars came back to us. They're friends as well as guests.'

She didn't realize quite how defensive she sounded until she heard Tony chuckle.

'Hey, I didn't mean to annoy you, kid. I was only making conversation. But I'd rather stay in the land of the living, if you don't mind, so let's go and have that little dance to remind ourselves that we're not past it yet. I've got a bottle of cider somewhere too. That'll cheer us up if anything will!'

'I don't drink cider,' Josie said automatically.

'Oh, this won't hurt you. It's just harmless stuff, not the old Somerset scrumpy that takes the hairs off your chest.'

Josie giggled. 'I don't have hairs on my chest either.'

'I'll have to show you mine then.'

A sudden shower of rain justified the Captain's words, and prevented her from giving any reply as they raced towards the shelter of the fairground and Tony's caravan. At least nobody could see her now, Josie thought, in relief. Once inside, they clung to one another as they caught their breath, and then Josie broke away in embarrassment as she became aware of the heat of their bodies through their thin summer clothes. She was suddenly nervous.

'Tony, I can't stay long, and I meant it when I said I don't drink cider.'

She didn't drink anything intoxicating at all. Donald didn't approve of it and had only agreed to a small amount at Charlie's wedding celebrations because it was the done thing to toast the bride and groom. Besides, Melvin would expect it.

'I'll tone it down with lemonade, then you'll hardly know it's there at all. It'll just give you a little kick. First of all, we'll have some music to cheer us up.'

Minutes later the tinny sound of the music coming out of the phonograph filled the caravan and Tony was bringing them each a mug of something sweet tasting and not alarming enough to make her head spin. Finally, she began to relax and enjoy herself. Nobody knew she was here, and she could stay for an hour without arousing any suspicion at home.

'Are you sure you're not mistaken, Captain?' Miss Hester Green, one of the elderly regulars asked him on his return to the hotel guest sitting room.

Captain Bellamy snorted. 'Well, I'm not so senile yet that I can't trust the evidence of my own eyes, madam. A pretty picture she looked too, holding on to the arm of a fine-looking young chap.'

Ruth Elkins looked in on the small group of guests assembled in the sitting room after their evening meal, to see if any of them wanted anything else, and smiled at the Captain and his companions. 'Still telling your saucy tales, are you, Captain?' she asked, with the familiarity of having known her regulars for many years now.

He chuckled. 'It's not saucy at all, dear lady. I was just saying what a pretty picture young Josie looked, walking along the promenade with a young man this evening. She'll be the next one to be wanting wedding bells, I fancy.'

'What nonsense you talk, Captain,' Ruth said, her fixed

smile hiding her annoyance. 'Now, if there's nothing else you require, I'll bid you all goodnight.'

Tony Argetti was content to bide his time. He could be aggressively lusty when he chose, but he also enjoyed the subtle art of seduction when it was required. And despite her brash manner and her almost exotic appearance, he had begun to realize that this girl was like a fragile bird, ready to take fright and fly the minute he put a foot wrong.

The more he thought about her, the more he wanted her. But not tonight – not until he had lulled her into a false sense of security. The thought was more exciting than trying to force her here and now and risk losing her. He preferred to think she would open up to him as eagerly and wantonly as he wanted her.

He had laced the sweet cider with twice as much lemonade to preserve the taste but to render it quite harmless. Tomorrow night it would be stronger, and after that . . . They danced to his music, and he didn't try to do anything other than nuzzle his chin into her neck and hold her close. He was aware of every delicious curve of her body, and she could hardly be unaware of the effect she had on him. But he never mentioned it. He never tried to press himself into her, nor to let his hand stray to the luscious places he so wanted to.

'I musn't keep you here too long,' he murmured into her hair a while later, taking the initiative about letting her go. 'I don't want your father coming to look for you now that the rain's stopped.'

Josie hadn't even been aware of it. As far as she was concerned, she could happily have stayed here, lulled by the romantic sound of the music and rocking gently in Tony's arms for the whole night. But his mention of her father brought her up short, and reluctantly, she wriggled free.

'You're right, I'd better go.'

'Shall I see you back to the hotel?' he offered, still the gentleman.

Josie shook her head quickly. 'There's no need. But I'll see you tomorrow night at the fair.'

'Good. And I'll arrange it so that I have some time off.'

He gave her a chaste kiss and let her out of the caravan

before he went back inside and let out a huge breath, wondering how he had held himself in check for so long. It wasn't bloody natural . . .

Josie sped back the way she had come, feeling alternately as if she was floating on air, and apprehensive at wondering if the Captain had said anything about seeing her. What a fool she had been to suggest meeting at the bandstand in the middle of summer where half the townspeople would be taking the air. She should have said in the centre of the town, near to where Barbara Venn was supposed to live. But Tony wouldn't know his way around Braydon. All he knew was the large field where the fair was held every year, and its nearness to the promenade.

Once at the hotel Josie intended to call out and tell her parents she was back before she slipped upstairs to her own room. But she was summoned at once from the family sitting room, and as soon as she went inside, she knew there was trouble brewing.

'Who have you been with this evening, Josie?' Donald demanded.

Her heart jolted. So much for the Captain's discretion then.

'I told you I was going to see Barbara,' she said nervously.

'So has this friend suddenly turned into the young man you were walking with on the promenade?'

With a sick feeling in her stomach, she thought quickly. 'He's Barbara's brother. I thought I'd walk along the prom first, and I met Tony by accident, and we went to their house together.'

'Does this Barbara really exist, or have you been meeting this boy all the time?' Donald thundered, and Josie realized at once how stupid the second lie had been, especially in giving him Tony's name.

'I haven't been meeting this boy all the time,' she stuttered, knowing that this, at least, was true. 'He's Barbara's brother, and she's not well, and I think it's perfectly mean of you not to trust me.'

She rushed out of the room and up the stairs, fully expecting her father to come storming after her. When he didn't, she could only guess that her mother had stopped him for the sake of not creating a row in the hearing of the hotel guests. For once, she was more than thankful for their presence.

But her whole evening had been spoiled, and she hated herself for adding more lies to the ones she had already told. It surely wouldn't be long before her father demanded to know where Barbara Venn lived, and asked Josie to bring her home to meet the family. Short of killing her off, Josie didn't know how she was going to get out of this one now. But the one thing she didn't intend doing was missing the chance of being with Tony again.

Her heartbeats gradually slowed. She lay on her bed and breathed more easily, gazing up at her ceiling as the daylight faded and remembering how they had danced and held one another, and the moment they had kissed when she had tasted the sweetness of cider on his lips.

Her bedroom door clicked open and then closed, and the next moment her sister had come swiftly across the room and was sitting down heavily on her bed.

'What idiotic stories have you been telling now?' Charlotte stormed. 'Are you completely barmy? It was bad enough that you had to have an imaginary friend as if you were six years old, but now you've given her a brother as well. Is she going to have an entire family next?

Josie curled up on her bed, completely mortified as Charlotte railed at her. 'I didn't know what else to do. The Captain saw me and Tony on the prom and he told Mum and Dad, so I had to think quickly.'

'And that meant more lies. You're a fool, Josie, and the best thing you can do is to keep right away from the fair and that boy.'

'What do you know about anything?' Josie hissed at her. 'He's sweet and kind, and nothing like —' she stopped abruptly.

'Like what?'

'Like Melvin Philpott. *He*'s more of an oaf than Tony could ever be, and I don't know how you can think of marrying him and living with him and his horrible father. They're both pigs.'

Charlotte felt her blood boil at this insult. 'If that's what you think, you'd better stay away from my wedding then. I don't want anyone there who doesn't support me the way a chief bridesmaid is supposed to do.'

She turned and flounced out of the bedroom before they really began shouting at one another and woke up everyone in the hotel. All the current guests, except the regulars, were due to leave in a few days, but the last thing her parents would want was for them to think they had come to a madhouse instead of a genteel hotel. She went to her own room and sat at her dressing table, trying to stop the hammering of her heart and wondering how she had ever come to say such awful things to Josie.

It would break her mother's heart to think there was a such a rift between her two older daughters and, despite what she had said, Charlotte knew it would break hers not to have Josie at her wedding.

She caught sight of her flushed face in the dressing-table mirror. It was a picture of misery and no way for a bride to look on the brink of her wedding. Behind the reflection of her face was that of her wedding dress, the symbol of the day that was going to change her for ever. She tried to revive the excitement she should be feeling at the thought of being Melvin's wife, and waited for the thrill to wash over her; but it never came. There was only the feeling of dread that not only was the day going to be ruined because of the state she and Josie were in and the fact that Josie had drawn her into her stupid conspiracy, but also because she wasn't sure she wanted to marry Melvin at all.

She realized she had been biting her lips so tightly she could taste blood. It was pre-wedding nerves, she told herself feverishly. It was nothing more than that. It was also the first and only time she had allowed the thought to form properly.

It wasn't too late to stop it, whispered a little demon inside her. She could go to her mother, and her mother would understand. Her father would be furious, but secretly relieved as well. Josie would get her way and Milly wouldn't have to wear the bridesmaid dress.

She heard creaks on the stairs as her parents came upstairs to bed, and she shook herself angrily, wondering why on earth she was letting her imagination get the better of her, because of course she was going to marry Melvin; she had loved him for too long to change her mind now. It was no more than pre-wedding nerves, she kept repeating to herself, over and over.

*   *   *

Josie lay in bed, seething. It had been an awful argument with Charlie, but Charlie was going to end up as staid as the Misses Green if she was prepared to spend her life with that dull old yokel Melvin Philpott, and Charlie couldn't possibly understand the kind of excitement Josie felt whenever she was with Tony.

All the same, she wished desperately that she'd never invented Barbara Venn, nor her brother. How was she going to get rid of them now! As soon as the fair left, she'd have to gradually stop seeing Barbara. She stared at her ceiling, thinking how boring life was going to be once this magical week was over – and that included being Charlie's bridesmaid, she admitted grudgingly, because of course Charlie hadn't meant it when she told her she had better stay away from her wedding.

Josie shivered, imagining the outcry if she did just that. Would they go ahead with it if she was temporarily missing, or would it would prevent Charlie making the biggest mistake of her life?

She sat bolt upright in bed, her head spinning, and her heart thumping so fast she thought she was going to die as the possibility entered her mind. She couldn't do it. It would break the family in two. It would be as terrible for them all as when the old Retreat had flooded and they had faced ruin. But it would save Charlie from a fate worse than death, Josie thought dramatically. She could save her from being hitched to that awful oaf for life.

She lay down again and gradually pushed the thought out of her mind, because of course she wouldn't do it. Charlie still said she loved Melvin, even though Josie didn't think it was anything like the way she once felt about him. Surely you should love a person more when you were about to marry them? You couldn't bear to go through all that lovey-dovey bedroom stuff with someone you didn't love completely.

Her thoughts switched at once to Tony and the way he had behaved so tenderly towards her that evening. He might look a bit rough and foreign in his fairground clothes, but at heart he was a gentleman, which was more than she could say about Melvin Philpott.

*   *   *

'You are not to go to the fair again, Josie,' her father said firmly at breakfast the next morning. 'From now on, it's out of bounds to you. And you will stay indoors this evening, so if you were thinking of seeing your friend Barbara, I'm afraid she'll have to do without your company.'

Josie almost howled in dismay, and then she saw how Charlie was eating her toast very deliberately without looking at her. No amount of arguing with her father did any good, and once the sisters were in the guest dining room, clearing away the breakfast plates, Josie turned on Charlotte.

'What have you told them?' she said furiously. 'Why would they stop me going to the fair if you hadn't said anything?'

'I haven't told them anything about your little charade. I just said that one of the fairground chaps seemed to be taking an interest in you, that's all.'

'Well, thank you very much. That would be all Dad needed! You've managed to spoil everything for me now.'

'Why? What were you planning to do?'

'It's none of your business. You don't tell me everything, so why should I tell you?'

Charlotte banged the pile of dirty plates down on the table, looking alarmed. 'Josie, please don't do anything silly. You don't know this boy properly, and if Dad finds out you went there against his wishes, you'd be in real trouble.'

'He won't have to find out then, will he? Unless you're sneaky enough to tell him.'

Charlie put her hand on her sister's arm. 'You know he's too old for you. He's too much of a worldly sort too. He's only playing with your affections, and next week he'll be amusing himself with some other girl in some other town.'

Josie shook her away. 'You don't know anything about him, and he's a real gentleman, so there.'

She knew she sounded as childish as Milly now, but she didn't care. Her emotions were all over the place, and she was blaming Charlotte for preventing her from seeing Tony. She knew only too well that long before next week he would be gone from Braydon, but by then she hoped to hear him say he loved her. She felt instinctively that he did. And now she was to be kept indoors like a naughty child, and unable to see him at all.

'I'll do what I want, and you won't stop me,' Josie snapped, then flounced out of the dining room with the pile of plates and marched to the kitchen.

But misery swept over her even as she said it. How could she ever get away to see Tony now, with everyone watching her like a hawk? And what was she doing that was so wrong? What was so different from the way Charlotte had been walking out with Melvin all these years? It seemed it was all right for some people, but not for her. She swallowed hard to stop herself wallowing in self-pity.

Ruth eyed her sympathetically. 'You know you've brought all this on yourself, don't you, Josie? If you changed your attitude towards your father he wouldn't be so hard on you. We're all a bit tense in these last days before the wedding, but please try not to upset things any more.'

'Even if I turned into an angel overnight, I doubt that Dad would let me go to the fair again!'

'Is it so important?' Ruth said with a half-smile.

'Not to you, maybe, but I've been looking forward to it all year. It's the only bit of excitement around here – and Clover would have understood.'

She didn't know why she brought her gran's name into it, but it was true. Clover always understood the need for excite-ment in a girl's life. It was part of being young, and in Clover's case the feeling had never left her.

'I'd have thought your sister's wedding was excitement enough,' Ruth said mildly. 'But if you promise to toe the line for the next couple of days I'll see if I can persuade your father to let you go to the fair on the last night it's here. I can't promise any more than that.'

Josie caught her breath. It wasn't enough. It was far from enough, but it would have to do. But, never one to miss an opportunity, she pressed on hopefully.

'Do you think Dad will let me go to see Barbara tonight then, even if it's only for half an hour or so? She's really poorly, Mum.'

Her lips trembled with shame at what she was saying. Her mother would probably think it was over concern for her friend, but Josie was realizing even more the enormity of the lies she had started. They could spread like the ripples in a pond, and she didn't know how to stop them.

Seven

In their school lunch break Milly Elkins and her friend Dorothy Yard were contemplating what it meant to get married, especially the awfulness of having to undress in front of a man and do all the yukky things that married people did, the details of which they had unearthed in a well-thumbed medical book. It had been loaned to them by a girl in their class who had sneaked it out of her older sister's bedroom. And they were sworn to secrecy about it.

'Well, I'm not getting married if you have to do all that!' Milly said flatly. 'It's not hygienic.'

Dorothy giggled nervously, impressed by Milly's words as always, and wishing she could think of them so quickly.

'Do you think your Charlotte will have to do it with Melvin Philpott then?'

Milly scowled. 'I suppose so, and she'll hate it, I bet. She's always fussy about washing and making herself smell nice, and you can't say that about *him*.'

'I bet they kiss each other, though.'

'That's different. You don't have to get undressed to kiss people.'

Dorothy stared into the distance. They were walking around the school playing field, oblivious to the shouts and laughter of anyone else, and more consumed by the enormity of what Charlotte Elkins and Melvin Philpott would be doing on Saturday night.

'You have to do *it* to have babies, don't you?' Dorothy said at last. 'That means your mum and dad had to do *it* three times, didn't they?'

Milly stopped walking and pinched Dorothy's arm so hard that she squealed. 'That's a horrible thing to say, Dorothy Yard, and I shan't be your friend any more if you don't shut up about it.'

Dorothy clamped her lips shut, and they carried on walking in silence. But Milly knew she was right, of course. You had to do *it* to have a baby, and that was something else the book had described that made them shudder, even though it was all written so clinically. And she definitely didn't want to think about her parents doing *it*. She had to accept that the human race would have died out if people didn't, so she supposed it must be all right if it was with somebody you loved. And Charlotte loved Melvin, so she could probably overlook any little problems like him not washing himself as often as he should and smelling like a pig.

'Are you mad with me now?' Dorothy said humbly.

Milly's mouth twitched. It was far too nice a day to be bothering their heads about such things, and she didn't want to be bad friends with Dorothy either. Dorothy said she was coming to the church on Saturday to see Milly in her bridesmaid dress and give her moral support, and you couldn't say fairer than that.

'Course I'm not mad,' she said cheerfully. 'Providing you promise not to try to make me laugh on Saturday. My mum says I've got to be dignified.'

'Oh yes,' Dorothy hooted. 'You and Charlie Chaplin, I suppose!'

That started them giggling, and when the bell rang for lessons, they ran back to their classroom, arm in arm, each determined that if she was going to think about the wedding on Saturday, it definitely wouldn't include the honeymoon. But there wasn't going to be one, Milly remembered. Charlie was just going to move into Melvin's house with him and his father, and that would be that. Poor Charlie.

To Josie's relief, Donald agreed that, since she was behaving herself and carrying out her hotel duties cheerfully now, she could visit her sick friend on Monday evening, but she had to be back within an hour or he would come looking for her. Since he didn't know where the fictitious Barbara lived, and she didn't want to create another lie by inventing an address, Josie promised she'd be back well within that time.

'If you're going to see that boy again, you're mad,' Charlotte said as she was getting ready. 'The fair is out of bounds to you, and there will be plenty of people there who know you, Josie.'

'They don't all know I'm not supposed to be there, so they're not going to come here reporting me to Dad, are they?'

She saw the unease in her sister's eyes and spoke more calmly. 'Look, Charlie, if I don't turn up, Tony will think I've lost interest, and I won't stay long, just long enough to tell him I can't see him until the last night of the fair. If you had so few chances to see Melvin, wouldn't you take them? Please don't think badly of me.'

Charlotte's face softened. 'I don't think badly of you – well, not too badly. Just be back in good time tonight.'

But as she neared the fair and heard the usual music blaring out and smelled the distinctive smells of a fairground, Josie began to feel more frustrated by the minute. If she told him the truth, Tony would think she was being treated like a schoolgirl, so there was only one thing for it, and that was to let him think that the fictitious visit to her friend Barbara was because Barbara was really ill, and that her mother had insisted on her not letting Barbara down.

'So I can only stay a little while,' she said breathlessly, seeing him frown, 'and I won't be able to get away for the whole evening until your last night, Tony.'

'Bloody hell, I was taking half the evening off tonight, but I suppose it can't be helped if you've got to keep your mother sweet. I'll arrange it so that I don't work at all on our last night instead.'

She was weak with relief. 'You do understand then?'

'Course I do. We'll just have to make up for it on Thursday.'

The cars on the dodgem ride slowed down, and before she knew what he was going to do, he had grabbed her around the waist and kissed her soundly.

'That's just to be going on with,' he said with a grin, before he swung away from her to help a couple of giggling girls out of their car, his arms around both of them as he made some cheeky remark to them.

Josie chewed her lips, not wanting too see how they were responding to his nonsense, or hearing his usual patter. It meant nothing, she told herself. It was just the friendly way the fairground folk were. She hadn't realized her eyes were blurred until she blundered into someone, who steadied her with a laugh.

'Whoa there, Josie, or you'll be walking up the aisle behind your sister with a broken ankle on Saturday,' Steve Bailey said.

She felt her face go red. 'What are you doing here?' she said stupidly, unable to think of anything else to say at that moment. She was still smarting from the way Tony had been flirting with those other girls. It may not have seemed important to him, but it darned well was to her.

'You're not the only one who enjoys the fair. Where's Charlotte tonight? You need someone to keep an eye on you with some of these flashy chaps around.'

Josie's face burned now. The damn cheek of him! 'I don't need anybody keeping an eye on me, thanks,' she snapped. 'And I've no idea where Charlotte is. Probably out with her *fiancé*, if that doesn't bother you too much.'

To her surprise she saw Steve Bailey's mouth tighten.

'It *does* bother you, doesn't it?' she said. 'Well, she's not married yet, so if you want to do something about it, you haven't got long!'

'Why on earth would I want to interfere with Charlotte's plans?'

'I don't know, unless you're in love with her yourself.'

Steve gave a short laugh. 'You've been seeing too many Hollywood pictures, Josie. I hardly know your sister.'

As he began walking around the fairground, she fell into step beside him, glad to get away from the sight and sound of Tony still flirting with those other girls. 'I've seen the way you look at her, and I think you should sweep her off her feet at the last minute, and stop her marrying that awful Melvin.'

He burst out laughing now. 'And I think you should curb such a vivid imagination, because I've no intention of doing any such thing.'

'I bet you'd like to, though,' she persisted.

'Whether I would or not is no business of yours,' he said lightly. 'Now clear off before I get really mad.'

He strode off, more nettled than she knew. Of course he'd damn well like to stop Charlotte marrying that oaf Philpott. He was more than halfway in love with her, and had been so since the first time he'd set eyes on her. But only a cad would come between a man and his girl on the eve of their wedding, and Steve was no cad.

Josie walked around the fairground for a while until she could decently go back home saying that Barbara wasn't up to visitors after all.

'Perhaps I could send her something,' Ruth said generously, making cocoa in the kitchen. 'Or I could visit her with you one evening.'

Josie almost panicked. 'Oh! Well, that would be nice, but I'm not sure I shall be going there myself too often in the future, Mum, and I'd rather not talk about it if you don't mind.'

Charlotte and Melvin were in the family sitting room, and Josie heard Charlotte choke with laughter as she went inside.

'What are you going to do, kill off the little beast?' Charlotte chuckled.

Josie saw Melvin grinning, clearly well aware of what was going on. 'You've *told* him,' she said furiously. 'You had no right to do so, Charlie. It's private business.'

'It's crazy business,' Melvin snorted. 'I always thought you were a wild one, but I didn't think you were as daft as your grandmother.'

There was a small silence in the room and then Josie found herself railing at him while he roared with laughter at her futile blows. 'Help! I'm being attacked by a wild woman.' He mimicked an ape, throwing his arms about and honking. The air was none too sweet as he flailed about.

Josie was incensed now, ignoring him and turning to her sister. 'How can you think of tying yourself for life to this pig? He stinks to high heaven, and I thought you had more self-respect. It's obvious what he thought of Clover too and I don't know how you can listen to that.'

'Well, it's no secret,' Melvin snapped. 'The whole town knew she was crazy. I'm just thankful my intended hasn't turned out as crazy as you and her.'

Charlotte let out the breath she had been holding while these two wrangled around her. 'Melvin, you'd better go,' she snapped.

'Why? Because of her? We've still got things to discuss before the wedding. That is, if you're sure there's going to *be* a wedding. I'm beginning to wonder about tying myself to such a crazy family now,' he sniggered, still not seeing how serious and upset she was.

'Of course there's going to be a wedding,' Charlotte said tightly. 'Everything's arranged, but right now I want some time alone with Josie.'

He shrugged. 'Don't I get a goodnight kiss from my girl then?'

As Josie turned her back on them, Charlotte offered her face to his, trying not to agree that he really did smell unwholesome. If he didn't bother too much with personal hygiene now, what was he going to be like in six months' time, or a year, or five years, when the first gloss of marriage had worn off?

He banged the door shut behind him as he left, and she flinched. He was like a sulky boy when he didn't get his own way, and that would certainly include wanting his wife whenever he felt the need, no matter what her feelings were. He'd made that plain enough in the past.

'It's not too late, Charlie,' she heard Josie whisper.

She rounded on her. 'Shut up and leave me alone! You've done enough damage already.'

Alone in her room, Josie felt distraught. She honestly hadn't intended any of this to happen. Everything seemed to be spiralling out of control, and in the midst of all the family problems, they still had to put on a cheerful face for the hotel guests. She groaned, thankful that the temporary ones would be leaving on Thursday morning. But sometime on Thursday evening they were expecting her great-aunt Mary and cousin Freda from Exmoor, who had deigned to travel to Braydon for the wedding, and would be staying for a few days afterwards. Josie groaned at the thought. They saw them so infrequently, and they hadn't even bothered to turn up for Clover's funeral, but Ruth was a stickler for keeping the family informed about events, and Freda had sent several letters since learning

74

of the upturn in the Elkins' fortunes, Josie thought cynically. The women rarely left their Exmoor smallholding, where they presumably scraped a living, but they had responded quickly enough to the wedding invitation, no doubt wanting to have a good nose around the new hotel. They would turn up in their old jalopy that was good enough for the rough Exmoor tracks but which Donald undoubtedly thought lowered the tone of the hotel.

Josie knew that all this derision she felt towards her relatives was simply to keep her mind off the most important things in her life: the fact that she didn't dare try to see Tony until the last night of the fair, and the awfulness of being such bad friends with Charlie at a time when everything should be exciting and happy for her. She hated what was happening between them, but when she'd knocked tentatively on Charlie's door earlier, she'd been told to go away. The voice was so muffled that Josie was sure her sister was crying, but Charlie had locked her door and Josie had had no choice but to do as she was told.

It was probably true what people said about absence making the heart grow fonder, because as the days went on, all Josie could think about was Thursday evening, and seeing Tony again. Until then she behaved herself as well as she could, considering that Charlie was barely speaking to her and the fact that she bitterly resented being treated like a child by everyone. She was nearly seventeen, capable of having a job outside the family business, and in her own eyes she was grown-up and should be allowed to see a boy without being made to feel she was doing something criminal. The resentment didn't abate, but she somehow managed to hold it in check, knowing that the minute she burst out with fury, she'd have no chance to go out at all.

'Be careful,' Charlie told her briefly on Thursday. 'You know what I mean. And if you don't, you shouldn't be going out at all.'

Josie flashed her a look of anger. 'Do you know how I hate that word? I shouldn't do this, and I shouldn't do that! I'm such a disappointment to everybody I sometimes think I shouldn't have been born at all!'

'Now you're being silly, and I'm not getting at you, Josie. I'm concerned about you, that's all.'

'Well, you needn't be. I'm old enough to take care of myself, and I'm only going to the fair, for God's sake. I daresay you and Melvin will be there later as well, so you can keep an eye on me,' she added sarcastically.

But not if I have anything to do with it, she thought.

'We've got more important things to think about than to follow you about.'

Josie was too wrapped up in her own excitement about the coming evening to notice the strained note in Charlotte's voice. She just wanted to get through this day, when she could change out of her day clothes into something prettier for Tony's benefit. She tried to stay calm and not to get ruffled when Milly taunted her about trying to look like a film star, and not to snap back when Donald told her she had better be home by ten o'clock at the very latest. Even that was a concession, he told her, since she'd been a good girl all week and behaved herself, which made her squirm still more.

But at last the day was over, her work was finished and she could get ready to go out. She sneaked a bit of Charlotte's face cream, pinched her cheeks to make them rosier, and dabbed a touch of lipstick on her lips. Not too much . . . and in any case, Tony was soon going to kiss it off . . .

The bubbling excitement couldn't be controlled any longer and, not wanting to be seen by the family in her soft blue dress and make-up, she slipped out of the hotel while the others were in the sitting room, calling out that she wouldn't be late.

A short while later Charlotte had also left the hotel, ignoring the raucous sounds coming from the fairground as she passed it, and cycled out of the town. She was now facing Melvin across the kitchen table of the smithy house. He looked at her in disbelief.

'I don't know what the hell you're talking about, Charlotte. We've had our differences lately, but this wedding has been on the cards for long time now. Are you telling me, at this late stage, that you're having second thoughts?'

Naively, she had never expected him to be so angry. But why wouldn't he be? she thought feverishly. He didn't deserve this. No man did; and besides, she wasn't saying the wedding was off, just that maybe they should think about what they were doing and be absolutely sure it wasn't a mistake. Even as the words came into her mind, she knew how feeble they sounded – how feeble *she* sounded. She loved him, she always had, and yet, and yet . . .

'I'm not having second thoughts, and I'm not saying I want to call it off,' she stammered miserably. 'I just want us both to be sure, that's all.'

'Christ Almighty, haven't we been sure about this for the last couple of years? You haven't seen me sniffing around any other floozie, have you?'

She hated his choice of words. It separated them as much as anything else could have done. But she knew that. She knew him and his way of life. She knew his crudity and his passion, and she had loved him for it and thrilled to it. Now, she wasn't sure. *Now*, when it was far too late . . .

'You haven't been getting ideas about some other chap, have you?' Melvin said, suddenly suspicious.

'What other chaps do I know!'

'Well, that newspaper bloke, for a start. I reckon he took a fancy to you after your old gran died, and for all I know you might have been seeing him on the sly.'

'My God, Melvin, sometimes I wonder what I ever saw in you! I have *not* been seeing Steve Bailey or anyone else on the sly, and you can't think much of me if you can't trust me.'

His eyes narrowed. 'There's no smoke without fire, so why has your face gone all red if there's nothing in it?'

Charlotte scrambled to her feet, close to tears. 'I'm not listening to any more of this rubbish. I'm going home, and I just hope you're in a better mood the next time we meet.'

She was shaking now, knowing that the next time they met would be in church when she would vow before God to love, honour and obey Melvin until death did them part. As if he remembered it too, he came around the table and grabbed her to him, nearly knocking the breath out of her.

'We're both getting in a state for no reason,' he said, his voice persuasive. 'We seem to have the knack of upsetting one another lately, but it'll all be all right after Saturday, sweetheart. Once we're wed and your home is right here with me and Dad, it won't matter a damn about the rest of the world.'

She let him nuzzle into her neck and responded to his kisses, but her stomach felt hollow, wishing he hadn't added his father's name to their future. It made her feel that she wasn't just marrying her long-time sweetheart but his father too. They were a package that came together, and it wasn't something she relished.

She cycled home with her head bent, still trying to convince herself that it was just pre-wedding nerves, and desperately hoping it was nothing more. As she passed the fairground again, the music blaring out and the sounds of people enjoying themselves only seemed to mock her more.

Walking through the crowded fairground, Josie didn't know what to do at first. Tony said he wouldn't be working at all that evening, and true to his word, she saw that one of the other young chaps was working the dodgem rides. Was she supposed to knock at Tony's caravan door, or hang around waiting for him to come and find her? His replacement saw her hovering near and waved her over.

'Are you Josie?'

She nodded, finding herself at a loss for words for once. Was she going to get some message that Tony didn't want to see her after all? Had all this week's anxiety been for nothing?

'He's waiting for you in his van. Said to tell you to go right on over,' the chap said next, clearly not too interested.

Josie did as she was told, feeling oddly put out. He could have waited for her here, knowing it was where she would come. She was nervous too, remembering Charlotte's warnings. But she wasn't going to back out now, having waited all this time to be with Tony, so she took a deep breath and walked through the various stalls and vehicles to his caravan.

He must have been watching for her, because he opened the door at once and ushered her inside. He was as freshly turned-out as he'd been on Sunday evening, and there was music playing on the phonograph, just as it had been before. She breathed more easily, forgetting any fears. This was what she had wanted for so long, wasn't it?

'I've prepared a little feast for us, love-bug,' he said. 'First we'll have a drink, then we'll dance, and then we'll eat. And then we'll start all over again. How does that sound to your highness?'

With a flourish he uncovered a checked cloth on the tiny draining board and Josie gasped at the tray of hunks of bread and cooked sausages and pickles.

'It looks good, but I hadn't expected a feast,' she said, her mouth watering at the piquant smell of the food.

'I always aim to please,' he murmured, re-covering the food and pouring them each a mug of cider before handing one to her.

Josie wrinkled her nose. 'This smells a bit stronger than the last time.'

Tony smiled easily. 'You're used to the smell now, that's all. But I'll add a drop of lemonade to it, until you get more used to the taste. Once you get the full flavour of it, you'll really enjoy it, and it won't do you any harm.'

'Well, as long as you're sure.'

'Trust me,' he said, smiling the smile that was guaranteed to turn girls' heads. He topped up her mug with lemonade and she tasted the sweet cider, running her tongue around her lips as she did so. It was quite mild, and the more she drank, the more relaxed she felt. When they had finished the first mugful they danced as they had done on that other evening, and she relaxed even more, caught up in the excitement of an experience she had never known before.

'Tony, I've got to be back before ten o'clock,' she told him, annoyed at having to say such a thing at all. 'In fact I should probably go earlier, as we've got relatives arriving for the wedding.'

Now why did she say such a daft thing? She was hardly thinking sensibly, what with Tony's arms around her, and the sweet taste of cider on his lips that she remembered so well.

'You could always go and say hello to them and come back later,' he said lazily. 'I'm sure a clever girl like you knows a way of sneaking in and out of the hotel without people knowing. Your gran used to do it, by all accounts.'

'Good Lord, how do you know that?'

'Word gets around, darling. She was a bit adventurous, your gran, wasn't she? I was hoping you took after her.'

'I do. At least, I think I do.' It was hard to think of anything at all with his hands roaming up and down her back and making her tingle. But she felt a glow at just remembering Clover, and knew how she would have loved all this. She might not have approved officially, but in her soul she would have loved the risks, the intrigue, the excitement. Josie giggled.

'Thinking about it, are you?' Tony said. 'Coming back later, I mean? We can dance all night if you like, and nobody around here is likely to tell us to stop.'

She giggled again, thinking how very bohemian it sounded. How foreign and exciting compared to her normal, ordered way of life.

'Perhaps. I'm not promising anything, mind,' she said archly, unaware of how she was inflaming him, and making him more determined than ever that tonight he was going to give her more than cider and sandwiches.

Eight

Josie was back at the hotel before half past nine. The mud-spattered jalopy was parked haphazardly outside the hotel, and she grinned, imagining her cousin Freda's determined and erratic driving to get it here. She was in high spirits now, and her excitement made her extra cheerful about seeing her relatives. Not that she had anything against them, and they had always been agreeable on the few occasions they had met. Coming here for the wedding had apparently taken some organization with neighbouring farmers to see to their animals while they were away.

She allowed the solidly-built, fresh-faced countrywomen to give her token hugs, and knew she had her father's approval at being the dutiful daughter. It made the prospect of what she intended doing later all the more exciting.

'Freda's brought me a corn dolly,' Milly shouted. 'It's supposed to bring me good luck.'

'Did she bring one for Charlie as well?' Josie said with a grin. 'She's the one who needs it.'

Charlotte ignored the barb as she continued preparing supper and cocoa for the Exmoor relatives with their heathy country appetites.

'We've had a look at Charlie's dress, and Milly's too,' Freda told Josie next, her red cheeks beaming like a beacon. 'Can I see yours as well?'

'Course you can. Come up to my room and I'll show it to you.'

It might be boring, but it was better than sitting here making small talk, when she was on fire at knowing all that was going to happen later. Her cousin followed her upstairs and into Josie's bedroom and plonked her bulk down heavily on the bed, then gave a sigh as she fingered the soft silk of Josie's bridesmaid dress.

'I thought of getting wed once,' Freda said, to Josie's surprise.

'Did you?' she said, trying not to imagine the lumpy woman in her early forties catching a young chap's attention.

'Oh, you needn't scoff. I never had many chances, Josie, but there was a farmhand once who took a fancy to me, and I thought about it a lot. I'd have liked babies too, probably more than I wanted a man, but you can't have one without the other, can you? Anyway, I knew Mother needed me more than he did. We're content enough as we are now, and men always bring complications. Have you got a young man yet? I bet you have, a pretty girl like you.'

Once Freda was away from talking to the sheep and chickens, there was clearly not much to stop her rattling on. But Josie started at the question, all the same. And Freda looked so eager to know, to share in whatever kind of romance her young cousin was having, that she smiled and spoke confidentially.

'Well, there is a chap, but he'll be going away tomorrow morning and I won't see him until next year. He works at the fair, and you're not to say anything, mind. Dad would kill me if he knew I'd been seeing him,' she added nervously, immediately wishing she'd never said anything at all. Freda wasn't exactly the sort she would choose to confide in, although she wouldn't suspect her of being a blabbermouth either.

81

'I'd never tell on you, Josie. What's he like then?'

Josie realized her cousin's eyes were shining now, even more intrigued by the thought of this romance that Josie's father was not supposed to know about. In Josie's opinion Freda didn't have much of a life in the wilds of Exmoor with only her mother and the animals for company – and the occasional local farmers who came to help the two countrywomen in bad weather.

'He's a bit foreign-looking,' Josie said dreamily, 'and he not only works on the fair. He owns the dodgem ride and has his own travelling caravan.'

'Must be worth a bit then,' Freda said practically.

Josie laughed. 'I've never thought about that. I just like him a lot. In fact—' She looked at her pudding-faced cousin, so obviously frustrated from having any normal kind of life, and decided she could do with a bit of excitement. She would think Josie was very sophisticated to have a secret young man, to say nothing of an imaginary friend called Barbara who had proved to be such a good alibi.

'Can you keep a secret?' she asked.

'I never tell nothing to nobody except my sheep,' Freda said solemnly, which made Josie giggle again until she realized Freda was deadly serious.

It was totally bizarre, Josie thought a long while later, when everybody had gone to bed and she was sneaking quietly downstairs and out of the side door. To be confiding in her cousin Freda was the last thing she had expected, but there had been something so thrilling in the telling, and also something so achingly sad about the way Freda was drinking it all in. It was as if Freda was truly living on Josie's dreams because she no longer had any of her own.

Josie shivered in the coolness of the night air, because however wrong this escapade was, it was surely better to enjoy yourself than to live a sterile and unfulfilled life. In fact, it was a person's *duty*, she thought, not to waste the life God had given them. And she had discovered an unexpected affinity with this plain older woman, whom she could confide in far more easily than her own mother.

But everything else was forgotten as she sped along the

quiet streets later that night until she reached the fairground. She walked through the maze of silent stalls and rides, many of which were already being dismantled and stacked or already loaded on the wagons for an early-morning departure. She knocked tentatively on the door of Tony's caravan and he pulled her into his arms at once.

'I knew you'd come back,' he said softly. 'Now we can carry on where we left off. I've been waiting impatiently for my girl.'

'Have you?' she said nervously. She shuddered deliciously in his arms. This was an adventure that not even Clover could have dreamed about. Then, as he kissed her again, she put all thoughts of Clover and anyone else out of her mind.

'We'll have some music to dance to,' Tony went on, 'but first we'll have another drink to warm us up.'

'I'd better not have too much,' Josie said, giggling again.

'I told you it's quite harmless, darling, just like me.'

All the same, she was sure the cider tasted stronger than before. She thought there might have been something else in it too, some spirit or other, but since she didn't know much about spirits, and since every sip she took was interspersed with kisses, she knew she wasn't going to bother her head too much about it.

There wasn't a lot of room for dancing in the caravan, but half an hour later it seemed a lot easier to stay on her feet and sway in Tony's arms rather than give in to the giddiness she was starting to feel. She needed his arms to hold her up. She needed to stay attached to him so that she wouldn't actually fall over.

'You're a beautiful girl, Josie. I bet you've got half the chaps in Braydon after you,' Tony whispered in her ear. His breath was warm and sweet, tickling her skin, and she couldn't seem to stop the inane giggling, or the way her legs didn't seem to want to dance any more but were starting to feel heavy and leaden.

'I don't have any other chap,' she murmured back. 'There's only you, Tony. I've been waiting all year for you.'

Her voice was thick and muzzy inside her head as she said the words, and she had the strange sensation of playing a part in a romantic movie. She was the beautiful, innocent young heroine, and he was the gallant, handsome hero. It was all so romantic, and so inevitable.

'Is that right? You've never had a chap before?'

She was vaguely aware of the mingled urgency and excitement in his voice, and while he still held her close he reached behind her back for her half-empty mug of cider. 'We should drink to that, Josie.'

'Should we? What are we drinking to?' she said, giggling again. And obeying him without question, because the cool, sweet taste of the cider was doing such delicious things to her.

'To me being the first. That's a very special event in a girl's life. It deserves being celebrated.'

She gazed up at him lovingly. The gas lamps in the caravan lent an even more seductive air to the place as they popped and flickered and lit his face in a soft shadowy light, adding to the illusion that they were taking part in a passionate movie where the hero was about to swear his undying love for her.

'The first?' she said vaguely. 'First young man, you mean?'

He laughed, and somehow he was steering her towards the curtained-off part of the caravan. She was in danger of losing her footing now. She knew she would have done so if he wasn't keeping hold of her so tightly . . . then suddenly, the supporting arms weren't there any more, and the hands that were pushing her towards the bed were no longer so gentle. She fell on to the bed, the breath almost knocked out of her as Tony's body weight was on top of her.

There was no light at this end of the caravan, and she gasped as she felt his fingers fumbling beneath her skirt, tugging at her stockings and tearing them. She felt sudden fear, and his breath was no longer warm and sweet, but hot and threatening. This wasn't the way the movie was supposed to end . . .

'What are you doing? Stop it. Please, Tony, *don't*! I don't like it,' she almost sobbed in sudden panic.

His reply was to smother her face with kisses again, while he almost growled in her face and she couldn't mistake his lust now.

'Come on, darling, you're not that innocent. Why did you come back tonight if it wasn't for what you've been teasing me with ever since I laid eyes on you? Just relax and enjoy it.'

Relax? How could she relax when his fingers were hurting her? And not only that . . . oh God, what was that? She wasn't totally innocent, and she knew the difference between a man and a woman's body, but it was all theory, and she had never imagined this – this *thing* – prodding and stabbing at her, and hurting her . . . She wasn't even aware of how he had produced it or how her lower limbs were suddenly chilled, and there seemed to be hardly any clothes between them now, and she was so dizzy with the cider and the hurt of it all that it was impossible for her to resist anything any more . . .

The pain was swift and tearing, and Tony gave a strange whoop of pleasure as if he had reached some sort of goal. And then he became the exciting lover she always knew he could be, his kisses covering her face again, his hands fondling her breasts, and after a moment or two he was moving slowly inside her, whispering against her mouth that she was the most wonderful girl he had ever known, and that she should relax, relax, relax . . .

Without realizing it, she slowly did as she was told, and the feelings were less painful and became more sensual and exciting. Her body began to feel almost weightless as he continued his rhythm, faster and faster, harder and harder, until she felt an enormous thrust, and all she was aware of was Tony's feral noises before he lay more heavily on her, taking her breath away. And then she knew no more.

There was a rare June dampness in the early-morning air on Friday. Fairground folk were habitually about their tasks early, none of them displaying their public cheerful faces as they dismantled the remainder of the stalls and rides and stacked everything into their wagons with the speed and expertise of having done the tasks many times before. At least the week of the fair here hadn't been ruined by rain, but it meant that by the time they had packed everything up and were ready to hitch their caravans to the wagons while most of Braydon was still sleeping, they were in a foul mood and more than ready to move on.

Tony Argetti had one more thing to do before he could

leave, and that was to get the girl out of his caravan. She had totally passed out last night, and he hadn't had the heart to waken her, so he had let her sleep it off in the bed beside him. But now he had to rouse her, give her a few bob, and tell her he hoped to see her again next year. She was a good kid, and he had enjoyed her, but it was time to say goodbye. He opened the door of the caravan and stepped inside. Either she'd gone already, which he hoped, or she wasn't up yet, which could be a nuisance. He heard a whimpering noise behind the curtain and he pushed it aside impatiently.

Josie was curled up in the bed, her knees drawn up tightly. Her head throbbed so badly it felt as though a team of demons were hammering away inside it. Her face was white, her face tear streaked.

'What have you done to me?' she choked.

Tony felt a stab of alarm. He liked the girl, he really did, and he'd truly thought she'd known what she was coming here for, but he hadn't anticipated the real fear in her face now.

'Hey, come on, darling, we had a good time, didn't we? Look, you can't stay much longer. We're moving out of here this morning, and we're not allowed to stay camped on this field once our time is up. I'll make you a cup of tea and then you'll have to go home.'

'I don't want your damn tea! And how can I go home or anywhere else like this?' she screamed.

She pushed back the bedcover and showed him her ripped stockings and the dried bloodstains on her legs and torn dress. He gave an uneasy scowl.

'That wasn't meant to happen. I was considerate enough and you weren't objecting. You came here of your own free will, and you knew what to expect, so don't go trying anything on,' he said warningly. 'If things got a bit rougher in the end, we still had fun, didn't we? You'd better stay where you are for a minute, and I can probably find you an old shawl to cover yourself with to get you back home.'

'An old shawl?' she almost screamed. 'Since you don't have a woman in the caravan does it belong to another one of your conquests?'

His face hardened and he spoke roughly. 'No, it bloody

well doesn't. But you've got two choices, kid. Either you get out of here in ten minutes, or you'll have to come with me. I've got to get my outfit on the road and I can't wait around any longer for you to make up your mind.'

'Do you mean that?' Josie said shrilly.

'That I've got to go? You're damn right I do.'

'No, that I can come with you,' she said wildly.

It was a bad idea. She shouldn't even think about it for a second. She didn't want to go on the road, as he put it. She no longer thought of it as being the least bit glamorous. It would be an awful thing to do to her family, to simply disappear when none of them knew where she had gone. It would hurt Charlotte so much. It would drive her father mad and her mother would be devastated and humiliated if Josie wasn't there to support her sister at her wedding. Besides which, it would worry them all to death. But how could she even think of trying to get back to the hotel that morning with her clothes in tatters, her face swollen with tears, her head feeling fit to burst, and the fact that they would know she had been out all night?

Tony hadn't said anything for a minute, but now he spoke sharply. 'Look, I can see you're upset, so you can come with me to our next stop until you're feeling better, then I'll get you some clean clothes from one of the women and put you on a bus back to Braydon. It's the best I can do. You'll have to go back eventually, mind. I don't take passengers, and I don't want anybody to come looking for me with a shotgun.'

Josie hoped he was trying to make a joke of it, but she glared at him furiously, her eyes full of tears. She felt young and terrified at what she had allowed to happen. And it was true, she thought bitterly. She *had* allowed it to happen – well, more or less. He hadn't forced her to come here, and she had given him every encouragement. And despite all, he was still the handsomest young man she had ever known, and he must have loved her to do what he had, she thought naively – even if it seemed he didn't really want her now.

'Do you promise you'll do that?' she said tremulously. 'I've got no money for bus fare.'

'Don't you worry about that,' he said, trying not to show his relief. 'I'll see that you get back home.'

He'd do that all right, he thought grimly. He didn't want the encumbrance of a permanent resident in his caravan, though remembering last night and how responsive she had finally become, he wouldn't mind keeping her a few more nights. He'd have to see how things went before he suggested anything of the kind, though, and she did look in a sorry state right now. He leaned forward and put his arms around her, holding her close for a few moments and speaking less harshly.

'You'll be quite safe inside the van once I've hitched up, Josie. It will rock about a bit once we're on the move, but you just stay where you are and go back to sleep until we set up again farther down country. I'll cook us a hot meal then, and by the time you get home again, your folks will hardly know you're gone.'

Josie doubted that. Her stomach gave a wretched lurch every time she thought about it, but what choice did she have? If she stayed away until Saturday was over, she might even save Charlie from marrying Melvin Philpott. She wouldn't let herself think about Charlie getting ready to go to church in her lovely dress, and Milly racing around excitedly, and the discovery that Josie's bed hadn't been slept in – although they'd have found that out already. She wouldn't think about ruining Charlie's big day, only that she'd be saving her. She could hardly think sensibly at all, with the throbbing pains in her head and the soreness down below.

Once Tony had left the caravan, she tried to make her mind a total blank. To do that, you had to imagine sinking into black velvet or something, she thought shivering, but she couldn't do it. She was mentally exhausted and physically sore. She was also bitterly ashamed and full of guilt. She had let everybody down. But it was so difficult to concentrate on anything because the unaccustomed drinking had given her such an atrocious headache. Tony was going to take care of her, she told herself almost desperately, and with that single hope drumming through her head she curled up in the bed again, and knew no more.

The kitchen of the Phoenix Hotel was less noisy than usual on that Friday morning. Milly had gone off to school, despite begging to be allowed to stay home because they had relatives staying with them. Aunt Mary and cousin Freda were inclined to make a pet of Milly, and she wasn't averse to using their presence to try to get her own way. But it didn't work today, and she was packed off as usual.

'She's a little treasure,' Mary said with a chuckle. 'And such a bright little maid too. She'll do you proud, Ruth.'

'All our girls do us proud,' Ruth put in, dispensing yet more cups of tea, and marvelling at the capacity of the two country women for drinking so much liquid. By the time the morning was half gone they had already drunk copious quantities, and it would soon be time for elevenses. She was thankful that Donald had gone out on business of his own, or he'd have been raising eyebrows and making some teasing comment, and Ruth wasn't sure how much of a sense of humour these two rather dour women possessed.

'Are the older two still lying abed?' Freda asked now.

'That's right. We told them there's no need for them to get up at the usual time today, and that I would see to the regulars' breakfasts. Charlie needs to be calm for tomorrow, and I daresay Josie's still tired after the fair last night. I didn't hear her come in, but once she's asleep it's like the sleep of the dead.'

Freda smiled. 'Your Josie's quite a girl, isn't she?'

'You could say that,' Ruth said, surprised at the thought that there could be any affinity between the two of them.

'Oh, we had a lovely chat yesterday. She's just the sort of help we could do with at the farm,' she said, almost wistfully. 'She's young and strong and she'd certainly liven things up a bit for us old 'uns.'

'You're not old,' Ruth protested with a laugh. 'You're younger than me, and I'm certainly not thinking of myself as old yet!'

'Mother is, though.' Freda glanced to where Mary was wandering off to the guests' sitting room to join the regulars, who were her contemporaries. 'I worry about her a lot, especially with the harsh winters on the moor. I'm still capable of coping with the work and the beasts, but I sometimes wish we had a younger person to give us a hand. The time will come when we'll have to think about it.'

'Can't you get a farmhand on a daily basis?'

Freda shrugged. 'Maybe. But they all have beasts of their own to look after, and the young farmhands get married and have their own families to fend for. That's something I never had, not like you, Ruth.'

She looked so gloomy now that Ruth had to chivvy her along.

'My goodness, Freda, you're here for a wedding, so cheer up. Your mother certainly isn't as agile as Clover was, but they were sisters, so I daresay Aunt Mary is just as hardy underneath.'

'I hope you're right. Now then, I'll help you with this washing-up.'

'No you won't. You're a guest.'

'No I'm not. I'm family, and I'm not used to being molly-coddled.'

Their amicable wrangling ended when Charlotte came into the kitchen and another late breakfast had to be served up, even though she protested that all she needed was toast.

'A piece of toast isn't enough to put meat on your bones, girl,' Freda admonished her. 'It's all right for these fashion plates at the pictures, but normal young girls need fattening up a bit to stay healthy.'

Charlotte laughed. 'The thought of being fattened up doesn't thrill me at all, Freda, and when did you last go to the pictures to see any fashion plates?'

'Oh well, not lately,' Freda admitted – which probably meant never, thought Charlie, feeling an odd rush of affection for the plain-faced woman who was clearly revelling in sharing the excitement of a family wedding.

They were all enjoying the thought of it, thought Charlotte determinedly, and it was going to be a lovely occasion . . .

'Where is everybody this morning?' she went on, before she thought too deeply about the one person who wasn't quite as enthusiastic as she should be. 'I suppose Milly didn't get her way about staying home from school or she'd be rushing about, and Josie's so quiet I think she must be hibernating.'

She didn't notice the flicker of alarm in her cousin's eyes at that moment. Freda continued drying up the plates and cutlery, trying to ignore the uneasy feeling inside, and she didn't say anything until she had finished. Then she spoke quickly.

'If there's nothing else you want me to do, Ruth, shall I go and see if Josie's awake? Mother's already settled with the regulars in their sitting room, so she won't need anything until they're ready for their elevenses. It's nice for her to have people to talk to instead of sheep.'

Freda tried not to gabble, especially as it wasn't her usual way. And until she was sure, the suspicions in her head were too monumental to share with anyone at the moment. She could still be wrong. Josie might simply be doing as Charlotte said and having a lazy lie-in. But Josie had shared her secret with Freda, and Freda couldn't ignore her growing unease as the morning went on.

'I think it's best to leave her,' Ruth said lightly. 'She's been in such a funny mood lately, so we'll let her wake up in her own time. There's nothing special for her to do, anyway, but if you really want to help, Freda, we can start preparing the food for tomorrow.'

Charlotte muttered something about Josie doing the best thing and keeping out of everybody's way, and then said she was off to the florist to check that the bouquets and button-holes would be delivered first thing in the morning. Short of insisting that she went to waken Josie, there was nothing for Freda to do but to give in and wait.

Nine

Even though the early-morning drizzle had long cleared up, Steve Bailey wasn't in the best of moods. How could he be, when tomorrow he would be an unwilling addition at the wedding of the girl he was more than half in love with, and had been from the day he first saw her? She was beautiful and intelligent and sparky, and far too bloody good for that blacksmith. But Steve wasn't in the business of wrecking people's lives and tomorrow he would have to be strictly professional and see that the Elkins and Philpott wedding had a good write-up in the local paper.

He hadn't expected to see Charlotte that morning, and he couldn't help noticing that she didn't exactly look like the happy bride-to-be. There were shadows beneath her eyes as if she hadn't been sleeping well. Rex, accompanying him as usual, had leaped with joy at seeing his adored one coming towards them, and Steve only wished he could afford the uninhibited reaction of his dog as he leapt all around Charlotte and was rewarded with a laugh and a hug.

'I thought you'd be too busy to be about this morning,' Steve greeted her.

'I've been to the florist to check on the flowers,' she told him.

'Everything's ready then?'

God, why did he have to sound so stilted, as if this occasion meant no more to him than an official duty? But it was better so, he reminded himself. There was no point in complicating things now, even though he knew there had been more than a spark between them at one time, or could have been if the bloody blacksmith hadn't been on the scene.

'My mother is preparing food even as we speak,' Charlotte said lightly. She lowered her eyes, aware of a tension between them that she couldn't explain.

'I'll be at the church with a photographer to cover it for the newspaper,' Steve said. 'But I might call round later today for a few details in advance, if it's not too much of an imposition; then I shan't need to be in evidence for very long tomorrow. And I hope you'll be truly happy, Charlie.'

'Why shouldn't I be?' She was bemused by his use of her nickname. It was over-friendly. It was too intimate for a virtual stranger. But he wasn't really a stranger. He had been a good friend during the family troubles, and when she had burst out with the news that the hotel was going to be saved after all, there had been that one exuberant kiss that she could remember, even now.

'You should be, and I hope you will be,' he repeated. He gave a lopsided smile and spoke more teasingly. 'But if it all goes wrong, you can always count on my shoulder to cry on. I'm kidding, of course!'

'I should think so too. But thanks for the offer. I'll remember it if I ever need it,' she answered just as lightly, wondering why such a silly remark made her feel oddly depressed. But she couldn't stand here talking all day, much as she would like to. And she would, she thought. With a twist of something like pain in her heart she knew that she would like to very much. She bent down and ruffled Rex's rough hair, avoiding looking into Steve Bailey's eyes as she said goodbye to them both.

'Where's Josie?' Donald said at once when he came into the kitchen soon after midday. 'I've got a job for her to do.'

Ruth looked at the kitchen clock with a start. She and Freda had been so absorbed in seeing to the regulars' and Mary's needs and baking all morning, they had lost track of time. Charlotte wasn't back from the florist yet, and was no doubt chatting about the wedding to any number of acquaintances.

'Good heavens, I'd forgotten all about her,' Ruth said now.

'Don't tell me she's not up yet?' Donald exclaimed. 'That girl really needs to be kept in line, Ruth, and not to use this place as – as—'

'As a hotel?' Ruth said with a laugh, and covered it quickly as she saw him frown. Josie wasn't his favourite person at the moment, and if she did one more thing to upset him, there'd be trouble tomorrow, and none of them wanted that.

'I'll go and wake her up,' Freda said hastily, not wanting to be in the middle of these two if they were going to have words.

She left them before they could object and went upstairs to tap gently on Josie's bedroom door. When there was no reply, she knocked a bit harder and then opened the door quietly. Freda wasn't stupid, but she stood completely still for a few moments, as if unable to take in what she was seeing. The room was empty, the bed was unslept in, and there was no sign of Josie.

Freda's heart thumped uncomfortably, knowing she was the keeper of a secret she had sworn not to tell, and praying with all her might that it wasn't going to be necessary to do so. Any minute now, she thought desperately, Josie would come sneaking up to her room and then they could join the family downstairs together as if she had just been having a lazy morning. Quite how her cousin would accomplish that Freda didn't have the gumption to work out, since her brain seemed to have turned to mush in those few minutes.

But she couldn't remain staring at an empty room for ever. She turned and started to go back downstairs to the kitchen, taking as long as possible and trying not to anticipate the eruption below when she had to report that Josie was missing. Not that she would choose to use that word, she thought hastily. Perhaps she could suggest that Josie had gone out early somewhere, and just as quickly she knew it wouldn't work. Ruth and Donald were always early risers and would know at once that it wasn't true.

As she dithered on the stairs, Freda realized that Charlotte had returned to the hotel. She could hear her talking to her parents about some chap called Steve whom she had met on the way back. He had wished her well, and had promised to be at the church tomorrow with a photographer.

'I suppose we have to have him there,' Donald said with a frown.

Charlotte defended the chap at once. 'If we want a little piece in the newspaper about the wedding, then of course we do. He might also call around sometime today to get some details, then he won't have to stay long tomorrow. I'm sure that will please you, but you know Steve would do us proud, Dad. He didn't let us down when he did that lovely piece about Clover, and you've said yourself that we've got a lot to thank him for.'

'For a girl who's getting married tomorrow you seem very partial to the newspaper fellow,' Donald said sharply.

'I like him, that's all. I don't have to stop liking other people because I'm getting married, do I?' Charlotte said.

Working in lonely isolation on her Exmoor farm, Freda might not need too many social skills, but she was fairly perceptive and in Freda's opinion Charlie spoke far too defensively about this Steve person. But perhaps she was wrong, and who was she to judge the emotions of young girls, when she was an unmarried woman with only an elderly mother and sheep and chickens for company?

As she came down to the kitchen, Donald frowned even

more when he saw that his daughter wasn't with her. He could be a jovial host at the hotel, but he was a strict father and disciplinarian too, and Freda dreaded what she had to say.

She took a deep breath. 'Josie's not in her room at the moment.'

Donald spoke angrily. 'Not in her room? Then where the devil is she? She can't have gone out without telling anyone. Have none of you seen her all morning?'

Charlotte looked at Freda, and Freda swallowed hard. Then a sudden inspiration came to her from nowhere.

'Perhaps she went out to see that friend of hers that she was telling me about last night. Barbara, isn't it? I understand she hasn't been at all well.'

Freda knew she was a hopeless liar. She wasn't used to lying and she had never had any cause to do it before. Her voice was husky with embarrassment, and her normally robust complexion had become blotchy.

'That could be it, I suppose,' Ruth said dubiously, trying to think that such a solution was reasonable, while being very aware of how Donald's face was darkening even more.

'No, it's not,' Charlotte said flatly. 'There is no Barbara. She doesn't exist.'

Ruth tensed, sensing that something was going on here that she didn't understand and didn't want to acknowledge. She spoke quickly.

'Don't be silly, Charlotte. Of course Barbara exists. Josie's been seeing her for quite a while now.'

'Have any of us ever seen her, Mum? Do we know where she lives? Do we know how old she is, or where Josie met her, or what's wrong with her?'

'I think you had better explain yourself, young lady,' Donald thundered, turning on her. 'What do you know about this Barbara that you're not telling us?'

Charlotte felt her stomach begin to heave. Too late, she realized she was as much to blame for this conspiracy about the fictitious Barbara as her sister. She was what the detective stories would call 'an accessory after the fact'. And already churning at the back of her mind was the thought that if Josie hadn't been with Barbara, which she couldn't possibly have been . . . then where was she now, and where had she been all night?

'I only know what I've already said, Dad,' Charlotte stammered. 'Barbara was an imaginary friend that Josie invented.'

'Are you trying to imply that Josie was an idiot? Only infants invent imaginary friends. I could understand it of Milly a few years ago, but not Josie.'

'I'm afraid it's true, Donald,' Freda put in nervously, seeing how distressed Charlotte was becoming. 'Josie told me about it last night.'

Donald faced her slowly, almost apoplectic now.

'I seem to remember you were the first one to suggest that Josie had gone out to see this Barbara who hasn't been well, Freda. Is everyone in this house turning into a liar now?'

Freda flinched, but Donald brushed aside her stumbling apologies.

'We'll go into all that later. The important thing that we're all overlooking, is where is the girl now? Can anyone tell me that, or is the truth too much to ask of any of you?'

'Donald, please don't get yourself in such a state,' Ruth said fearfully. 'I'm sure there's a simple explanation for all this.'

But Ruth was completely out of her depth. She longed more than anything for Josie to come breezing into the house, saying she'd gone for walk, or to the shops, or *anything* but the dread that was creeping into her thoughts now. That her daughter was hotheaded had never been in question, but that she had done something wicked was something Ruth didn't want to imagine.

Freda's basic honesty wouldn't allow her to keep silent any longer. 'Donald, I think I know what may have happened, although I didn't think for a moment that it would end like this,' she said shakily.

The silence was ominous, and then he strode across the room and gripped Freda's wrist so hard that she cried out.

'Tell me at once what you know, Freda.'

'Well, she was going to see her young man late last night.'

'What young man? She doesn't have a young man,' he roared.

'Tony somebody.'

Nobody spoke for a moment, and Freda rubbed her arm where Donald had gripped it so cruelly. Her face was full of misery; she was clearly wishing herself anywhere but here, and preferably back on her isolated farm with the sheep and chickens. Donald snapped at her.

'I was given to understand a few days ago that *Tony* somebody was *Barbara* somebody's brother, but that is obviously not the case. Is it, Charlotte?'

It was Charlotte's turn to jump now as her father's full wrath was turned on her. She stammered out the words: 'He works on the fair, Dad, and Josie took a liking to him. I would hardly call him her young man. He's just a pleasant boy.'

It sounded feeble, even to herself, and remembering the way Tony Argetti's flashing dark eyes had flirted with every female he saw, she knew her words were very much an understatement.

'A fairground chap!' Donald exclaimed, more scathing than angry at that moment. 'Well, that's all I need to hear. How could she do this to us? Especially to you, Charlotte, at such a time.'

'I'm more concerned with what's happened to her than with how she's let down the family and your precious hotel!' Charlotte said shrilly.

'Do you think that's all I care about?'

'Well, don't you?'

For an instant she thought he was going to strike her, then Ruth put her hand on her husband's arm, holding back her own tears.

'Donald, please let's think about what's most important right now, and that is, where is Josie? Don't you think we should go to the fairground and see if she's still there? They may not have moved on yet.'

'I'll go,' Charlotte said at once, even though she knew it would be hopeless. Everyone knew the fairground people habitually moved out of the town before dawn, leaving their mess behind them for others to clear up.

'I'll go with you, Charlotte,' Freda said. 'It will be quicker if I drive us there. Please let me do this, Donald, as I feel partly responsible.'

'Just bring her back,' he almost growled, and even though Charlotte had taunted him about his snobbery and how furious he was with Josie, she knew how painful this must be for him.

She and Freda left the hotel and climbed into the ancient jalopy. Freda's driving was no better than ever that morning, but it was the last worry on their minds as they lurched and bumped towards the moorland field.

'What do you think, Charlie?' Freda said hesitantly.

'I don't know what to think, but I've got a nasty feeling about it.'

'It's too bad of her to stay away like this right before your wedding.'

Charlotte stared ahead. 'I can't even think of that right now, Freda. All I can think of is that something might have happened to Josie. I don't know any other reason why she would stay out all night.'

They didn't look at one another, but both were thinking the same thing, the thoughts that nobody had dared to put into words, that perhaps there was something more sinister about Josie's disappearance than just high jinks. For all her brashness, Josie was still a vulnerable and sometimes gullible young girl.

They reached the fairground, empty now except for the flattened grass and churned-up mud from many heavy vehicles, and the usual flotsam and debris left behind that the birds and dogs were picking over. The two women sat in the car in silence, not knowing what to say or do next. And then Charlotte spoke tightly.

'Will you take me to the smithy, Freda? I have to talk to Melvin.'

'You're not going to do anything rash, are you?' Freda said nervously. 'Do you think he can help?'

'I'm going to do what I have to do. Please, Freda.'

Melvin looked up from his work as the clanking old car approached. He'd never seen it before, and at first he assumed it was a farmer arriving with a job to negotiate, so he put on his professional face as he straightened up. His expression changed as he saw Charlotte step out. The plain-faced woman behind the wheel also got out and stood beside the car, folding her arms tightly around herself.

'Couldn't keep away, eh? We're not meant to see one another until we meet in church, and I thought you'd be busy with girlie things today,' Melvin grinned.

She was tongue-tied for a moment. It was such a trite, harmless remark, and yet it was so unintentionally insensitive that she could have burst into tears. But it wasn't time for that yet . . .

'Josie's missing,' she said brutally, because there was no other way to say it.

He didn't see how serious she was, and his face broke into a wider smile. 'What do you mean, missing? How can she be missing? Or is this a joke, finding an excuse to come out here and check up on me? If I know your crackpot sister, she'll be hiding away somewhere, dolling herself up in her fancy bridesmaid dress and planning to outdo the bride.'

The smell of him was rank with body odour from his exertions. The added stink of the hot metal at the forge was bitter and acrid, and in an instant Charlotte knew she couldn't bear to spend the rest of her life with him. She had known it in her heart for a long time, but she had never been willing to accept the truth. And she knew exactly what she had to do, even if her insides were turning upside down.

'Are you completely stupid?' she almost screamed. 'My sister's missing, and all you can do is make stupid remarks like that!'

'Charlie, love,' Freda began nervously, but Charlotte didn't heed her.

'If I'm so bloody stupid, I wonder you can bring yourself to marry me at all,' Melvin snapped, aggressive in an instant.

'Maybe I can't. Maybe that's the most sensible thing you've ever said!'

He didn't take long now to catch on to her mood, and he was quick to match it. 'Is that what you want then? To call the whole thing off? Suits me if I have to spend my life with a temperamental little tart like you.'

They stood facing one another, both boiling inside, while Freda gasped and unconsciously backed away. This was none of her business, though her heart was thumping as hard as she was sure theirs must be.

'It is what I want, and I think I must have wanted it for a long time,' Charlie said, suddenly choked at the enormity of what she was saying.

Melvin's mouth tightened and he snarled at her. 'So that's

it, is it? Even if your precious sister turns up at the last minute from wherever she's hiding out?'

'She's not hiding out, and even if – *when* she turns up, it won't make any difference. I'm sorry, Melvin. I have to do this.'

She dragged the engagement ring off her finger, and offered it to him. She was shaking all over, and she felt worse than she had ever felt in her life, except that deep inside she knew she was doing the right thing. The only thing.

'Keep it,' he said, turning his back on her. 'Maybe it'll serve as a reminder in future that not many blokes will want a girl who's a second-hand tease.'

Charlotte dropped the ring and turned away, her eyes blinded by tears and hardly aware that Freda was helping her into the car. They were both thankful to leave the smithy behind and Freda drove back to the hotel in silence until Charlotte gave a huge, shuddering sob.

'Oh God, Freda, what have I done?'

As they reached the hotel yard, Charlie prayed that Josie would have returned and that at least one trauma was over, but one look at her parents' frantic faces told her nothing had changed. And now she had to tell them what had happened between herself and Melvin. She knew Melvin would never beg her to reconsider, and it wouldn't make any difference if he did. Guiltily, somewhere deep inside herself was an undeniable sense of release at knowing that she didn't have to go through with it, but it was far too soon to even acknowledge that feeling.

Right now she had to cope with the outcome of what she had done. Even if they were moments away from learning of it, she knew that all her parents' plans for tomorrow were in ruins. The wedding was to be a modest affair, but friends and acquaintances would have to be told; the vicar too – the entire day cancelled. Donald would be doubly humiliated by his two daughters' actions, and she simply didn't know how she was going to tell him. In the end, it was Freda who took the initiative, ordering Charlotte to sit down before her legs crumpled beneath her completely.

'What have you discovered?' Ruth burst out. 'There's obviously something to tell us, and if it's bad news, please let us know at once.'

They both realized too late that their appearance had made Ruth fear the worst about Josie, and Charlotte felt aghast to realize that for the last ten minutes she had given no thought to her sister at all. But this was her problem, not Freda's, and before her cousin began to speak, she broke in quickly.

'It's not about Josie, Mum,' she said, still in that thick choked voice. 'We haven't found out anything, and the fair has already gone from Braydon to wherever it's going next; but there's something else I've got to tell you.'

'Not more trouble?' Donald grated.

'It rather depends on how you look at it,' Charlotte said, with something like hysteria welling up inside her. She didn't know whether she felt like laughing or crying, or whether she even had the option, since she seemed to have lost control of her emotions. She felt Freda's firm hand on her shoulder and glanced up at her cousin, letting her continue.

'Charlotte's done a very brave thing, Donald, and it's not something that many young girls would do on the eve of their wedding.'

'What the devil are you talking about, woman?' he said angrily.

'I've called off the wedding, Dad,' Charlotte babbled, knowing she couldn't let Freda do this for her. 'We've been to the smithy and I've seen Melvin and told him I don't want to marry him, whether or not Josie comes back in time. We had the most awful row, and I know I've upset everything, but I won't change my mind. I don't want to marry him, now or ever.'

She turned and ran out of the kitchen and up the stairs to her bedroom, unable to face her parents a second longer. She fell on to her bed and sobbed uncontrollably. She had meant every word, but that didn't mean she wasn't distraught about it. She had loved Melvin for so long, and she couldn't even pinpoint the moment when she had begun to fall out of love with him. But she knew it would be a sin to promise to love, honour and obey a man for whom she had no true feelings any more.

A short while later she heard the click of her door handle, and then Ruth came swiftly across the room to her and sat down on the bed with her arm around her daughter's heaving shoulders.

'My poor darling,' she said softly. 'This is a terrible time for you.'

'I'm so sorry, Mum,' Charlotte said, muffled into her pillow. 'Maybe if Josie hadn't been missing, it would never have come to this. She always said I was making a mistake, but I wouldn't believe her. I know she was right, though, and I'm just sorry it has taken this to make me realize it.'

'Charlie, if you're sure about the way you feel, then it's far better for you to know it now, because there would be no turning back once you were married. I can't say that your timing is perfect, but I would never wish any of my girls to marry a man they didn't truly love.'

Charlotte sat up and looked at her mother with red-rimmed eyes. 'But Dad must be so angry and ashamed of me.'

Ruth gave the ghost of a smile. 'Your father has had enough setbacks in his life to be able to deal with this one. If you're quite certain about this, then we have a lot of work to do before tomorrow, and at least it will take his mind off Josie for a while. Go and wash your face and then we'll decide how to go about things.'

Charlotte hugged her mother, praying that her father was going to be so understanding, and knowing she might as well be wishing for the moon.

But by the time they went back downstairs, Freda had clearly told him all that had happened at the smithy. Their faces were so set that Charlotte wondered what her blunt-speaking cousin had also told him about his strict paternal ways. When he spoke it was in a gruff monotone.

'Are you so afraid of me that you can't even look at me, Charlotte?'

'I know I've shamed you, Dad. You've been so good about my marrying Melvin even though you didn't care for him, and now I've spoiled everything.'

He grunted. 'Well, he was never my ideal choice for a son-in-law, but if he was your choice for a husband, I wouldn't have stood in your way. Now that you've seen sense, I can hardly say I'm sorry that I don't have to go through the farce of giving you away to that oaf.'

She gave a small cry and flew into his arms. It was so much more than she had expected and relief flooded through her.

They still had to face so many people, but this was the worst moment, and it was over. Donald's rare bout of understanding and not condemning her must be an omen, she thought tremulously. Clover would certainly have thought so, since she'd set a lot of store by such things. The next thing to happen would be that Josie would return, contrite as ever. But with Charlotte's decision, their father would surely be able to overlook Josie's foolishness.

Charlotte held on to that thought when the family went into the guests' sitting room in force to tell Aunt Mary and the regulars that there was going to be no wedding tomorrow. Once the first shock was over, Ruth set about making lists and strategies for informing everyone as quickly as possible, and to word it all with as little fuss as possible. The vicar had to be first, of course . . .

Into all of this activity Milly came whirling home from school in the middle of the afternoon, having been let out early on account of the big day tomorrow. She kicked off her shoes and threw down her satchel, announcing as she did so that the newspaper chap was here and that Charlie had said it was all right for him to call.

Before Donald could make the expected reply that this definitely wasn't a good time for anyone to call, Steve had already followed Milly inside the hotel and he could see by their tense and anxious faces that something was seriously wrong.

Ten

'I'm sorry if this is a bad time, and I can always come back later if you prefer,' Steve said. He hesitated, but he couldn't ignore the fact that Charlotte's face looked red and tearful and nothing like the blushing bride she should be. 'Forgive me for asking, but has something happened?'

'If it has, it's a family affair, and nothing that concerns outsiders,' Donald said curtly.

He was being unusually rude and, like everyone else, Milly was silent for once, knowing that something was wrong but not yet knowing what. She moved to her mother's side and put her small hand in Ruth's.

Charlotte broke into the silence, her voice tight. 'I think he should know. He's come here for details about the wedding, so he might as well know that there isn't going to be one.'

'What?' Steve said, startled. 'I'm sorry, but I don't understand. Only this morning when we met . . .'

She gave a brittle laugh. 'Oh yes, this morning. I was checking on the flowers at the florist, wasn't I? Well, we won't be needing those now, either. Add that to your list of things to cancel, please, Mum.'

'Charlotte dear, please don't get upset,' Ruth said uneasily.

She turned on her mother. 'What would you expect me to be? I know I made the decision, and I'm going to stick by it, but that doesn't mean I'm not upset about it. And aren't you all forgetting the other little thing that's happened?'

Milly leaned heavily against her mother. She didn't like what was going on here. She didn't know what had happened, but everyone was looking as unhappy as they had done when her gran had died, and as worried as when the hotel had been in danger of collapsing after the storm. It had frightened her then and it was frightening her now.

Steve turned away from Charlotte, finding it hard to resist the urge to take her in his arms and console her. He knew it would be the very worst thing he could do right now, but he couldn't deny that he felt a rush of relief at whatever had gone on between her and the oafish Melvin Philpott to break up their marriage plans, even if they were only postponed. He did his best to smother those feelings, and spoke directly to Donald.

'Mr Elkins, I'm here to help if I can. This has clearly been a traumatic day for you all, and I assure you that whatever you tell me won't go beyond these four walls. I might be a reporter, but I'm not inhuman.'

He saw Ruth give her husband a small nod.

'Josie's gone missing,' Donald said starkly. 'She didn't come

104

home last night and we don't know where she is. We're hoping and praying that she didn't go off with one of these fairground people she'd taken such a shine to.'

They had almost forgotten Milly was there until she gasped. 'You don't think she's gone away with that Tony, do you?'

'What the dickens do you know about it?' her father snapped.

Milly's face went a deep red. 'She writes things in her diary.'

'Oh, Milly,' Ruth said sorrowfully.

Donald raised his hand. 'Never mind "Oh, Milly". And for now we'll overlook the fact that you did wrong to snoop into your sister's property, young lady. Where is this diary?'

'I don't know! She puts it in different places.'

Seeing that the child was about to burst into tears, Steve took control.

'Mr Elkins, has anyone checked to see if Josie took any extra clothes with her? It may help to decide whether she chose to stay away last night, or even longer. Or whether she didn't.'

'Are you implying that she may not have stayed out all night of her own free will, Mr Bailey?' Ruth said nervously.

'I don't mean to alarm you, ma'am, but in my job we come across all kinds of eventualities, and I think you should look for the obvious before you take things any further.'

'Before we inform the police, you mean,' Donald stated.

Milly began to sob. 'Is Josie dead?'

'Of course not,' Charlotte said swiftly, alarmed at the sinister turn it was all taking now. 'But Steve is right, and we should have thought of it before. Milly, you can come and help me look in Josie's bedroom to see if any of her clothes are missing, and tell me where you last saw her diary.'

'I didn't mean to look at it!'

Charlotte tried to boost Milly's flagging spirits. 'Never mind that now. It's important that we find it, and you could be the only one to give us some clues.'

She glanced back at Steve as she and Milly left the room and went upstairs. She was enormously thankful that he was here, since he was the only one whose emotions weren't involved, and the only one to help keep them all sane. It might be what her father had called a family affair, but sometimes an outsider was the best one to see things clearly. But her father's mention of informing the police gave her a great jolt. She supposed it would have to be done . . . but she still couldn't believe that Josie had been so heartless as to go off like this, and that only led her to a more alarming conclusion.

She and Milly were upstairs when they heard a new commotion downstairs.

'Do you think Josie's come back?' Milly said joyfully.

The next minute they heard Melvin's voice bellowing up the stairs, and Donald trying to remonstrate with him.

'I want to talk to you, Charlotte,' Melvin roared. 'If you don't come down I'm coming up, no matter what anybody says.'

'Over my dead body!' Donald snapped. 'Just remember where you are, young man, and if you can't keep a civil tongue in your head, I'll have the police on you.'

'It's all right, Dad,' Charlotte said in a shaky voice from the top of the stairs. 'Come into the small sitting room, Melvin, and say what you've come to say.'

'What the bloody hell do you think I've come to say?' he said, beginning to bluster. 'We're due to be married shortly, and you're telling me the whole thing's off just because your stupid sister's run off. Good riddance to her, I say.'

The blow at the side of his head spun him round before he had a chance to see who had struck him. Charlotte gasped, and came running down the stairs, but not before she had seen the glint of satisfaction in her father's eyes at the way Steve Bailey had moved so swiftly. From the guests' sitting room they could all hear the excited twittering of Aunt Mary and the regulars at what was going on, but that was no one's concern right now.

Steve still held Melvin by the scruff of his neck. 'You'd better apologize for that insensitive remark, you bastard, before I throw you out of here,' he snapped.

'What the devil gives you the right to tell me what to do?'

'I do,' Charlotte said, coming right down now. 'I told you there'll be no wedding, Melvin, not now or ever. Josie is just fine, and this had nothing to do with her,' she lied, 'and Steve is here as a friend of the family.'

'A friend of the family, is he?' Melvin sneered. 'I reckon

from the looks of the two of you, he's already more than that. It's not only your sister who's the flighty one, is it, sweetheart?'

Without another word, both Steve and Donald had grabbed hold of him, lifted him off the ground and removed him bodily from the hotel.

'One more word,' Donald grated, 'and you'll be hearing from my solicitor for defamation of character. Charlotte has made her wishes clear and I would advise you to go home and salvage what little dignity you have.'

'And I'll have her for breach of promise,' Melvin shouted back before the door slammed after him.

Charlotte slumped against her father. 'Dear God, do you think he'll do that?'

Donald snorted. 'I do not. His sort wouldn't want it bandied about in public that he was jilted. Now let's forget him and set about what we need to do to get people alerted about the change of plans.'

It was a poor way of referring to this terrible day, but Charlotte knew it was his way of dealing with it, and for the briefest time it kept their minds occupied with something other than Josie. She'd known instinctively it was best to lie about Josie being fine, otherwise who knew what gossip Melvin might have spread? But Steve was part of it by now, and volunteered to inform the police that a girl was missing. Once he had gone, they could get down to other urgent business.

The telephone was a godsend now, and even if it was hardly the height of etiquette to use it to inform the vicar, the florist and other folk that the wedding was off, it was the quickest and least traumatic way to do it, and between them Donald and Ruth saw to it all.

It was less easy to explain to Aunt Mary and the regulars, and even less so to Milly, just why the wedding had been cancelled. Milly was still upset at the hurtful things Melvin had said about her two sisters and was being comforted by Freda.

'Don't you love Melvin any more, then?' she whispered to Charlotte.

'Not enough to marry him, darling. I know you'll be finding it hard to understand—'

'Well, I wouldn't want to live with a smelly bloke like him, either, nor his smelly old dad,' she said, her voice suddenly vicious.

Charlotte and Freda exchanged small smiles. Perhaps Milly wouldn't be as upset as they had thought she would. Not about the wedding, anyway.

'So where's Josie?' she went on, as if she could read their thoughts. 'Has she really gone off with Tony?'

'We don't know. That's what we have to find out,' Charlotte said. 'If she has, I'm sure she'll be back soon. She won't want to stay away for ever.'

Just until the wedding day had come and gone, perhaps, Charlotte thought with sudden clarity. If that was the case, Josie had a funny way of trying to force her sister's hand, but it had worked, she thought, with a small sob in her throat. It had definitely worked. She took a deep breath.

'Let's look on the bright side,' she said, to the group of miserable faces around her. 'Mum and Ruth have been baking all morning, and we're going to have a real feast of things to eat for the next week!'

The Misses Green sniffed back their tears and nodded simultaneously. 'You did such a brave thing in cancelling your marriage, Charlotte. There could be nothing worse on earth than being married to a man you didn't love and having to live a lie.'

The Captain cleared his throat as usual and patted her hand. 'We're all very proud of you, my dear, and once young Josie comes home we should make it a bit of a party with all that lovely food that's been prepared – if you don't think it's too presumptuous of me to suggest it.'

'Not at all, Captain,' Charlotte said, tears stabbing her eyes. 'That's exactly what we'll do, and thank you all for being so understanding.'

It wasn't really Steve Bailey's place to inform the police of Josie Elkins' disappearance, and since it was less than twenty-four hours since she had gone missing, he assured the sergeant that the family was anxious not to make it sound like a full-scale alarm.

'Bit out of your way to come here on their behalf, isn't it,

Bailey? Or are you angling for another bit of gossip for that scandal rag of yours?'

'This is a private matter,' Steve replied coolly. 'I'm acting as a friend of the family and not as a reporter, and I'll ask you to keep this news under your hat for the present. Mr Elkins wanted to alert you in case any action needs to be taken, and he'd like a word with you this evening. You'll understand why he doesn't want to leave the hotel himself, in case his daughter is trying to contact him by telephone.'

He elaborated the reasons, since the cancellation of the wedding wasn't the sergeant's business, but if Josie hadn't returned by then, she would have been gone far too long for comfort, Steve thought grimly.

'All right, I'll call around about seven and see what the situation is then.'

'Make it eight,' Steve said, not caring for the man's attitude, and knowing it would change pretty quickly if anything bad had happened to Josie. He tried not to think about that as he left the police station and hesitated, wondering whether to go back to the Phoenix or go home.

He chose home, knowing he had to feed Rex and take him for a walk, but his footsteps inevitably took him back to the seafront. He didn't expect to see Charlotte, nor anyone else, and he deliberately kept well away from the hotel, lest they should think he was snooping. He couldn't stop wondering what was going on inside that hotel now, though, and although he ached for Charlotte, he couldn't deny his joy that she wasn't going to marry the smithy after all. This wasn't the time to tell her how he felt, but he had a feeling that she knew anyway, and he had to settle for that for now.

The police sergeant turned up at the Phoenix promptly at eight o'clock that evening. By then, the atmosphere inside had changed. The first shock of Charlotte's decision was over, and everyone had been frantically busy in informing the people who should be told. Milly had wanted to race along to her friend Dorothy's house to tell her the news, but she had been prevented from dramatizing the situation any further by being allowed to speak briefly to Dorothy on the telephone while her mother supervised the conversation.

109

'Come into the sitting room, Sergeant,' Donald told the man. 'We've got trouble enough here, and it's best that it's discussed between us and my wife first, though no doubt you'll want to speak to more of my family in a little while.'

Not too sure what this was really all about yet, Sergeant Hawkins followed him into the small sitting room, where Ruth nodded briefly. She was pale and upset, the sergeant noted, and Elkins looked fit to explode.

'I understand from Mr Steven Bailey that your daughter has been missing for a while, sir?' he said, since neither of them seemed to know where to begin. 'I trust it's not the bride who has taken herself off?' he added, in order to inject a bit of levity into the room. He knew at once it had been a big mistake, cursing himself for fitting so neatly into his policeman's size ten clodhoppers.

'My daughter is no longer getting married, but she is not the reason you're here,' Donald snapped. 'It's our second daughter, Josie, and we have reason to believe she may have gone off with the fairground people.'

Normally the sergeant would have sent a constable to deal with a missing-person enquiry initially, but the Elkins were important people in the town. Even so, Hawkins didn't have much love for the hotel owner and his superior manner, but he managed to resist a low whistle now. The poor buggers, he thought, as if they hadn't had enough to deal with recently, what with the collapse of the old hotel and the grandmother's cuckoo behaviour before she'd died.

'Have you any grounds for believing such a thing?' he asked cautiously.

Donald gave a heavy sigh. He hated airing his family business in public, and it had become all too frequent in recent times. He quickly related what Charlotte, Freda and Milly had told him of Josie's activities, and he smarted at having to reveal his daughter's deceit.

'May I see these other people to confirm what you've told me?'

He saw Ruth put her hand on her husband's arm, as if to ward off another explosion. Damn it, he wasn't implying that he didn't believe the man, Hawkins thought irritably; it was procedure, that was all. Elkins nodded and strode off to fetch Charlotte and Freda.

'My daughter Milly is only a child,' he said. 'These two will give you all the corroboration you need of what I've already told you.'

The discussion was swift, with the sergeant jotting down everything in his notebook, including the tearful state of the two women. Like most folk in the town he knew the older one was due to be marrying the smith tomorrow; he concluded that this cancellation was due to the other one's disappearance, and he chose not to put questions in that direction. But by now, his face was grave.

'We don't often deal in cases of this kind, Mr Elkins' – he kept his gaze away from the women – 'but there are clearly several possibilities here. Your daughter has either gone away of her own accord, in which case you may ask why she hasn't contacted you or left a note. Or she has been abducted by persons or persons unknown – or even by someone known to her, since you seem to be aware of the identity of this fairground man,' he added. 'The thing is, what do we do next?'

'Well, that's what you're here for, man!' Donald snapped.

'I was told you didn't want to make it sound like a full-scale alarm,' he said, repeating Steve's words.

'That was hours ago, and Josie's still missing.'

'Sergeant, we just want her brought home safe and well,' Ruth put in, speaking for the first time. 'Whatever you have to do to find her, please do it.'

He stood up. 'If you give me a full description and any photographs you have of the girl, I'll see that bulletins are sent out this evening to a wide local area. The fair usually follows a regular pattern and we'll contact the police in those towns first. Don't worry, ma'am, if that's where she's gone, we'll get her back for you.'

'And if she hasn't?' Donald said.

The sergeant shrugged. He didn't intend to say in front of the womenfolk that they'd be searching the coastline and the lanes and ditches next, but that was what it usually entailed, he thought grimly.

'I'll be in touch just as soon as there's any news, and meanwhile if she contacts you, please let us know.'

*   *   *

111

Once the fairground wagons had finally stopped, Josie rose stiffly from the bed at the back of the caravan. She felt sick and ill from the unaccustomed motion. She hadn't seen anything of Tony, who had been driving the towing vehicle all this time, but now she could hear the shouts of the men and women outside as they began to leave their caravans in preparation to set up their stalls and rides in the next town they were visiting.

Everything was alien to Josie. She didn't want to go outside. She felt dirty and unkempt. She hadn't washed or combed her hair since she had left home, what seemed like a lifetime ago now. She smothered a sob in her throat, remembering that this would have been Charlotte's wedding day.

Perhaps it still was. Perhaps her sister had decided to go ahead with her wedding after all, and Josie's disappearance hadn't put a stop to it. This would all have been for nothing then. She sobbed again, knowing she was deluding herself if she thought that was the only reason she had left home, because of course it wasn't. It had been to be with Tony, for the thrill and excitement she felt whenever she thought of him.

She didn't feel like that about him now. He had done things to her she hadn't wanted, and she knew to her bitter shame that she was as much to blame for it as he was. She was a bad girl, and nobody would want her now. Her family certainly wouldn't, and every time she pictured her mother's face she wanted to weep.

The caravan door was suddenly wrenched open and Tony came inside. 'You're awake then,' he said cautiously. 'Well, you'd better get back beneath the covers and pretend to be asleep, because we've got cops swarming all over the place looking for you.'

'*What?*' Josie rammed her fist into her mouth in a fright.

'Don't worry, I won't let them in here. Do as I say and get back to bed. If anybody asks, you're my sister and you've got mumps, all right? No blokes will come near you for fear of catching it, and my mates will back me up, so all you've got to do is keep your mouth shut.'

For a moment, Josie felt like shrieking that she didn't want to tell any more lies and she just wanted to go home, but through the window she caught sight of several blue uniforms roaming about between the vehicles and she simply took fright and dived back beneath the bedcovers.

By the time Tony came back he looked relieved, saying the cops had believed his story. He told her she was a good girl and that he was going to cook her that hot breakfast now. She thought it would probably choke her, but she also realized how long it was since she had eaten properly, and that her stomach was gnawing.

'Here,' he said, tossing her a colourful garment. 'One of the women said you can have this to wear. When you've eaten, you can wash and change while I get on with setting up the dodgems for tonight. We always get a good crowd here.'

She couldn't believe he could talk so calmly, or that he didn't realize what a nervous state she was in.

'I don't want to wear that old thing,' she said, eyeing the dress fastidiously.

Tony's eyes flashed. 'You asked to stay, and if you don't want to walk about in the state you're in, you'd better not be so bloody fussy.'

'Do you think I'm going outside to be gawped at, and to have everybody knowing I'm here with you?' she almost wept. She felt humiliated, and all she wanted was to be back where she belonged.

He spoke shortly. 'I told you I'd see that you got home again. Once the cops have left the site I'll take you to the bus stop, if that's what you want.'

She didn't have the faintest idea where they were now, but it registered that it must be in a reasonably sized town if there was a bus going back to Braydon.

'We're on the outskirts of Minehead,' he said, reading her mind. 'We're only here for three days, working afternoons and evenings, and then we go further south, so you can either stay until we move on again or go today.'

She felt sick. Where was the dashing bloke she had always thought him to be? He had been so tender and loving on that first night . . . It seemed ages ago, and she felt that she had grown up so much in that time.

As if realizing just how distressed she still was, he reached

113

out and put a hand on her shoulder, and she flinched back with a little cry as he did so.

'Christ, Josie, I'm not going to hurt you. I'm not a monster! Look, do as I say and get back to bed. I'll cook us both a good breakfast in a little while and you'll be feeling as right as rain.'

She doubted that she would ever feel right again, but if she didn't want to be hauled out of here by the police and become even more humiliated, she knew she had to do as he said. When he left her she burrowed beneath the bedcovers and prepared to wait it out. A short while later she heard the caravan door open again and Tony speaking to someone who she presumed was a policeman, and then they went away again. His story of his sister with the mumps had evidently satisfied them. She seemed to slump into the bed, knowing she was living a lie now and that things were going from bad to worse. She longed for her mother, for home and normality – had never realized before how important it was.

'Feeling better now?' Tony asked her an hour later.

The police had left the site, she had been given a mug of strong tea, and the caravan was filled with the succulent smells of fried bacon and mushrooms. While she was on her own she had washed, resisting the urge to scrub herself where he had touched her, knowing it would only make the soreness worse, and she had tentatively changed into the dress he had brought her, accepting that it was clean if hardly to her taste in clothes.

She accepted the plate of food, dipping a hunk of bread into the bacon fat and eating ravenously. She felt a mite more human once her stomach was full.

'So what's it to be?' he asked her. 'Do you want to go today, or do you fancy a couple more days here? It's up to you.'

She was suddenly aware that he couldn't hide the hot, lusty look in his eyes, any more than she could resist responding to it. She was weak, and stupid, but the wickedness had already been done, and she was no longer the girl she was when she'd first come to his caravan. She had ruined her sister's wedding day, and it might be wiser to give her family a few more days to let things settle down. So what harm could a couple more days do?

114

'If I stay,' she said hesitantly, 'do you promise to let me go before you move on from Minehead?'

'Of course. I didn't kidnap you, did I?' he said, hiding his relief that she wasn't going to be a clinger as he had half-feared. She was a sweet kid, but he liked his freedom too much to want her around permanently. Besides, for a while now he'd been thinking of selling the ride and the outfit altogether and moving to Ireland, where he could be a real king of the road without having to kowtow to idiot yokels.

Eleven

Tony wasn't going to tell Josie or anyone else of his plans. The fewer people who knew of them, the fewer could track him down if he wanted to melt into the land and just disappear, which was something that had always appealed to his Romany nature. While his father had been alive it couldn't be done, but now he had the whole world ahead of him to choose from. Meanwhile, there was Josie Elkins, and he wasn't going to waste the opportunity of having her here.

'I'd suggest that you could help me on the ride, sweetheart, but it's probably not a good idea in case the cops decide to put in another appearance any time,' he said, almost ruefully.

She flushed at his use of the word 'sweetheart'. It reminded her of how often she had thought of him during the year before the fair's arrival, and how much she had dreamed of his kisses, and more . . .

'I think it's far better if I stay inside,' she stammered. 'If you want to show me where everything is, I could cook us a meal sometime.' She didn't have much experience at cooking, but she was willing to try.

'There's no need. I can do all that, or I'll get fish and chips from the town,' he said with a smile, with no intention of starting a more domestic arrangement. 'There are some books in the cupboard and a pack of cards, and when we close down tonight we can go for a walk. You'll need to get some exercise.'

And later, there would be a different kind of exercise, he thought, feeling the familiar surge of pleasure in his loins. She would know what to expect now. It wouldn't be the first time, and he would teach her to enjoy it.

He left the caravan, and since Josie had nothing else to do, she opened the cupboard and was surprised to find such a collection of books inside. She had never taken him for a reader, but there were lots of map books and several classics as well as some cheap rubbish, enough to keep her absorbed.

She also found it interesting enough to be behind the net curtains in the caravan and watch the comings and goings of the fairground people. She could see them, but they couldn't see her, and she felt as if she was in a secret little world of her own. She could shut them all out, while all the time she was desperately trying to shut out that other world as well, the one she had left behind. Despite herself, she kept looking at Tony's clock and as the time for Charlotte's wedding approached, she couldn't stop herself imagining what should be happening at home right now.

She would be helping Charlie into the lovely white wedding dress and arranging her hair for her and handing her the bouquet of roses. When her mother saw Charlie in all her finery, with Josie and Milly dressed up to the nines as well, she would be hiding a few tears and her father would be clearing his throat every bit as noisily as the Captain. Freda would have got all soft and soppy and so would the Misses Green, while Aunt Mary would probably still be her stolid, no-nonsense self.

'Stop it,' Josie told herself angrily, as her eyes filled with tears. 'It's too late now to change anything, and if Charlie's gone ahead without me there, good luck to her; but I hope and pray that she hasn't married that oaf. If I've saved her from that, then it will all have been worth it.'

She gulped. Talking to yourself was supposed to be the first sign of madness, wasn't it? If that was the case, then her grandmother Clover must have been totally mad. But so she was, according to everyone except those who'd loved her. Josie swallowed, knowing the full truth of that old saying that she had made her bed and now she must lie in it.

But not for long, she thought slowly, knowing at last that she could never live like this, in this cramped and claustrophobic atmosphere. If it had taken this madness to show her that, then perhaps Tony had done her a favour after all. She knew she was clutching at anything to defend what she had done. In an attempt to blot out everything she tried to interest herself in the map books and tracing how far they had travelled.

It wasn't such a great distance on one of the larger maps, but on one of the Ordnance Survey maps it seemed a very long way from Braydon to Minehead. Even so, it wasn't as far as she had come emotionally and physically, Josie thought, trying hard to smother the guilt that kept washing over her.

Tony came back to see how she was from time to time, and each time the door opened she leapt back in panic. He made her strong tea and brought her biscuits, and he was being kind and considerate, she told herself desperately. She couldn't blame him for thinking she had come here for the same purpose as he had in mind. He couldn't have known she was so inexperienced, and by the end of the day she was blaming herself for everything.

By the time the fair had ended for the night and the raucous, tinny music had stopped, they went for a walk in the sweet summer evening air and she breathed in deeply, knowing that whatever had gone on at home now, Charlie's future had been decided. There was nothing she could do to change it, and she might as well make the best of these few days and nights she was going to share with Tony. After that, she had the strongest feeling that she would never want to see him again – but that was something she wasn't prepared to acknowledge just yet.

'This little adventure isn't so bad, is it, love?' he said softly, his arm around her as they walked close together in the moonlight.

'Is that what this is then – a little adventure?'

He gave a throaty laugh. 'Well, it's what you wanted, isn't it? A bit of excitement? It's what we both wanted.'

She couldn't deny it. Nor could she deny that he had given her all the excitement she had ever dreamed about. She remembered the heady sensations when she had drunk the sweet, seductive cider, and then dancing and floating in his arms, and she remembered the way she had yearned to grow up so that he would no longer see her as a child visiting the fair year after year. Oh yes, how could she deny that she had wanted an adventure? She was so very much Clover's granddaughter.

'We should go back now,' he said. 'I don't want you getting cold.'

As they turned around, he twisted her into his arms and his mouth was cool on hers. It was the first time he had kissed her since he had almost devoured her with kisses on that first night. For a moment she tensed, and then she let herself relax in his arms as the familiar thrills began shooting through her at his touch.

'Don't hurt me,' she found herself whispering against his mouth.

'Nothing's going to hurt you, sweetheart. I only want to pleasure you,' he whispered back.

Ruth Elkins tapped on her daughter's bedroom door tentatively. Charlotte had been in there for so long now that everyone was getting alarmed. Eventually Donald had insisted that his wife should take her a cup of strong sweet tea and ask her if she needed the doctor.

'Of course I don't need the doctor,' Charlotte replied sharply. 'I'm not ill, Mum, but I know I've upset everyone terribly by doing what I did, and on top of Josie – well, I'm so, so sorry.'

Ruth walked across the room swiftly to where her daughter was sitting at her dressing table. She put down the cup of tea so that she could put her arms around Charlotte for a moment, knowing that any more would probably finish her.

'Darling, you did what you felt you had to do, and none of us is condemning you for it. I've already told you that, and you have to believe it. I'm not pretending that there won't be gossip in the town, but we can rise above that. We've done so before, haven't we?'

Charlotte nodded.

'So please come downstairs and have some food. I don't know what you've been doing up here all this time on your own, but I'm sure it's not good for you.'

'As a matter of fact it is good for me. I've been reading.'

Ruth looked at her in surprise. It wasn't the answer she had expected to hear. It sounded far too normal, when the girl should have been in a state of distress. But seeing the dark puffy shadows beneath Charlotte's eyes, she knew she had been too hasty in thinking that she wasn't suffering.

'Before you think I've become heartless, Mum, Milly discovered Josie's diary and gave it to me. I know you'll say it was the wrong thing to do, but that's what I've been reading, and it tells me so much about Josie that I never even knew. Or rather, that I didn't take the trouble to find out. She's not a child any more, and none of us ever gave her the benefit of recognizing that.'

Ruth bit her lip. 'Well, I know I should be cross with you for reading her diary, but in the circumstances, if it tells us anything of her plans, I think you did the only thing you could, darling.'

'It doesn't tell us much about that,' Charlie admitted. 'But it does reveal how deeply she felt about Tony, and how much she hated the thought of me marrying Melvin. You know how dramatic she could be,' she said, with the ghost of a smile, 'and she says in here that I'd be selling my soul to the devil if I married him. I can't help wondering if she went off with him just to stop me doing so.'

'Oh no, Charlie, she thinks far too much of you to ever do such a thing!' Ruth said, then paused as the possibility sank in and Charlotte went on almost feverishly.

'But what if she did? What if all this disappearing act was nothing more than that? It certainly had the desired effect, didn't it? It did stop me marrying Melvin and making the biggest mistake of my life. And Freda told us she was sneaking out to see Tony last night, so it is possible that she stayed with him and went off with the fair, isn't it? I know that Barbara was a fictitious friend, and I'm ashamed at having told you lies about her – but on the other hand Josie could be staying somewhere else, or hiding out somewhere quite near. It could all be far more innocent than thinking she's gone off with this Tony!'

She desperately wanted it to be true. She didn't want anything bad to happen to Josie, and she knew just how seductive a sweet-talking boy could be. She knew it from her own experience with Melvin, which she bitterly regretted now, but she thanked her lucky stars it had never gone too far.

'If that's what you truly think, then we should repeat all this to your father,' Ruth said. 'I don't think for a moment he'd agree to calling off a police search and giving Josie another day or so to contact us, but I suppose you could just be right.'

'I think we should give her the benefit of the doubt. I want to believe that she was doing this for my sake, to save me from marrying Melvin, however misguided it might have been. Lord knows she tried to tell me often enough that he was wrong for me, and I would never listen.'

'And do you truly believe you've made the right decision now?'

'I know I have.'

'Then leave the diary here and let's go and talk to your father. I don't think it's right that either of her parents should read it, and when she returns I shall strongly advise her to burn it. In fact I shall insist on it.'

Charlotte noticed the deliberate way she used the present tense. But of course Josie would return, and soon. Neither of them would consider any other possibility.

On Sunday morning Freda took her mother back to their farm, and returned in the evening, doggedly digging in her heels and prepared to stay until Josie turned up, saying that her mother could manage perfectly well with the help of local farmhands. Lord knew how that old jalopy didn't fall apart over the rough Exmoor ground, Donald told Ruth, but they were all glad of Freda's presence. While they had her and the regulars to cater for, they had to show a reasonably bright front. And at the end of next week they would have new guests to think about.

All that came to an end when the police sergeant turned up again with a constable very late that night. The family had all gone to bed, and thankfully Ruth had taken a sleeping pill and hadn't woken. But the minute Donald came downstairs and opened the door he could see that something was wrong. For a start, the sergeant wasn't bringing his daughter.

'What is it, man?' he said hoarsely.

'Can we come inside, please, sir?' Sergeant Hawkins said briefly.

They went into the kitchen and the sergeant motioned Donald to sit down.

'Tell me at once what you've come to say, for God's sake,' Donald said harshly. 'If it's bad news, don't pussyfoot around it like an old woman.'

The sergeant bristled and then remembered the man's anxiety. 'Mr Elkins, a young woman's body has been found in one of the Somerset rhines several miles from here. At this point, we've no reason to believe it's your daughter, but the physical description is not dissimilar. I'm afraid I have no option but to ask you to accompany us to identify her.'

They heard a cry from upstairs, and looked up to see Charlotte gripping the banister. Donald told her harshly to go back to bed and not to disturb the others. She came down in a rush, pulling her dressing gown around her tightly.

'I'm going with you, Dad. You can't do this alone, and besides, if it's Josie, I want to see for myself. I can't bear to wait here now, not knowing.'

'It's probably best if the young lady does come with you, sir. It will be a shock either way,' the sergeant said quietly.

Donald looked undecided for a moment and then nodded. 'We'll be dressed in a moment,' he said, and Charlotte knew she had his consent.

Ten minutes later they were being driven away in the police car to some unknown place. Everything seemed unreal, and neither of them could really believe that they were being taken to view a girl's body that may or may not be Josie. They sat close together in the back of the car, their hands clasped.

'I keep praying that it's not her, Dad,' Charlotte said, through chattering lips. 'And if it's not, then when she comes home, I shall forgive her anything, and so must you. All we want is for her come home safely, isn't it?'

He didn't answer. He just sat there with his head bowed, and she couldn't tell what his feelings were. But they must surely be as agonized as hers. So short a time ago he'd been raving about Josie's tardiness, and now all they wanted was to be assured that she was alive and well. If the body they were about to see wasn't Josie's, then they still had hope.

Charlotte had to fight down the hysteria that she could even be thinking in those terms. But there must have been some substance in the police bringing them here, some likeness to Josie's description, and she was so very afraid now. The car stopped and they were taken inside a darkened building, their hearts thudding painfully. An elderly man in a white coat asked them to follow him into a small room. A sheet covered a shape on a table that could only have been a body. The room was very cold, and Charlotte clutched her father's hand as the man motioned them to come forward, then gently lifted the sheet from the young woman's face. As they gazed down at the glacial features in horror for a moment Charlotte felt guilty relief flooding through her so fast it was a sharp physical pain.

'Is this your daughter, sir?' the man asked Donald quietly.

He shook his head, unable to speak, and Charlotte took control.

'It's not my sister,' she gasped, fighting back the nausea.

He replaced the sheet over the young woman's face, and quickly ushered them into an ante-room, where they were offered a tot of brandy for their nerves, if they felt the need.

'I need fresh air more than brandy, man,' Donald grated. 'Let's just get out of here and go home.'

They found it difficult to speak on the drive back to Braydon, and once they arrived at the hotel, the police sergeant spoke apologetically.

'I'm sorry we had to put you and your daughter through that, Mr Elkins, but I'm afraid it was necessary. You'll also understand that I have to make a report about this young girl, and that it will go into the newspaper.'

'*Why*, for God's sake?'

Sergeant Hawkins spoke carefully. 'Whoever that young woman was, there will be people grieving over her, and needing to know what happened to her. You do see that, don't you, sir?'

Donald had to agree, however much he hated the thought of reading the details in the newspaper. But it had nothing to do with them, he thought thankfully. It would be some other poor family who would be crying over their daughter.

'You can leave us out of it, I take it?' he said gruffly.

'Of course, unless any other leads turn up. Your daughter is still missing.'

'Thank you for reminding me!' Did the plod think he didn't know that Josie was still missing? But he also realized what a sobering effect this night had had on him, and that it could just as easily have been his Josie lying under that white sheet.

As the sergeant opened the car door for him and Charlotte to get out, he spoke quickly before he changed his mind. 'Look, if you think it will be any help, you can mention that Josie has been gone from home for a couple of days, and that if anyone has news of her whereabouts we'd be grateful to hear it.'

'Are you sure? It'll mean that young Bailey reporting it, and it'll be all over the town in no time then.'

Donald gave a grimace. 'I know that, but I doubt that anything worse can happen to this family. Goodnight to you.'

He strode into the hotel, his head held high and with Charlotte still holding his arm. He tried to believe what he'd just said, but his stomach still turned to water every time he pictured that dead girl's parchment-like appearance.

They found Ruth and Freda in the kitchen, drinking cocoa, their faces tense.

'We heard you go out, and not even a sleeping pill could shut out the sound of that police car, Donald. Please tell us what's happened.'

'It's not Josie, love,' he said, going quickly to her side. 'The police found someone, but it wasn't her. I'm sure she's still safe.'

He glanced at Charlotte, knowing he would have to reveal everything that had happened, and also that he had consented to the news of Josie's disappearance being put in the newspaper, but he couldn't tell her now. Tomorrow morning would be soon enough for that, and Freda was already bustling around making more cups of cocoa, doing the ordinary domestic things to keep hands and minds busy.

Steve was at the hotel early the following morning. By then Donald had told his wife and cousin of the traumatic journey to the police morgue and that they must expect such things if

Josie didn't come home soon. They also knew now that there was to be a report in the paper, and they trusted Steve to report it as sensitively as possible. It didn't alter the fact, though, that a young girl had been left for dead in a ditch, and that it could have been Josie Elkins.

'So much for trying to keep it from Melvin,' Charlie said. 'Though I don't think even he would try to make capital out of this. He's not all bad.' She caught her father's sceptical look and gave a shaky laugh. 'Well, yes, he is, but we can only hope he doesn't go bragging that this is the only reason I stopped the wedding.'

'More likely he'll be saying he's glad he got out of being tied to such an unstable family, what with Clover and now Josie,' Donald said acerbically.

'I don't really care what he says any more,' Charlie told him, wishing she hadn't even brought up his name.

Steve cleared his throat. 'I've got the police report, Mr Elkins, and if I can just have a few words from you or Charlotte, I'll go back to the office and write up my piece for the paper. I'll bring it back for your approval this evening.'

'Stay and have some supper with us,' Ruth said without thinking. 'You're a part of all this now, Mr Bailey, and we can do with the company.'

'Well, thank you, if you're sure I'm not intruding,' he said, noting Donald's not-too-welcoming look at his wife's invitation.

'You're not,' Charlie told him. 'Mum's quite right. We can do with the company, and we can't sit here looking at one another with gloomy faces for ever. Please join us, Steve.'

When the evening was over, they all admitted that it had been better to have an outsider among them than surrendering to such dread in their hearts, and jumping every time the telephone rang, even though it was usually a query about a hotel booking. Normal life went on, despite all that was happening inside this small household. Not that any of them could truly consider Steve Bailey an outsider now. He had become a friend and support.

'You like that young man, don't you?' Freda asked Charlotte on Tuesday afternoon when she had offered to help in preparing the rooms for the new guests.

'We all do,' Charlotte replied.

'Yes, but you *really* like him, don't you, Charlie? Don't worry, I'm not a snitch unless circumstances make it necessary. I think he's very nice, and if that other chap's manners are anything to go by, I think you've definitely gone for the better choice.'

Charlotte straightened up from tucking in the bottom sheet and gave it a final tweak before she faced Freda with a small frown. 'Honestly, Freda, I haven't chosen anyone and it'll be a long time before I think of anyone in that way again.'

'Well, don't wait too long, dearie. Life has a habit of passing you by if you don't seize your chances when they come along.'

Before Charlie could ask what she meant by that remark, Milly, home from school, called out excitedly that there was a telephone call for Charlie. She groaned, wondering if it was Melvin about to give her more abuse. She was tempted not to answer it at all, and to tell Milly to put down the telephone without speaking. But where was the sense in that? If it was him, he would only try again. Thankfully both her parents had gone out to market for fresh fruit and vegetables, and couldn't overhear what she had to say to him. She went downstairs and was handed the receiver. Once she spoke, a man's voice she didn't recognize replied quickly.

'Josie will be home tomorrow.'

The line went dead and Charlie stared at the telephone in disbelief, her heart pounding, and wondering if she had actually heard those words at all. Just as quickly she wondered if the message was a true one or a cruel hoax and, even more, what she should do about it. She desperately wanted to tell someone, but she didn't want to raise false hopes if it wasn't true.

'Who was it?' Milly wanted to know, jumping up and down beside her.

'Nobody, and you're not to mention it to anyone, Milly. I'm going out for a while and if anybody asks, I've got an errand to do and I'll be back soon.'

She slipped out of the hotel before anyone noticed, and made straight for the newspaper office. There was only one person who could look at the situation dispassionately and that was Steve. He would know what to do. She found him in a small office which was in a state of total chaos, filled with newsprint, books and magazines and the smell of ink. Steve stood up at once when he saw her face.

'What's happened?' he said, steering her to a chair, from which he swept the papers on to the floor.

'Somebody phoned,' she said, her lips numb now. 'A man. I didn't recognize his voice. He said Josie would be home tomorrow. That was all, so how could I tell if it was true? I didn't know what to do or who to tell, so I've come straight here.'

He produced a small flask from a drawer and unscrewed the top. He pressed it to her lips and she tasted the bitterness of brandy coursing down her throat, making her choke.

'You came to the right place,' Steve said quietly. 'But we must go to the police with this information.'

'I can't! I haven't told my family yet.' Too late, she knew she should have waited for her father to come home. Donald wouldn't appreciate her having gone to Steve before him, and she didn't want to consider her reason for doing so.

'The police have got to be told, darling. They may be able to trace the call. In any case, let's be positive about this. If the message was true, then Josie will be home tomorrow.'

She realized he was chafing her cold hands. The day was warm, and yet she felt chilled inside. But he had called her 'darling' and that was the one tiny thread of warmth in her body right now.

'Let's tell my parents first,' she said huskily. 'I can't do this alone without them knowing what's happened.'

'All right,' Steve said, 'but you're not alone, Charlie. You do know that, don't you?'

Without warning, his lips brushed her cheek, and involuntarily she flinched slightly. It was too soon. He must know that. She had loved Melvin for a long time, even though she hadn't realized how slowly and surely she had been falling out of love with him. It took time to come to terms with that, and it wasn't even the most important thing on her mind right now. Josie was.

'I'm sorry, 'Steve said. 'Let's go and face your parents, and then I'm sure your father will want to go to the police.

126

Unfortunately the newspaper will be out this evening with the details we discussed last night, about finding that poor girl's body, and the fact that Josie is missing. It's too late to stop it. In any case, we don't know for sure whether your phone call was genuine or just a crank. I'm afraid these things do happen, Charlotte,' he added, seeing how her face had whitened.

Twelve

Tony Argetti had finally lost his nerve about having the girl in his caravan all this time. The fact that the cops had turned up at the fairground site did nothing to make him feel any easier about it. Josie was all right, but she had become a bit of a whiner, forever fretting now over what she was going to say to her parents when she went home. This also made Tony wary that she might change her mind and want to travel with him, and he had no intention of letting that happen.

He knew he was leaving her alone more than he should, but truth to tell he was getting tired of seeing her moping about, complaining that she didn't get enough fresh air, worrying about her sister, yet refusing to leave the caravan except with him late at night. He was already bored with her and, in his defence, he hadn't exactly begged her to come along. It had been her choice.

That was why, on Tuesday afternoon, he made the decision to telephone Charlotte, leaving the minimum of information and hoping it would reassure her family to know that Josie was safe and coming home the next day. It would ease her way, he told himself, and when his afternoon shift on the ride was over and he handed over to an assistant, he would tell her what he'd done.

He knew she would be pathetically grateful, and they'd have one final night's romp before he put her on the bus tomorrow morning. He'd already got the times of the few buses back to Braydon for her, and he'd be rid of her by ten o'clock the following morning. He was whistling cheerfully as usual when he went back to his caravan, ready for a cuppa and a hunk of bread and cheese to see him through the evening.

It was all quiet inside when he opened the door, and he assumed she was either curled up on the bed, sleeping or reading. He stood completely still for a moment, relishing the fact that, once she had gone, the caravan was going to be like this again. It took a moment to realize it was already empty. Perhaps she'd decided to take a walk after all, he thought uneasily, and immediately hoped the silly bitch wouldn't take fright if she came face to face with a copper.

It was then that he saw the note on the pillow. He read it quickly: 'Tony, I'm going home today. I've borrowed the bus money from the cupboard and I'll pay you back next year. Josie.'

He swore impatiently, knowing he needn't have made the bloody phone call at all now. Not a word of thanks for letting her come with him and the good times he'd shown her. Well, good riddance to her. He'd had his fill of her and it had been good while it lasted, but now he could put his long-held plan into action, put out feelers about selling his ride and his outfit and head for pastures new across the Irish Sea.

Josie had never felt so conspicuous as she did on the bus back to Braydon, nor so petrified at the reception she was going to get when she got home. It would be late afternoon by the time she got there, and although she had brushed her hair and made herself as tidy as she could, she still felt as if every eye was on her. She felt like a gypsy in the gaudy dress, especially with her bare legs, since her stockings had been torn and ruined on that first night with Tony. Just as she had been, she thought with a sob in her throat. Torn and ruined . . .

She was bitterly ashamed of it all now. She had hurt Charlotte and her parents, and for what? For a few stolen nights with a boy she didn't even like any more. It was tawdry and cheap, and she knew he had only been using her. The words of love on his lips hadn't meant a thing, only a means of getting her into bed with him. And she had fallen for it so easily, so shamefully.

A woman with two small children got on the bus at the next stop, and one of the children went to sit beside her and was quicky pulled away by her mother, adding to Josie's shame. It was as though everyone could see what she had done, what she had become.

'I won't bite,' she snapped at the mother, at which the woman tutted and commented to someone that these people shouldn't be allowed on public transport but should stay with their own kind.

Her eyes smarted. If her father could have heard it, he'd have been mortified. His own mother – Clover – had worn colourful garb and revelled in being thought an eccentric in the town, but no one had ever accused her of being little more than a gypsy.

Eventually the journey came to an end and she alighted from the bus in the centre of Braydon, wishing she didn't have to walk through the town to reach the seafront. But there was a taxi standing nearby and she went to it quickly.

'Will you take me to the Phoenix Hotel, please? Someone will pay my fare when we get there,' she said, as imperiously as she could.

The man looked as if he was going to refuse until she gave him her parents' names and stared him out. When he relented, she got inside gratefully, away from any curious eyes that might wonder why Josie Elkins was dressed in such a peculiar fashion.

It took only a few minutes for the taxi to take her home, and the driver stayed close beside her as she went inside, clearly determined to get his fare. She was shaking so much she could hardly put one foot in front of the other, and when she walked inside and saw her father behind the reception desk, her legs simply folded up beneath her and she collapsed in a heap.

When she came round she was bent double and for a moment couldn't think where she was. She seemed to be sitting down and someone was pressing her back very firmly. Her vision was obscured by a garish sort of material that she slowly realized was her dress. Beyond it were her feet and the linoleum of the entrance hall of the hotel. She struggled to sit upright and looked straight into her father's eyes.

'She's come round,' he said. 'Help me get her into the small sitting room.'

He took one of her arms and her mother took the other. She didn't seem to have the capacity to speak, and if she had, what could she have said?

'Give her a moment, Donald,' she heard her mother murmur.

'Here, Josie.' Someone thrust a glass of water into her hand, and she looked up to see Charlotte's anxious face with Milly hovering behind. And Freda too. She was still here then. Josie felt as if she had been away for weeks, instead of only a few days. She began shaking again, spilling the water over herself.

'I'm so sorry,' she wept. 'Oh Charlie, I'm so sorry.'

Her sister's arms went around her. 'It doesn't matter, Josie. Nothing matters except that you're home and you're safe,' Charlie said, just as tearfully.

'We'd better get her upstairs and into bed. She looks done in,' Ruth said decisively. 'There'll be time enough for explanations later.'

'The taxi driver—' Josie began.

'He's long gone,' her father said shortly. 'All right. Do as your mother says, young lady, and then we'll talk.'

She knew that tone of voice. Her mother and Charlotte might be glad to see her home safely, but her father wouldn't stand for any nonsense and would demand a full explanation. But there were some things he wasn't going to know. Some things she couldn't bear to tell him, or anyone.

Minutes later she was upstairs in her own room and curled up in her own bed, completely exhausted, and the others had gone downstairs and left her alone.

'What do you think, Donald?' Ruth said cautiously.

'I think I want a full explanation of what the girl's been up to,' he said angrily. 'I'm just as glad to see her back as any of you, but she has to know that this isn't the way I expect a daughter of mine to behave. We have a position in the town, and I'll not permit any more disgrace to come to this family.'

Charlotte felt her face redden. He might not be pointing a finger at her right then, but she knew she too had been the cause of a great upheaval during these past few days. Josie might have started it, but she had added to it by refusing to marry Melvin, now or ever. Her father hadn't wanted the wedding to take place, but it would have been a severe blow to his pride to have it cancelled in such a way. He couldn't help being a snob, but right now Charlie wished angrily that he would climb down off his pedestal now and then. Her voice was shrill when she spoke, hardly trusting herself to sound normal, when she too still felt anything but normal.

'Well, now that we're all happy to see Josie back, I'd better go and see Steve again and make sure he hasn't gone to the police yet about that phone call.'

'Stay here. If we have to have him involved, it's quicker to telephone him,' Donald snapped.

'Then I'll do it,' Charlie said.

Her father shrugged, seeing the glint in her eyes. Steve had been a good friend, and she had no intention of hearing her father's wrath spill over on to him.

Minutes later she was speaking to Steve on the telephone. It was the first time she had done so, and his voice was immediately close, intimate, concerned. She swallowed, and then said what she had to say. When she had finished, she turned to see Milly, round-eyed, behind her.

'Is Josie back for good now?'

'Of course she is, love,' Charlie said, pushing the caring sound of Steve Bailey's voice out of her mind – and the fact that the police would need to be informed that Josie was home, and would certainly want to come and question her soon.

'So are you going to marry Melvin after all, then?' Milly said, the two things obviously tied together in her mind.

'I'm not going to marry anybody. But listen, Milly, you do know that all this is private family business, don't you? Mum and Dad won't want it gossiped about, and you must promise not to talk to people about any of it.'

'I know – "It'll be bad for business,"' Milly said, mimicking him. 'Can't I even tell Dorothy that she's back?'

'Well yes, but not where she's been. All anyone needs to know is that she's just been on a little holiday because she wasn't well.'

It seemed the best solution, even though the police might want to probe further. But she hardly thought Josie was going to say exactly where she had been and with whom, and they couldn't force her . . . Before anyone else had a chance to talk to Josie she went to her sister's bedroom, where Josie was lying on the bed now in her old dressing gown, the garish dress thrown on the floor.

'You know you've been an idiot, don't you?' Charlie said matter-of-factly.

Tears rushed to Josie's eyes. 'I've been worse than that. I ruined your wedding, and I don't know if you're ever going to forgive me.'

'Well, I am, so you can forget any worries about that. I'm not going to marry Melvin, but I wish you hadn't gone to such extremes to make me do it, Josie.'

'I wish I hadn't, too,' Josie muttered. 'I've been such a fool, Charlie. I thought he loved me, and it was all so exciting – and then it was so awful. But how did you know where I'd gone?'

'Freda – and your diary, which Milly produced.'

'Oh God, don't tell me Mum read it.'

Although Charlie could see how much distress she was in now, she spoke briskly. 'She didn't, but I did, and it's been decided that you should burn it. And this time I think you should do as you're told. Think yourself lucky no one suggested showing it to the police, or both you and this Tony might have been in real trouble.'

'The *police*? she said, aghast.

'The police, and newspapers, already know about your disappearance. Don't think you're going to get out of this with just a smack on the wrist, Josie. We all love you and we're enormously thankful to have you back safely, but you did a bad thing, and after all the troubles we've had in recent times you'd do well to keep your head down for a while.'

If she didn't speak harshly, Charlie knew she would dissolve into tears herself. She hated to see her sister like this, being more the naughty child than the grown-up she always tried to be. But she had to be strong, for Josie's sake.

'I will, I promise,' Josie said huskily.

Charlie didn't know what her parents said to Josie, but they had been in her bedroom with her for a long time before her mother reappeared, and said Josie was going to have her evening meal in her room rather than joining them. By then Freda and the regulars knew that she was home safely.

Sergeant Hawkins had also been to the hotel and interviewed Josie and been given the story that she had been upset about various things and had gone to stay with a woman acquaintance who had loaned her the dress since her own had got badly torn. It was a feeble enough story, but she was adamant it was nothing more than that, and since her parents didn't wish it to be taken any further, the sergeant had to be satisfied. The less information they had, the less gossip could be bandied about, Donald had decided, even though people would put their own interpretation on things. But if they didn't know anything for certain, it was all speculation, and the family could live through that.

Freda asked to take Josie's meal upstairs to her, and Ruth had no objection. Josie was sitting up in bed now, looking dejected, but she gave her cousin a wan smile when she entered with the tray of food.

'I've made a real mess of things, haven't I, Freda?' she mumbled.

'You did it for what you thought were the right reasons, love, and as long as no real harm's been done, we'll all get over it.'

Josie bit her lip. She pushed the tray away, knowing she couldn't eat anything. The sight of the food made her feel nauseous.

'It depends what you mean by no harm being done,' she said in a small voice. 'I stayed with him, Freda. I thought he loved me, and I thought I loved him, otherwise I would never have – well, let things happen.'

She closed her eyes, wishing she'd never blurted it out, sure that she would have shocked and disgusted her cousin. Freda might be a simple countrywoman, but she wasn't slow-thinking. She felt her cousin pat her shoulder.

'Now you listen to me, Josie. You're not the first girl to be carried away by a good-looking chap with the gift of the gab and you won't be the last. So you let yourself be taken in and he had his way with you – that is what you mean, isn't it?'

Josie nodded dumbly.

'Well, I know you feel as if it's the end of the world now

133

and that you've been very wicked, but in a few days you'll be feeling better and back to normal. It's not the worst thing a girl can do, Josie. You didn't burn down the hotel or commit murder, did you? And I don't suppose it was all bad, was it? He was your choice, wasn't he?'

Josie managed the ghost of a smile by the time Freda had finished. She had such a lot of common sense, even though she was sure her parents wouldn't be so tolerant if they knew the truth of it all. But she had somehow managed to persuade them that she hadn't been alone with Tony all this time, but with one of the fairground families. It was lie upon lie, but there seemed no other way if she was to save her father from complete disillusionment with his daughter.

'Freda, I do love you,' she said fervently.

'Then eat your supper while I go downstairs and eat mine. And Josie, if you ever feel that you want to get away for a while, there's always room on the farm for you with Mother and me. I think you'd fit in well to country life.'

Josie had a lump in her throat as her cousin left her. She could no more imagine herself fitting in well to country life than – well, being on the road with the fair people, and she'd been charmed enough to think she could do that, though being cooped up all day in a small caravan hadn't been her idea of fun.

She looked at the tray of food her mother had prepared and her mouth suddenly watered. She was only seventeen; she had had an experience she didn't want to repeat, but she had come through it and she was home now. There was life after Tony after all.

The family had hidden the newspapers from Josie, but they omitted to tell the regulars as much, and she found a copy in their sitting room, where, with mounting horror, she read the account of her disappearance, and the finding of a young girl's body. It made her think anew what she had put her family through, and there and then she resolved never to do anything like it ever again. From now on she was going to be the perfect, dutiful daughter . . .

It couldn't last, of course. Josie was never going to be a quiet little mouse, nor could she sit around all day while the

134

rest of the world revolved around her. Freda had gone back to the farm, and she really missed her company and her no-nonsense talks, especially as there seemed to be a definite barrier between her and Charlie now that neither of them knew how to cross. Freda had promised to write to her, and as the diary had now been burned as promised, Josie thought she would write out everything in her letters to Freda, knowing she would understand, even if it seemed ironic that they had found such an affinity with one another.

She couldn't even think about work outside the hotel, certainly not to go back to Hallam's Stores. The very thought of Arnie Hallam's beady little eyes on her, wondering what she had been up to, made her squirm. She knew very well that everyone in town would have read about her in the paper, but she was getting so bored with twiddling her thumbs all day. Nobody seemed to know quite what to do with her, and everyone else seemed to be busy with the hotel getting ready for new guests that weekend.

'Can't I help, Mum? I could do some shopping for you,' she pleaded.

Ruth avoided her eyes. 'We think it best if you stay indoors for a week or two, Josie, but you could make yourself useful by writing out the menus.'

'I suppose it will be all right if I go for a walk after dark then, so that no one will see me, will it?' she burst out.

'Of course it will, and no one's keeping you a prisoner here, my dear, but we think it will be less embarrassing for you to stay indoors until the fuss dies down.'

'You mean it'll be less embarrassing for Dad and his precious hotel if his wayward daughter isn't seen about the town,' Josie said before she could stop herself.

Ruth looked at her coolly. 'That's one of the reasons, yes.'

Josie gasped, her eyes smarting at this unexpected response. 'Give me the menus then, and I'll start copying them out,' she snapped.

'Make sure you don't make a mess of them out of spite,' Ruth replied.

The tears stabbed Josie's eyes now. Milly had such clear, childish handwriting that she had often been given the job of writing out the weekly menus, and now Josie was being given the task. It was humiliating. Everything seemed set on putting her in her place. It was two days after she had returned home and she was just starting to realize how fragile and brittle she still was, and how nobody else seemed to realize it.

'I would never spoil the menus, Mum.'

Ruth gave her a small, apologetic smile. 'I know you wouldn't.'

Once the afternoon had turned to early-evening dusk, she told her mother she was going for a walk along the seafront. For a moment she thought Ruth was going to forbid it, but something in Josie's eyes must have begged her to trust her, and she merely nodded and told her not to be out too long. Once, Charlie would have come with her for a good gossip, but Charlie was out somewhere on an errand of her own. Besides, they had little to talk about now, Josie thought miserably.

The salt air was refreshing, the moon was rising, and the sea was rippling gently towards the shore as the daylight turned the water to a pinky hue. Josie breathed deeply, feeling slightly more relaxed for the first time since coming home. It was almost impossible to think that this time last week she had been at the start of what she'd thought was a great and exciting adventure, one which she was now prepared to see as a sordid little escapade. She knew what a gullible fool she had been to be taken in by Tony and his sweet talk, but it was over now and she was never going to be so foolish again.

She walked the entire length of the seafront and beyond it, going much farther than she'd intended, but just enjoying the sense of freedom in being outside and being alive. Learning about the girl's body they had found in a Somerset rhine had sobered her up considerably, bringing home even more forcibly how wicked she had been in putting her family through such distress. She shivered, not wanting to think about it. She was glad there weren't too many other people about that evening, and those she met merely nodded or said hello and went on their way. Any who recognized Josie Elkins and knew her story would merely note that she was apparently back home with her family again.

Some distance ahead of her she could see the outlines of two people and a large dog. Her heart jolted as she recognized Charlie as one of the couple. They seemed to be in deep conversation and she would have avoided them if she could, but they had clearly seen her now, and Charlie waved. She had no option but to wave back, and as they drew nearer she saw that the other person was the newspaper reporter, Steve Bailey.

Interesting . . . but also embarrassing, Josie thought swiftly, remembering how much he had been involved in their family affairs lately.

'They let you out then,' Charlie said evenly.

'I thought it was time I got some fresh air,' Josie said, thinking how trite this conversation was, when they had always been at such ease with one another.

The next minute the large dog rubbed his nose into her hand and, as she jumped back with a little yelp, Steve hauled the dog back with an apology.

'Sorry about that. Rex has a habit of being over friendly.'

'I'm glad somebody is, even if it's only a dog,' Josie muttered, feeling an idiot for reacting the way she had.

For a moment none of them said anything, and then Charlie linked her arm firmly in her sister's. 'Well, that's not the case where you're concerned, you ninny. Look, I've just asked Steve back to the hotel for a cup of cocoa or something, so let's all go back together and show a united front, shall we?'

'Why not? That's sure to please them,' Josie said, trying to sound as close as possible to her old self before she started wallowing.

But the first real glow she had felt since returning home was all due to the fact that at least Charlie seemed to have come out of it all right, if the way Steve Bailey was looking at her was anything to go by.

Thirteen

Before the new guests arrived at the hotel on Saturday, Josie decided to write to Freda. She still felt too awkward to be in her father's company for long, and she knew that, despite his attempts to act normally with her, he still hadn't forgiven her, and probably never would. She couldn't say any of this to her mother, nor to Charlie, who now seemed to have a life of her own, and she wouldn't trust anything with that little sneak Milly, after she'd betrayed Josie to the adults with her diary. She couldn't really blame her for that, though, she thought with a sigh. The kid had only done what she'd thought was right.

The only person she felt able to convey her thoughts to properly was Freda. Distance gave an extra sense of freedom in the writing, anyway, but even if she'd been here, Josie knew she would have been able to confide in her. Which was very odd, considering how very different they were.

But when the hotel was busy again, everyone had to pull their weight; there was not much time for dwelling on personal problems, and Josie found a small sense of normality in being sociable to the guests and making them welcome. For a long time she had hated the thought of doing this for ever, but right now it was just what she needed to restore her spirits and her self-confidence.

'I don't feel quite so awful now, Freda,' she wrote. 'Mum and Dad aren't quite so grumpy with me any more, and I can always ignore Milly. It's Charlie I care about most, and I didn't think I'd ever be saying that, because you don't go around saying out loud that you love your sister, do you?'

She paused after she had written those words, remembering how Charlie had said they all loved Josie and were enormously thankful to have her back. But Charlie was much more

138

mature than herself, Josie admitted, and it probably came easier to her to say such things. She continued with her letter.

'I think Charlie and Steve Bailey will get together some time soon. Well, perhaps not soon, but some time. It's easy to see from the way they look at one another that they're sweet on each other. I wouldn't mind him as a brother-in-law. He's a hundred per cent better than that awful Melvin Philpott. I could never fancy him in a million years. Not that I'm thinking of fancying anyone for years and years yet. I may even become a nun.'

She found herself laughing as her pen ran away with her, and she scratched out the words at once. They were still visible, though, so she left them like it and added that Freda could forget what she'd just scratched out, because she was sure she'd feel differently when the right man came along.

'I'm not actually looking for him, mind,' she went on, pouring out her thoughts the way she used to do in her diary, only in more detail now. 'I shall probably wait at least ten years before I think about getting married. I shall stay here and help Mum and Dad run the hotel, because if Charlie and Steve get hitched, as I think they might, she won't want to work here any more and then I'll be chief cook and bottle-washer – after Mum, of course. By that time Milly will be off somewhere doing whatever clever thing she intends to do.'

She paused, rereading what she had written. She couldn't really imagine herself ten years ahead. It seemed like a life-time away, and she'd be quite old at twenty-seven! But it wasn't that which made her think. It was referring to herself as being chief cook and bottle-washer. She wouldn't be second best to Charlie, and she wouldn't have to watch that little toad Milly being petted by the regulars and the guests. She wouldn't be the one in the middle any more.

She frowned, knowing she had never thought of it quite so brutally before. She was jealous of Charlie's good looks and self-confidence, and she was jealous of all the attention that brainy Milly got. It was shameful, but there it was, staring her in the face. She had even gone wild with Tony in order to prove to Charlie that she could get a chap too, and look where that had got her!

She finished the letter to Freda hurriedly, before she was

obliged to do any more soul-searching that she didn't like.

'I've got to stop now, Freda, but don't take too much notice of my rambling. Write back when you can, and you never know, I might take you up on your offer of a little holiday at the farm one of these days – if you really meant it. Love from Josie.'

She put it in an envelope, wrote Freda's address on it and sealed it quickly before she changed her mind about sending it. But that would be a waste, and it had felt good to get things off her chest. She didn't really think she would ever go and be a country yokel on the farm, tramping about in all that Exmoor mud, but it would please Freda to know she had thought about it.

A month or so later the general excitement about Josie Elkins' disappearance had died down. It was the end of the school term, and in Dorothy Yard's bedroom, she and her best friend Milly were wrangling as usual.

Dorothy folded her arms and glared. 'I don't know why you can't tell me everything,' she said.

'That's because there's nothing to tell, and besides they don't tell *me* everything. I'm always told to go out of the room when they want to talk about stuff. Even if I try to get the regulars to tell me things, the Captain says it's not for little girls' ears; but the Misses Green tell me bits.'

'What bits?' Dorothy persisted.

Milly sighed. She wished she did have something spectacular to tell Dorothy, but since Josie had come home and the hotel had got back to normal, it had all got as deadly dull as before. It was only when they were really busy and she helped out and got praise and occasional tips from the guests that it was worthwhile being at home at all. She much preferred it at Dorothy's house, where they didn't have strangers coming in and out all the time. There were always interesting things to discuss there, without people arriving to interrupt them.

Just before the end of the summer term they had learned the rudiments of reproduction. The grammar school was more progressive in that respect than most schools. Even so, the biology mistress had concentrated the information with particular reference to rabbits. There was only the merest passing reference to the fact that all mammals reproduced in the same way, including humans. It was enough to start excited speculation among the more knowing pupils, including Milly Elkins and Dorothy Yard, especially since Milly had two older sisters whose dealings with young men hadn't run the smoothest course that romance was supposed to do.

'I think Charlie's got a crush on that newspaper chap,' Milly said at last.

Dorothy snorted. 'Tell me something new! I'd rather hear about Josie. Do you think she did it with that chap from the fair?'

'Of course not,' Milly snapped. 'And even if she did, nobody's likely to tell me, are they? Anyway, I've been forbidden to mention anything outside the hotel, and it's only because you're my best friend that I tell you anything at all.'

'But you don't tell me anything!' Dorothy wailed.

'That's because there's nothing to tell.'

At that moment Josie was clearing away the guests' plates from the hotel dining room and becoming aware of a distinctly uneasy sensation in her stomach as the lingering smell of the food wafted into her nostrils. She was never ill, but right then she had to swallow several times as the unaccustomed nausea threatened to make her throw up. It would never do to disgrace herself in here, and without having time to say a word to Charlie, who was folding napkins at the other end of the room, she rushed upstairs to the bathroom and emptied the contents of her stomach into the lavatory bowl.

She rinsed her mouth and washed her face with shaking hands. Whatever had caused this must be something she had eaten, and she immediately prayed that it wasn't, since it would be disastrous for the hotel if there was any hint of food poisoning among the guests. But Charlie was all right, and so were her parents and the regulars, and Milly had gone off in high spirits to see that friend of hers, so it was obviously no more than an isolated incident. She breathed more easily, and once her stomach had settled down again she went back to the dining room, to find that Charlie had finished the work for her.

'Are you all right, Josie? You went out of here as if you'd

141

been stung. Either that or you devised some bright idea for getting out of working!'

'I thought I heard the postman,' Josie lied. 'Freda promised to send me some pictures of the farm.'

'Good Lord, you're not thinking of taking up farming and turning into another Freda, are you?' Charlie said. 'I know you and she hit it off, but I can't really see you in wellies and dungarees.'

'She's all right,' Josie said, defending her. 'I liked her, and we've been writing to one another ever since – well, ever *since*, if you must know.'

Charlie looked at her uneasily, realizing that her sister looked paler than usual. 'Josie, you are over all that, aren't you?'

'Of course I am! And since we're on the subject, you are over Melvin, aren't you? I didn't really ruin everything, did I?'

'You did me a favour, and I think you know that. I'd rather you hadn't had to go to such extremes to do it, but I'm happier now than I've ever been.'

'I wonder why,' Josie said.

She realized they were talking more or less as they used to do. Somehow they had recaptured at least some of their old easy footing. Being Josie, she could easily overlook the times they'd fought and argued. That was far behind them now. They'd been children then, and now they were adults, and if Steve Bailey was the one to put the stars back in Charlie's eyes, then it had all been worthwhile. She could even think of herself as a matchmaker. Whatever she had done, it had been the means for Charlie to ditch Melvin, and find true happiness with Steve. She smiled to herself, her old self-confidence gradually bubbling to the surface again.

When another bout of sickness happened the following morning, and the next, and the one after that, Josie began to get alarmed. Whatever was wrong with her clearly wasn't affecting the rest of her family, nor the hotel guests. Perhaps she had some terrible disease, she thought wildly, her imagination running away with her. Perhaps she was gradually going to pine away and die, and then they would all crowd around her bedside feeling desperately sorry for her and telling her how much they all loved her. She was putting herself into every sad story she had ever read – the tragic young heroine dying so young . . .

And then one evening while she and Milly were playing draughts, the familiar sensations began again, and she had to bolt out of the room and upstairs to the bathroom. She heard Milly shout out to her mother, and moments later, as she retched over the lavatory bowl, she heard Ruth's cool voice telling Milly to go downstairs, that everything was all right, and that Josie was just feeling unwell.

She finally straightened up, trembling, while her mother handed her a face cloth for her to wipe her mouth.

'Has this happened before, Josie?' Ruth said quietly.

'A few times, but never in the evening before.'

'In the mornings?' Ruth asked.

She nodded miserably.

'Oh Josie,' Ruth said, appalled. In an instant she knew she should have been forthcoming with her daughters about such intimate matters, but she had never been able to bring herself to do so. Now she saw how wrong that had been. It didn't excuse things – and it was Josie who had done wrong, if what she suspected was true; but the girl was still so naive, despite all her brashness. She might be seventeen years old, but beneath it all, right now she looked like the child she still was.

'What do you think it is, Mum?' Josie said fearfully. 'I haven't caught something dreadful, have I?'

Ruth closed and bolted the bathroom door quickly. Her heart thudded painfully, but she knew she couldn't let embarrassment stop what had to be said.

'Josie, have you noticed a change in things lately? Monthly events, I mean?'

'I don't think so. I don't know.' She blushed, knowing that too many things had been happening lately for her to keep a proper account of such things. Besides, without her diary, in which she kept dates and so on, how could she remember?

'Well, I think the best thing is for you and me to see Doctor Jacobs tomorrow, and don't mention it to anyone else until we find out what's wrong.'

Especially not Donald, Ruth thought with a sinking heart, if what she now suspected and dreaded was true. She daren't

143

speculate on his reaction. How *could* Josie have been so stupid and so wicked?

'You *do* think it's some serious illness then, don't you, Mum?' Josie said, suddenly shrill, and clutching her mother's arm in a fright.

'No, I don't, but I want you to tell me something truthfully, Josie,' Ruth said carefully. 'When you went off with that young man, did he – did he touch you? Did you and he spend the nights together?'

Josie felt her face flame now. She hung her head, never thinking in a million years that she would be standing here being questioned by her mother like this. She felt so weak, and her legs still shook, and she just couldn't lie any longer.

'Yes,' she whispered.

Ruth spent the worst night of her married life. She had never lied to Donald before, and she tried to tell herself that she wasn't lying to him now. She just wasn't confiding in him and sharing her worries with him as she had always done. Through all their troubles with Clover, and then facing ruin with the collapse of the old hotel, they had always shared everything. But this was too momentous for her to speak a word to anybody until she knew for sure.

As she listened to the rhythmic sound of Donald's breathing, she agonized over the fact that by this time tomorrow his heart would be breaking all over again. He had such pride in his daughters: Charlotte the pretty, fair-haired one; Josie, the darkly dramatic one, and Milly, the brainbox, who looked likely to turn out to be the prettiest of them all.

Had she failed them so badly? Ruth wondered. By not telling them the so-called facts of life at an earlier age, had she been so lacking in a mother's duty? She remembered her embarrassment at trying to tell Charlie something of it when she had first gone courting with Melvin Philpott, but she hadn't got very far at all. She hadn't even attempted it with Josie, and Milly was still far too young . . .

Donald turned restlessly, his arm reaching out to cover her. 'Can't you sleep?' he murmured.

'I will in a little while,' she whispered back.

She almost wished she could put off sleeping for the whole

night, so that she wouldn't have to face tomorrow and the doctor's visit with Josie. So far the girl seemed innocently unaware of what might really be wrong with her, but when she did realize, the panic would hit her as hard as it was hitting Ruth now.

The next afternoon, as far as anyone else knew, they were going shopping together. Instead, they arrived at Doctor Jacobs' surgery and waited their turn until he was free to see them. Thankfully, there were few people waiting, since illnesses were fewer at this time of the year than in the winter, and there was nobody there who knew them. By the time they went inside the small surgery, Ruth was the more apprehensive one, her thoughts already winging ahead and wondering just how they were going to cope with what she expected to hear.

'Now then, what can I do for you, Mrs Elkins?' the doctor said amiably.

'It's not me, it's Josie,' Ruth said in an oddly strangled voice.

'All right, so what can I do for you, Josie?' The doctor turned his attention to her, while registering that it was the mother who seemed more anxious than the daughter. He wasn't unaware of what had been happening to the family recently, and it was no surprise to him that a girl of her background should be feeling a reaction over her part in it.

'I've been sick a few times,' Josie said abruptly. 'In the mornings mostly, and then again last night. I think it must have been the smell of Mum's cooking,' she said, trying to make a joke of it when she saw the doctor's expression change slightly. It wasn't something really awful that was wrong with her, was it? she wondered fearfully.

The doctor asked her a few questions and then said she should lie on the couch while he examined her tummy. She went behind the curtain, took off her skirt as she'd been told and climbed on to the cold leather couch, pulling the blanket up around her. She began to feel increasingly alarmed as she heard the low voices of her mother and the doctor from the other side of the curtain. She couldn't hear what they were saying, but it had to be about her, of course.

When Ruth and Doctor Jacobs came to join her, he was rubbing his hands together to warm them, he told her jovially. Josie's frightened eyes met her mother's as he pulled down the blanket and began to press gently on her tummy. After a few moments he covered her again.

'Josie, I have to ask you a very personal question, and I want you to answer me honestly. Have you had intimate relations with a young man?'

She gasped. She wasn't prepared for this. It had nothing to do with the way she was feeling; but her mother was looking so distressed now that she could only nod, and turn her face away as she felt her lips trembling.

'Then I think there's little doubt, Mrs Elkins, that Josie is expecting a child.'

Josie gave an anguished cry and then burst into tears. Her mother's arms went around her tightly and they rocked together for a few moments while the doctor went back to his desk and left them to deal with the news.

'You knew, didn't you?' Josie wept against her mother.

Ruth was still hugging her tightly as if to protect her from whatever the future held. 'I guessed. I didn't want to believe it, but in my heart I knew it had to be true.'

'And now everyone will know how wicked I am. What am I going to do, Mum?' She couldn't stop shaking, and she couldn't stop crying. She felt complete and utter terror at what she had heard.

'Well, first of all we have to go home and talk about it,' Ruth said, unusually decisive in this moment of crisis.

'Will the doctor tell everybody?' Josie asked fearfully.

'Doctors never betray a patient's confidentiality. It's part of their code of honour.'

'I haven't brought much honour to this family, have I, Mum?' Josie said unhappily, starting to shake all over again.

'Now you listen to me, Josie.' Ruth held her by the shoulders. 'I'm not denying that this has been a shock, but since I suspected something of it, I'm able to face it more calmly than you are. It will be an even worse shock to your father, but we'll face that together.'

She quickly brushed aside the thought of Donald's reaction when he heard this news. They had faced disaster and scandal and ridicule, but this was something else that could rip the family apart, if they let it. Ruth had no intention of letting that happen. She wasn't an overly emotional woman, but she loved her husband and her family, and she wasn't prepared to see them torn apart by the wolves or by each other. She heard the doctor give a discreet cough in the background, and remembered that he would have other patients to see. Patients with bad backs and sore eyes and everyday coughs and colds, and with nothing as momentous as they were facing today. She swallowed the lump in her throat that threatened to choke her and led Josie back to where the doctor sat waiting for them.

'If the sickness persists, I suggest a cup of hot water and a dry biscuit before you get out of bed in the morning, Josie,' he said briskly. 'It will almost certainly pass in a couple of months.'

'A couple of months?' she said huskily. Her brain was so confused she couldn't think properly at all.

He paused, seeing her stricken face. 'You do know the facts of life, my dear?' he said, more kindly.

It was Ruth now who felt her face redden. She had never been able to bring herself to tell her girls more than the rudiments of their bodily functions, and never in any detail about how babies were conceived. She had shied away from anything so intimate and embarrassing. She felt a renewed sense of panic, thinking again that this was all her fault. She had failed her girls. Her head swam until she heard the doctor's voice again, sharper this time.

'Mrs Elkins, are you feeling unwell? Would you like a glass of water?'

'I'm quite all right.' Ruth spoke as steadily as she could, considering she had just learned the worst thing a mother could learn about her young daughter. 'But I think Josie and I should go home now. We have a lot to talk about.'

'Of course. But before you do, I'll let you have some leaflets for Josie to read. I'll see her again in a few months' time to check that all is proceeding normally, and then we must all think about the future.'

'I *am* here, you know,' Josie said in a hoarse voice. 'This is me you're talking about. And I don't want this – this thing – inside me. I want you to take it away!'

She heard herself suddenly shrieking as the sheer horror of what was happening to her sank in. She knew now just what Tony Argetti had done to her, what evil he had allowed to happen when he'd pretended to love her. All her feelings for him now were those of hate and disgust. She turned into her mother's arms again, wishing Ruth could put things right for her the way she had when she was a little girl. But not even Ruth could put this right now.

Doctor Jacobs spoke more gently. 'I shall ignore that remark, of course. She's overwrought, and understandably so. I'll give you a mild sedative for her, Mrs Elkins, so take her home, and encourage her to have a lie-down and think calmly.'

They were still talking about her as if she wasn't there, Josie thought. As if she wasn't a person any more, and nothing more than a – a cow or a brood mare, carrying its young. They didn't care about her feelings . . . but one look at her mother's anguished face as they left the surgery and she knew that wasn't true. Ruth was feeling this very deeply. The fact that she was a woman who had never been able to express her emotions didn't mean she wasn't tortured by what was happening. Josie took a deep, shuddering breath as they walked back towards the hotel, clinging to her mother's arm as if she was a very old woman.

'Mum, I'm really, really sorry,' she whispered. 'You do know how sorry I am, don't you? You know I never wanted this to happen. I never meant it to happen, and I didn't know it could happen. I didn't know,' she finished helplessly.

Tony had said he would never hurt her – but he had hurt her in the worst possible way.

'Let's not talk about it any more until we get home. It's happened, and we have to think about how we're going to deal with it.'

She sounded so strong, stronger than Josie had ever thought she could be. She was more understanding than Josie had ever imagined, too, even though they had never had to face a situation like this before, and she had no idea how Ruth might be feeling underneath that calm exterior. It was a certainty that her father wouldn't be as calm or understanding once he knew. He would want to break Tony's neck.

Her teeth chattered with fright all the way home, and her

head felt as if it was about to burst with all the shameful thoughts clamouring inside it. She had no idea how she was going to face her father . . . and Charlie . . . and Milly and the regulars, and the whole town . . .

Fourteen

When they returned to the hotel Ruth ordered Josie to bed for a couple of hours, saying she would bring her up a stomach powder. Instead, she mixed the mild sedative in a glass of water and took it up to the girl, saying there would be time enough for talking later. Downstairs, when Donald asked what was wrong with her, Ruth told him it was her unwell time, which was enough to stop any more questioning. The mystery workings of female bodies were as alien to Donald as the moon, and best left to them. Besides, the hotel didn't stop for personal business, and there were guests to be catered for.

Ruth was discovering she had a more devious side to her than she had ever believed. Charlie also accepted that Josie had the stomach cramps, and when she said cautiously that Steve had asked her to the cinema that evening, Ruth told her to forget her qualms at being seen in the company of another young man, and to go.

Then there was only Milly to deal with, and she had been begging for days to be allowed to sleep at Dorothy's house, now that the school holidays were here. To Milly's delight, her mother told her to go along and ask Mrs Yard if tonight was convenient, and was assured that it was. Josie was still sleeping with the aid of the sedative, and once the evening meal for the guests was over and cleared away, Ruth and her husband had a few hours to themselves.

Despite her fast-beating heart at what she had to tell him, she gave a tentative sigh of relief that they wouldn't be interrupted in the small sitting room. It was then that she realized Donald wasn't as oblivious to her machinations as she had thought.

'Out with it, woman,' he said with a smile. 'I know there's been something bothering you, but I'm sure it's nothing we can't deal with together. We haven't been through these last couple of years without knowing that we can beat anything.'

For one agonized moment Ruth wished so hard that she could keep him in blissful ignorance of what had happened to Josie. He would be furiously angry, appalled, and ultimately devastated at what that loutish young man had done to her. If she could have saved him from that, she would have done, but she knew it wasn't possible.

'Donald, I haven't been entirely truthful with you.'

He began to laugh. 'Well, don't look so tragic, my dear. Knowing you, I'm sure that whatever it is, it can't be too bad.'

When she didn't smile in return, the laughter faded, to be replaced by a frown. 'Is this something to do with Josie?' he said.

'I'm afraid it's everything to do with Josie. Oh Donald, I wish I could spare you this,' she said, suddenly overwhelmed by the secret she had to share. 'Josie and I didn't go shopping this afternoon. You know she hasn't been herself lately, and so we went to see Doctor Jacobs.'

He wasn't a dull-witted man, and even though he didn't want to accept what he realized was becoming blatantly obvious, he could see it all in his wife's face. 'Dear God,' he said hoarsely, 'are you trying to tell me that bastard has put her in the family way?'

Ruth felt the merest flash of relief that his instant thought was to blame the boy. But she knew it wouldn't last. It took two . . .

The sitting-room door suddenly opened and Josie stood there, her face white and frightened, clearly just aroused from sleep and swaying slightly on her feet.

'Daddy,' she said in a choked voice.

Whether she had intended to tell him herself none of them knew, because the next moment she had collapsed in a heap on the ground. Ruth rushed to her and lifted her on to a seat, pushing her head between her knees and wondering frantically just what was happening to her family. When the old hotel had been ruined amid all the gossip surrounding it and the eccentric Clover, there had been rumours that it was cursed. But what if it wasn't only the hotel, but the family itself?

She shook herself, realizing that Donald had left the room, to return a few minutes later with a glass of water, which he thrust at her and Josie.

'Is this the reason you so conveniently disposed of Milly for the night?' he snapped at his wife. 'So that we can discuss this girl's disgraceful behaviour in private?'

'It seemed best,' Ruth whispered, knowing how quickly his wrath had turned on Josie, whom he wasn't even referring to as his daughter at that moment, but as 'this girl'. All her motherly instincts wanted to shield Josie from him. She knew just how badly Josie had behaved, but having known it for a little while longer than Donald, she was more able to face it than he was.

She saw that Josie was recovering now and trying to sit upright, her whole body shaking.

'Daddy, please don't think too badly of me,' she stammered.

'I can hardly think worse of you, can I? You've shamed yourself and you've shamed your family by consorting with a common lout.'

'Don't you think I know that?' Josie hung her head, ashamed to look at him, the weak tears flooding her eyes.

He didn't say anything for a few minutes, but Ruth could see how tortured he was by the way his hands were constantly clenching and unclenching.

'What has the doctor said? Is it definite? There's no doubt?'

Ruth knew he was desperate for her to say there was a doubt, but she couldn't lie any more. She shook her head. 'I fear not. It will be next March.' She gave the expected date as delicately as she could, thinking for the briefest of moments what a sad welcome to the world this child was going to have.

'Then we have to decide what we're going to do about it.'

Josie's head jerked up. They were doing it again – discussing her as if she wasn't there; as if she had no feelings; as if her emotions weren't hurtling about in her brain with the now familiar feeling that it was going to explode again; as if her stomach wasn't churning because of this thing inside her. She couldn't think of it as anything else. It was a monster, a growth that was only going to get bigger and bigger and consume her . . .

Her anguished cry was like that of an animal, and then she was screaming hysterically, begging her mother, or God, or anyone, to take it away from her. She felt Ruth's arms go around her, holding her tight; and then she heard her father stamp out of the sitting room, slamming the door behind him.

'He wants to kill me, doesn't he?' she sobbed against her mother.

'I'm sure he feels like killing the boy,' Ruth said keenly. 'But he doesn't want to kill you, Josie. You're his daughter and he loves you, despite what you may think now. This has been a tremendous shock for him, and he needs to come to terms with it. You have to accept that.'

'What will he do? Will he tell the others? I can't bear to think of Milly and her gossiping friend knowing, *ever*.' Her voice began to rise again, as the implications of it began to hit harder.

'Josie, my love, this is something that can't be hidden away for ever.'

'You never told me anything much, did you, Mum?' she muttered. 'I don't know the first thing about babies.'

She knew how they began now, though. And she remembered seeing married ladies in the town hiding their ungainly lumps beneath voluminous clothes until they became too large to be seen decently in public. She couldn't bear to be seen like that, to be stared at and pointed out as the Elkins girl who had got herself into trouble and disgraced her family.

'I know I've been very lacking in such matters, and I know I've failed you in that respect,' Ruth said awkwardly. 'But of course I'll tell you everything you need to know, so we'll go up to your bedroom where we won't be disturbed.'

Donald tapped on the bedroom door a long while later. By then, a white-faced Josie had learned the rudiments of giving birth and the long nine months leading up to it. Ruth wasn't the most articulate of women when it came to explaining medical matters, but she managed to put her own inhibitions aside, knowing it was essential that Josie knew what to expect. Her heart ached for her daughter's ordeal, nor could she ignore the social impact it was going to have on them all.

'Can I come in?' Donald said.

Josie sat up on her bed, her knees up to her head with her arms clasped around them. Her long dark hair hung in unkempt strands about her face where the tears had matted it. She looked, and felt, about twelve years old, yet she knew she could never return to that sweet innocence again.

'So what are we going to do with you, Josie?' he said next.

Her heart leapt with fright. 'What do you mean?'

Donald tried to stay as calm as possible, considering that he felt as though the earth was closing in on him all over again. The shame and embarrassment of Josie's disappearance and then the cancellation of Charlotte's wedding had been about as much as he could take, but now this . . . this beat all.

'Darling,' Ruth put in with a warning glance at her husband. 'You must see what a stigma this is going to be for all of us. I know you're suffering, but something like this has far-reaching effects. It touches all of us.'

'We have to think what to do for the best,' Donald said, stony-faced.

Josie gasped, her eyes dark with pain. 'You want to send me away, don't you? You want to send me to one of those places where bad girls go. You don't want me here any more. I wish I'd never come back at all now.'

'You would have preferred to live the life of a travelling showman's doxy, would you?' Donald snapped, using the only word he could think of that wasn't totally alien to all his principles.

'No,' Josie muttered. 'But at least Tony wanted me.'

She knew it wasn't strictly true. He'd wanted her for a few nights, but after that she was pretty sure he'd got tired of her. He was glad to be rid of her. He was never going to be the sort to settle down with a wife and children. He hadn't really wanted her, and he wouldn't want this baby. Nobody did.

She felt a weird sensation at that moment. It wasn't a

movement from the thing growing inside her. Her mother had explained all about that, and it was far too early. It was more a sense of protection from somewhere deep inside her at the certainty that nobody in the world was going to welcome this unwanted scrap. It was almost certainly going to be taken away from her as soon as it was born and sent to some orphanage or other. It would be cared for by strangers.

She gave a great shuddering breath. 'I know I'm a terrible disappointment to you both,' she said in a cracked voice. 'I don't know how to tell Charlie, and I dread Milly knowing and watching me every minute with that awful friend of hers. So until you've decided what to do with me, could I go and stay with Freda for a few weeks? I know she'd have me.'

Her father made what sounded like a derogatory sound in his throat, and then muttered something about country hayseeds not knowing what time of day it was, let alone dealing with a situation like this.

'Is that all I am to you, Dad? A situation?' Josie said, still choked. 'And Freda's not a hayseed. She's kind, and I know she'd understand.'

He still looked sceptical, but Ruth spoke quietly.

'Why not agree to it if Freda and Mary will have her for a few weeks? Just until we clear the air.'

'Do you think a few weeks away is going to clear anything? There's still the problem, and it's a damn sure thing it's not going to go away in a few weeks, or have you forgotten the way procreation works?' he added sarcastically.

Ruth flushed deeply. 'I have not, nor have I forgotten how mixed up a woman's feelings and emotions are at such a time. Josie will be feeling all of that now and you're not helping. Have you also forgotten how to love your daughter?'

He glared at the two of them, and then he wilted. 'No, I haven't forgotten how to love my daughter,' he said heavily. 'It's because I love her that I'm grieving so much over what's happened. I'm not completely heartless, and it's not only the good name of the hotel that concerns me, no matter what you all think of me.'

Josie gave a sob, scrambled off the bed and rushed towards her father. His arms opened automatically to hold her and she wept against him, her whole body shaking.

'Daddy, I'm so sorry. I never meant this to happen. You know I never meant to be so wicked!'

Donald met Ruth's gaze above her head, and he gave a small nod.

'Then we'll telephone Freda's village post office and ask them to take a message for her to call us right away. You must ask her yourself if you can stay for a few weeks, and if she can come to fetch you as soon as it's convenient. You must make the explanations yourself, Josie. You have to take responsibility.'

'I know,' she mumbled. 'And I will.'

A few weeks would take them near to the annual carnival time, the time that Josie loved so much, as they all did. She wouldn't feel much like celebrating, but she would have to put on a show of being her usual self by then, even if she thought she would never feel normal again.

'You must only stay a few weeks, though, Josie,' Ruth said firmly now. 'You can't put upon your cousin for ever. You must be here until Christmas, anyway.'

It slowly dawned on Josie what her mother meant. Now that she knew the workings of a woman's body when she was carrying a child, she presumed she wouldn't be too fat and ugly by Christmas. She wouldn't need to be hidden away until after that, for the final three months until the baby was born. But where would she be sent then? She still couldn't bear to think how they were going to keep it all from Charlie and Milly and the regulars.

Her whole life seemed to stretch ahead of her in one gigantic deception, in which she had unintentionally and so wickedly involved her parents. There was no joyous future event to celebrate in the way she had seen in young married couples in the town. There was no husband, no ring on her finger. There would be no welcome for this child, and she felt a weird, grudging sadness for it.

But the immediate thing to do was get in touch with Freda, and give all of them a bit of breathing space. Freda was her lifeline, and she knew Freda wouldn't let her down. Hearing her cousin's cheerful voice on the line telling her it was no problem and she'd get one of the local farm lads to help out for the day while she fetched her, Josie could have wept. Freda sounded so normal that she almost blurted out the truth, but somehow managed to hold her tongue.

By the time she went to bed that night she felt totally exhausted, but it had all been arranged. Freda was coming the day after tomorrow to collect Josie, and only when they were safely at the farm was Josie going to tell her the real reason for her being there. She was nearly asleep when she heard her door open, and Charlie's cautious voice asked if she was awake.

'I am now,' she muttered, guessing that Charlie would have learned everything from her mother now.

Charlie came across the room and put her arms around her. 'You poor, stupid, little idiot. It's not much good saying I warned you umpteen times not to get involved with that chap, so I'm not going to say it. I'm just so sorry for you, Josie.'

'I'm sorry for myself. It's such a mess. I know I've let everybody down, and I'm never going to get over it.'

For a moment she sounded so much like the old theatrical Josie, and Charlie hid a smile. However desperate she might feel now, she was quite sure that Josie *would* get over it. But Charlie dared to ask the question that nobody else had actually put into words yet.

'What are you going to do about the baby?'

Josie felt a small flash of anger. 'What do you think I'm going to do about it? I can't change things, and I'm not going to some back-street woman to get rid of it. I've heard that's what some girls do, but it sounds too awful to think about.'

'I wasn't thinking anything of the sort. But you have to face up to what's going to happen when the time comes, Josie. I believe there are special places to go to where you'll be taken care of, and people who know what to do for the best,' Charlie said carefully.

'Is that what you and Mum and Dad have been talking about downstairs?' Josie said, sitting bolt upright and suddenly wide awake, 'where to send me until the time comes so that I won't be a total embarrassment to you all? And where the baby can be taken away and things can go on just as they were before?'

Charlie folded her arms. There was a time to be gentle and a time to face facts. 'Well, darling, think about it. Can you see yourself walking around Braydon pushing a pram next spring, with everyone knowing you don't have a wedding ring on your finger, and whispering about you? And what about the baby? Do you want the busybodies of the town looking in the pram and pretending to be interested, and all the time wondering who the father is?'

'Why don't you just stick a knife in me and be done with it?' Josie snapped.

Neither of them said anything for a moment. Josie knew her parents would never have said anything like that – not yet, anyway. Her father would be too angry, and her mother too embarrassed. She fought to keep the tears down, because for the first time she had been forced to look ahead and think of the child growing inside her as a real person, a tiny someone who cried and demanded to be fed and clothed, and who would depend on her for everything. Someone who hadn't asked to be born at all. Anyone with a shred of decency left in her couldn't possibly hand him over to strangers in the way Charlie was suggesting, she thought fiercely.

'Josie?' Charlie said.

'I'm keeping him,' she replied. She realized that, for her, there had never been a choice from the moment Doctor Jacobs had told her the truth. 'He might never have been wanted, but he's mine, and I shall look after him. I owe him that much.'

'Oh Josie, for God's sake think what you're saying,' Charlie said in distress. 'I came up here to try to help and I seem to have made things worse.'

'Well, how would you feel if it was you?'

'I wouldn't have got myself in this situation!' But she bit her lip as soon as she'd said it, knowing she could have done. There had been plenty of times when she and Melvin had got carried away, and if he had had his way, it might just as easily have been herself and not Josie facing this awful prospect now.

'Oh yes – Saint Charlotte!' Josie said bitterly.

'I'm anything but that, but arguing about it won't make things any better, will it? I do feel for you, Josie.'

'So I suppose they sent you up here to try to make me see sense,' she said.

'Not really, although it was mentioned.'

Josie drew a deep breath, changing the conversation quickly. 'Oh Lord, Charlie, what about Milly? I can't bear for her to know.'

It wasn't the time for Charlie to say she couldn't avoid knowing if Josie remained at the hotel. But her sister would only feel worse once the news was out in the open.

'For the time being, she's not going to know anything except that you've got a small stomach complaint and the doctor's treating you.'

'It's not going to be a *small* stomach complaint for long, though, is it!' she said, as if determined to be difficult, Josie-like.

The unlikely sound of uneasy laughter filled the bedroom and then they were hugging one another with tears in their eyes.

'We'll get through this, Josie,' Charlie said firmly. 'You have these few weeks with Freda as you've arranged, and I'm sure you'll be able to think more clearly about things after that.'

She avoided her eyes then, but the unspoken message was that Josie must surely see the sense of having the baby in one of those places where they sent bad girls. The baby would be taken away from her and she could return home as if nothing had happened. Presumably her father would find out from the doctor where such places existed, preferably far away from here, and no one would need to be any the wiser.

'There is one other thought, of course,' Charlie said cautiously. 'You don't want Dad to find out where Tony's gone with the fair, do you? He should take some responsibility for this.'

'Absolutely *not*,' Josie snapped. 'I never want to see him again and I don't want anyone looking for him. I shan't be visiting the fair next year, I can tell you!'

'Good. That's what we hoped, but we had to be sure, Josie.'

Strangely, now, the fact that they had all been discussing her and making plans and suggestions for her was somehow washing over her. Let them say what they liked. She had always been a bit of a rebel, just like her grandmother, and she would be a rebel in this. Not that wanting to keep her own child should make her a rebel, she thought indignantly.

Instead, she would think of herself as a tragic figure, sacrificing her life for that of her unborn child.

The brief noble thoughts disappeared just a quickly as the contents of her stomach threatened to erupt once more. She clapped her hands to her mouth and scrambled out of bed, rushing out of the bedroom and into the bathroom.

'So much for keeping things quiet,' she gasped weakly to Charlie standing behind her with a face cloth and towel.

They would have to do it, though. For her own sake, and her parents', and the reputation of the hotel. She finally knew that it meant something to her as well. You were never completely isolated in this world. Those who were were the unfortunate ones. At least she had people who cared about her, and still did, no matter how bad she had been.

'There's one thing you can be sure of,' she told Charlie when she had recovered. 'I'll never do anything like this again. I'm off men for ever now.'

'And pigs might fly,' Charlie said dryly.

Milly learned that Josie had a mild stomach complaint and was going to spend some time on Freda's farm.

'Can I have your room while you're away?' she said at once.

'No, you can't,' Josie said crossly. 'You're like a little vulture, always wanting to pounce where you're not wanted. I'm only going for a couple of weeks, and you're not to touch anything of mine while I'm gone.'

At least there wouldn't be a diary for her to pry into, Josie thought with a small shiver, because she'd decided to give up recording her thoughts and feelings for good, except in her letters to Freda. And she wouldn't need to do that any more, once she was at the farm. For the first time, however, she felt a twinge of doubt. It was one thing pouring out everything in letters, knowing the recipient was miles away. It was another to be talking face to face about intimate things – especially to an unmarried woman like her cousin.

But it was too late to change her mind now. The arrangements had been made, and Freda arrived at midday on the appointed day, in time for a bite to eat, and then they were bundling Josie's things into the old jalopy. There were quick hugs and kisses, as unemotional as they could all make them, before the car turned out of the yard of the Phoenix Hotel and began its journey to Exmoor.

Fifteen

'I hope this old bone-shaker don't do you any harm,' Freda remarked when they were well away from the town and on the twisting open roads. 'It's been known to give Mother the gyppy tummy before now, to say nothing of the squits.'

'I'm sure I shall be all right,' Josie murmured, trying to ignore the graphic images. It was probably quite normal to speak so frankly in farming communities, she supposed, where they were often dealing with sick animals and had no time for the niceties.

Freda glanced at her. 'On the other hand, perhaps a bit of bone-shaking might be all to the good, to dislodge what's really ailing you, eh, love?'

'What do you mean?' Her heart began to thud.

'Josie, love, I wasn't born yesterday. A mild stomach upset and a face as pale as death, and that frightened look in your eyes? To say nothing of your folks acting like scared rabbits, afraid to say a word out of place in case they give the game away. Don't you think I can guess pretty well what's wrong with you? *And* how your pa has been taking it,' she added.

'Well, nothing like as calmly as you seem to be,' Josie stuttered.

'Oh, I'm not saying I approve, but I'm not saying it's the end of the world neither. I've seen one or two young girls in your situation before, and with a bit of help, they usually get by.'

'What kind of help?'

As the ancient car rattled along, Josie thought this must be the most bizarre conversation she had ever had with anyone.

160

And it was probably only her plain, no-nonsense cousin Freda she could possibly have been having it with.

'Well, what do your folks say about your having the babby? I daresay they want you to dispose of it like an unwanted parcel when the time comes. They'll be saying all kinds of things like the best thing you can do is to give it a good home with folks who really want a babby, but all that talk is just so they can hold their heads up again in the town without you being an embarrassment to them. Is that about right?'

She glanced Josie's way, realizing she had shocked her into silence.

'It sounds about right,' Josie managed to say at last. 'I just never expected to hear it put so bluntly.'

'There's no other way as far as I'm concerned, my dear. And I bet they haven't asked what you want to do either, have they?'

'I told Charlie I was keeping it. I said it without thinking. I don't suppose I can, or if I really want to. I feel all tangled up inside.'

'Well, of course you do. Anyway, you've got a few weeks away from them to get your thoughts untangled. Your pa's a good man, but he don't have much time for sentiment, does he?'

Josie gave a small smile. She'd never thought Freda had much time for sentiment, either. 'What's your opinion, then, Freda? Everybody else has got one, so what's yours?'

'It makes no difference what I think. You're the only one who can decide if you want to give the babby away or bring it up by yourself – and that's always assuming your pa will agree to it. Could you face the town, knowing what they'd be saying about you?'

'I really don't want to talk about it any more,' Josie said sharply. 'This jolting's making me feel sick, if you must know, and I'd rather keep quiet.' And she didn't want to have to face such pointed questions, either.

Freda had no objection to keeping quiet, and Josie tried to take an interest in the passing countryside, if only to stop her imagination going where she didn't want it to go. They passed quaint little villages with thatched cottages, where old-fashioned hollyhocks and honeysuckle grew in colourful profusion in the gardens; they passed the familiar square-topped Somerset churches, and tumbling streams crossed by tiny, ivy-covered ancient bridges. Here and there an old inn displayed the name of the Dog and Duck or the Rose and Crown.

The car rumbled and jolted along, covering the miles between Braydon and Gulliford, which was little more than an isolated hamlet itself, where Freda's sprawling farm nestled in a hollow on the moors. In the summer sunlight it looked surprisingly picturesque, but anything would have looked inviting to Josie after having travelled all this way, she thought feelingly.

'It's pretty,' she said, thinking she should say something.

Freda gave a sniff. 'I'll grant you that. It's not so pretty in midwinter when the winds blow and the snow comes.'

'What the dickens do you do then?' Josie said, thinking it must be even more like the back of beyond than it was now.

'We snuggle down for the winter when we're not seeing to the beasts. They can't be left without shelter and fodder, so their needs come first. Me and Mother get by, and neighbours come to see that we're all right. We're hardy folk on the moor, and we all muck in – more than townsfolk do, from what I've seen.'

It sounded like hell on earth to Josie, stuck up here on the moors with no entertainment, no shops except what the small village provided, and so few *people* . . . though there was a kind of attraction in that, she conceded.

'How do you fancy being here in winter, Josie? Mother's not getting any younger, and we could do with an extra pair of hands,' Freda teased her.

She pulled a face. 'A fat lot of use I'd be, waddling about like a whale!'

'I've never seen a whale waddle,' Freda commented. 'And I'm half serious. If you want a place to be away from your folks when your time comes or before it, you'll always be welcome here.'

'Can you see me as a farmhand?' Josie said jokingly, more touched by the simple words than she had expected to be. And even more so by the way Freda had just accepted what had happened, and was neither condemning nor lecturing her. She was the first – and only – person who had. Not that the

162

doctor had been too unpleasant, but she could guess what he'd been thinking.

'Why not?' Freda went on. 'I wasn't born to tend sheep, nor feed hens and collect eggs, any more than you were born to be a hotel-keeper's daughter. We become what we choose to be.'

Josie couldn't quite believe that, since this tumbledown farm had been in the family's hands for several generations. It had just been passed down . . . and how the two women managed to make a living out of it, she couldn't imagine. But she supposed Freda could have left while her father was still alive. She could have got married, had babies, as she had once wanted to do . . .

'Think about it, Josie. You don't have to be a townie all your life. You rather fancied being free of it and going on the open road not so long ago.'

Josie flushed. 'That's hitting below the belt, Freda.'

'And look where that got you!'

For a moment Josie didn't answer, not expecting a dry sense of humour, but when she heard Freda chuckle, she relaxed her face into a smile.

'That's better. If you're going to spend the next few weeks with a gloomy face, you might as well have stayed at home.'

It was time for Josie to say what had been on her mind for a while now. 'Freda – what about Aunt Mary? She'll think I'm a terrible person if she hears about this. Can we keep it from her?'

'I doubt it. Mother might not say much, but she's as canny as I am, and she'll soon guess that something's amiss, especially if you start throwing up every morning. I might not have had babies myself, but I know what's what. But don't you worry. I'll tell her and then it'll either be forgotten, or brought out in the open whenever you want to talk about it. You did wrong, and you're paying for it, but we shan't spend the time moping over something that can't be changed.'

She was like a breath of fresh air, Josie thought again. Of course, she was a step removed from Josie's own family, so it didn't affect her quite as much. But she seemed to have such a different outlook on life, and a way of making Josie feel that, just as she said, it wasn't the end of the world.

* * *

163

Aunt Mary fussed around her for a few minutes, then told Josie to show her to her bedroom and let the girl get acquainted with the place.

'She won't bother you much,' Freda said with a grin as they went up the creaking staircase. 'She sees to the house and I see to the beasts, and neither of us has ever been much for conversation.'

'You seem to be doing pretty well at it today.'

'That's because I'm fond of you, Josie. I was that pleased when you said you wanted to come and stay, and I'm even more pleased now that I know why.'

'Good Lord, are you?'

Freda didn't reply as she pushed open the door to a small bedroom at the back of the farmhouse. The lattice window looked out over a wide expanse of heather-clad land where the wild moorland ponies roamed freely. A patchwork quilt covered the single bed in the room. There was a small chest of drawers with a mirror above, and an old-fashioned wardrobe. On the floor there were rag rugs. There was also a small wicker chair, and a washstand.

'We don't run to a bathroom,' Freda said, apologizing. 'I know it's not what you're used to, Josie. There's a lav in the outhouse, but in winter we generally use the chamber pots rather than go out there at night.'

'Oh!' Josie said, not liking the sound of this at all.

Freda spoke quickly. 'Don't look so worried. We decided a while ago that we should have an inside affair, on account of Mother's getting on a bit, so a couple of the village chaps are seeing to it. They've already knocked a wall down, so that we'll be able to go through from the scullery to the brand new lav without going outdoors. It'll all be fixed in a couple of months.'

'That'll be too late for me,' Josie said, still poking around her new bedroom, and grudgingly charmed by it. 'I suppose I'll just have to make do in the meantime, however awful it sounds.'

She realized how ungracious that was and quickly turned to apologize, surprised to find Freda staring at her almost wistfully.

'I know you'll have to get used to our country ways, Josie

love, but me and Mother will try to make you as comfortable as we can. I'll show you the animals and take you down to the village tomorrow. You can telephone your pa from the post office there whenever you like. If I had my way, I'd like you to stay here for ever, but I know you wouldn't want to do that.'

Josie began to smile. Of course she wouldn't want to stay here for ever. This was a temporary visit. It wasn't home.

'You wouldn't say that when I go off in one of my bad moods. And don't forget why I'm here, Freda. From next March my life won't be my own, whatever is decided. You wouldn't want to be stuck with a screaming infant, any more than I would, not really.'

It occurred to her that she was talking more easily about the baby than she had done until now. She still hated the thought of what had happened and, as yet, she had deliberately shied away from the frightening thought of actually giving birth to it. But she couldn't deny its presence.

'I love all small things,' Freda said simply. 'I love the lambs in the spring, and the chicks, and the new ponies on the moor, and the ducklings on the village pond. What's so different about loving a baby?'

Just for a moment Josie let herself wonder about that too. And just as quickly she closed her mind to it. It wouldn't do to get attached to the idea. She had told Charlie she wanted to keep it, but she was already seeing how impossible that was. The only way was to do as her father implied, even if he hadn't actually said it yet.

She would have to go away to some proper establishment in good time before the event, to avoid the embarrassment of her condition, and be sure to ask not to see it before it was taken away from her. Oh no, she thought with a shiver, she wouldn't want to see it. Once she did, she wasn't sure what conflicting emotions she would have, and it would be too late. Some other woman, respectably married, would be glad to adopt it. Either that, or it would go to an orphanage.

She sucked in her breath. It was wicked and awful to think of her baby as an orphan. It would have a mother, even one who had never wanted it, and somewhere in the world it would have a father too. She pushed that thought aside, but it was still almost blasphemous to think of it as an orphan.

'Let's go downstairs and have some tea. You'll be glad of a cup, I'm sure, and Mother will have brewed it by now, and got out the cake tin,' Freda was saying.

Josie turned to her almost blindly. 'Is it so terrible of me to want to be rid of it as soon as it's born, Freda?'

'I think you're the only one who can answer that, and there's time enough for you to ponder on it.'

'But what do *you* think? I really want to know. I wish you'd tell me!'

She almost stamped her foot as the old Josie might have done when someone was being so irritating. But this was far more important than asking someone's opinion about a new dress or a pair of shoes.

Freda spoke carefully. 'I told you, I love all small things. It's the way we're meant to be, the strong looking after the weak. I could no more harm a tiny creature than fly, nor give away the runt of a litter or be rid of something that wasn't physically perfect. And your baby will be perfect, God willing. He'll already be growing into a real little person inside you now, and there's nothing that can be done to stop that, no matter what the future holds for the poor little mite.'

She turned abruptly and went down the stairs. Shocked at her vehemence, there was nothing else for Josie to do but to follow her.

Later, she discovered that Aunt Mary had accepted the situation. It seemed that here on the moors people thought differently about life and death and everything in between. It wasn't that they lacked morals, but in the town everyone seemed so intent on making good impressions with neighbours and visitors that people's feelings and frailties were sometimes overlooked.

She felt guilty at putting her own family into that category, but it was true, Josie thought sadly. Even Charlie had been shocked, and Milly was to be kept ignorant of the facts for as long as possible, if not for ever. Josie herself had wanted that, not able to bear seeing the little toad watching her slyly at every opportunity to see if her waistline was expanding yet. She shuddered, knowing she would have to face all of them once this haven of peace was over. But not yet. For now, she could relax, knowing that her cousin and aunt didn't seem to think ill of her. She had never thought to have such a confidante as Freda, but she was unbelievably grateful for her understanding.

During the next few weeks she joined in the workings of the farm with her cousin, revelling in the clear moorland air while they saw to the animals and fed the clucking hens as they squawked and clamoured around their feet in the mornings.

She telephoned her father once a week from the post office, and when she spoke to him and her mother, she felt close to them and at the same time oddly removed. When they asked how she was feeling, it was as if they enquired about a stranger. They all skirted around the most important fact in all their lives, that of the baby.

The farmhand from a neighbouring farm who came to help out twice a week was called Ned, and Josie suspected he was a bit sweet on Freda. She could imagine how Charlie might smile at that, and how Milly would hoot as if it was a scream that anyone Freda's age could possibly attract a chap. The farmhouse was often quite noisy with the local workmen busily constructing the new indoor lav alongside the scullery now. They hadn't gone so far as putting in a proper bath, but Freda was told it could be done any time in the future if they wanted it.

'They think we're made of money,' Aunt Mary said with a mild grumble. 'I never had a bath all my life and I don't aim to start now. A good wash down is all that's needed to keep a body clean, though I daresay when I'm gone Freda will have these newfangled things put in – a telephone too, I wouldn't wonder.'

The other two grinned at one another. Mary was definitely Clover's sister, Josie thought with rough affection and more than a surge of nostalgia for her eccentric old grandmother.

The workmen lingered rather longer one morning, and Josie saw them gabbing together and glancing her way. She felt a flush of embarrassment, wondering if they could possibly tell; but she was still as flat as a sixpence, and since the morning sickness had all but stopped now, she could almost pretend this thing wasn't happening to her at all. Except that it was – and it would.

167

'Go on, Walter, ask her before you lose your nerve,' the older one said 'She'll be gone soon, and you'll have missed your chance. She won't bite.'

Josie suddenly realized why they were looking at her. It wasn't that they suspected her condition, she thought, relaxing slightly. Walter, the younger chap, all tousled hair and ruddy cheeks, wanted to ask her out. And since she was definitely off men, she *definitely* wasn't going to say yes!

'There's a Saturday night hop at the village hall,' Walter said, pushed forward by his grinning mate. 'I wondered if you fancied coming wi' me. It don't matter if you say no, but I'd be mighty pleased if you said yes.'

From what she had seen of the village hall it was about the size of their hotel dining room. She spoke without thinking.

'No thanks. I don't know how to dance.'

'Well, no more do I. But that's all right. We can bumble around together. Everybody does. It won't be up to the standard of your townie dance halls, but it's always a bit of a lark. What do you say, miss?'

She had an instant vision of how they would look. Walter, all gangling arms and legs, and herself, trying to be elegant, trying to fit in with the village characters at a Saturday night hop. Her father's daughter, snobbish to the last . . .

'All right,' she heard herself say. 'And for goodness' sake call me Josie.'

She hadn't meant to agree at all, but the words were out before she stopped to think, and the beaming look on Walter's face made her hope uneasily that he wasn't going to get the wrong idea.

Freda was charmed. 'Walter's a nice boy, and a *good* boy,' she enthused. 'You'll have no trouble with him, Josie, and it'll do you good to get out, instead of being around we two old 'uns all the time.'

'I never think of you as old! I feel a bit awkward about it, though. I mean, he doesn't know anything about me, does he?'

She blushed even deeper now, and Freda gave her a quick hug.

'He knows you're a pretty girl, and that you're here for

168

a bit of a change, that's all. He knows you're a townie, of course—'

Josie burst out laughing. 'Oh, you country folk! I don't feel like a townie at all. Braydon's nothing like Bristol – and I'm sure it's nothing like London with so many people rushing about, and all that traffic!'

'Be that as it may. He doesn't know anything else about you, Josie, and I wouldn't dream of telling him. But if he did, he'd take it in his stride. We country folk do,' she said, tongue in cheek. 'There's more than one babby around these parts who was born the wrong side of the brush. It's all to do with nature, see.'

'Is it?' Josie said, still bemused at how matter-of-fact she was.

'Anyway, what are you fretting about? You're only going to a Saturday night hop with a nice boy. You're not setting up home with him, are you? And next week you'll be going back to your folks, so you'll probably never see him again.'

It gave Josie a funny kind of jolt to think about going home. She had settled in here so easily, far more so than she had expected. She had thought of it as a bolt-hole, to get right away from the shame of facing her family while they got used to the idea that she was having a baby. Freda never made her feel ashamed. And when Aunt Mary had been told, she had merely said she suspected as much when she'd heard Josie throwing up of a morning.

Somehow, she had been able to put the horror of it aside for these few weeks, but once she returned home she would have to face questions and make decisions, and no matter what they said or how much they loved her, she would never be allowed to forget the disgrace she had brought on her family.

But she wasn't going to think about it now. She had given her word about this dance on Saturday night, and for the rest of the week, while the workmen were in and out of the farmhouse and going about their tasks, she could hear Walter whistling as cheerfully as if he'd found the Holy Grail.

'You see what you've done for the lad, Josie girl,' his mate Perce said cheekily. 'He's that excited about taking you he'll be all left feet on Saturday.'

'Well, that will make two of us,' she said with a grin.

She still thought it would have been better to have said no. But her heart gave a small flip of pleasure at seeing the way Walter smiled at her now and then, and at the thought that she would be going out and doing the normal things a seventeen-year-old girl did.

The only person she told about it was Charlie, and that was in a letter.

'I know I shall be home next week, Charlie,' she wrote, 'and it feels quite funny to be thinking about it. I've loved being here. Freda's a lovely person and I enjoy the animals and the farm, though I never thought I'd be saying so quite so enthusiastically.

'A young chap who's working here has asked me to a dance in the village on Saturday night. I said yes, and before you get alarmed, he's got Freda's full approval as a *good* boy, so I'm sure I shan't come to any harm. You needn't worry that I'm going to get myself into any more difficult situations. Anyway, I can't get any worse, can I? Don't tell Mum and Dad anything about this, Charlie, but I thought you'd like to know that I'm not completely bored stiff here, and that I feel more able to face the future now.'

She signed it 'Your loving sister, Josie'.

She walked down to the village and posted it before she changed her mind. Saturday would have come and gone before Charlie received it, but that didn't matter. In a way, it was how she used to feel when she put all her feelings into her diary. The diary had taken the place of a confidante then, and she still felt the need to confide those feelings to someone. Charlie was the only one in her family she felt able to trust – apart from Freda, of course. She knew she could tell Freda anything and her confidence would be respected. She would miss her so much when she went home. But home was where she belonged.

By the time Saturday came she was all of a twitter. She told herself she was stupid to feel this way. It wasn't exactly a posh garden party – not that she had any idea of such an event! It was just a village hop.

Walter arrived at the farm to walk her the short distance down to the village. He was spruced up in tidy clothes, his

hair slicked down for the occasion, and he looked quite present-
able, Josie thought. For a moment it flashed through her mind
that he was about as different from Tony Argetti as it was
possible to be, and if anything was going to make her warm
her towards him, that was it. She said goodbye to Freda and
Aunt Mary and they set off for the village hall. They had to
cross a couple of stiles, where Walter held out his hand to
help her, the perfect gentleman, and her nerves began to relax.

'I've never been to a village hop before,' she told him. 'I
suppose you've been to lots of them.'

'Well, only with a couple of mates. I've never taken a girl
before.'

'Really?' She looked at him to see if he was joking, but
the telltale colour in his cheeks told her he wasn't. 'So did
you mean it when you said you couldn't dance, either, or was
that just to make me feel better?'

'Oh, I meant it! I hope you know the steps, then you can
teach me.'

Josie laughed. 'Is that the only reason you asked me then?'
she teased.

She didn't mean to be provocative, but his colour deepened
even more.

'I wouldn't be so rude. I asked you because I like you, and
because you're the prettiest girl I've ever seen.'

'Oh!'

'I haven't offended you, have I?' Walter said hastily. 'I don't
really know how to behave with a girl, Josie, and that's the
truth.'

She felt strangely protective towards him. He was a few
years older than her, but despite the way he larked and joshed
with his mate when they were working at the farm, he hadn't
lost his youthful innocence. He wasn't being arch or devious,
either; he was simply speaking in the only way he knew, with
complete honesty.

'Well, I think you're doing just fine,' she told him softly.

Sixteen

It was too much to expect that Donald Elkins wouldn't try to trace the Argetti boy. He had no plan about what to do even if he did discover his whereabouts. It was more a case of feeling he must act the way a father should. His first thought was to contact the local police and ask if they knew the route the fair people took each year, but he was loath to get them involved. The fewer people who knew of his daughter's acquaintance with the boy, the better.

Help came from an unexpected quarter. Steve Bailey was a frequent visitor to the hotel now, and it was tacitly accepted that he and Charlie were walking out. They didn't make a great show of it in the town, since it was not so long ago that she had called off her wedding to the blacksmith, and she had no wish to be thought of as a hussy. But inside the hotel, with the regulars and the family, Steve was quickly becoming a favourite.

'He's *so* much nicer for dear Charlotte than the blacksmith fellow,' the Misses Green were often heard to remark to the Captain.

And it was Steve who was able to give Donald the information he needed. 'I've got contacts with other newspapers throughout the south-west,' he told Donald. 'It would be a simple matter to get in touch with them and find out the next locations of the fair, if that's what you want, sir.'

'Are you sure that it is, Donald?' Ruth asked anxiously. 'What are you going to do with the information when you get it?'

He gave a scowl. 'All I want is to get on to the local bobbies wherever he's likely to be and ask them to go the fair and make enquiries about him. If that's enough to put the fear of God into him, and make him think I'm about to come after him

172

with a shotgun, I'll be satisfied. I certainly don't want him having anything more to do with Josie.'

He knew it was probably a futile thing to do, but it would give him some satisfaction, at least, for what that bastard had done to his daughter.

It was a relatively simple matter for Steve to find out the locations from his newspaper contacts, since they always advertised when the fair was due to be in their town and the dates never varied from year to year. It was also arranged that the local police would do as Donald Elkins asked and get back to Steve with any information. Shortly before Josie was due home, he had something to report.

'It seems the bird has flown,' he told Donald. 'He's sold his entire outfit and vanished. There was some vague reference to him having gone to Ireland, but nobody was really sure. The only thing they did know was that he'd left the fair for good. I'm sorry.'

'I'm relieved, rather than sorry. It means he won't be coming back to Braydon with the fair next year and Josie will never have to fear seeing him again. We wanted nothing from him, and this is the best thing that could have happened.'

'I hope she'll think so too,' Charlie told him later when she and Steve were alone and sitting close together in the small sitting room. 'She was so crazy about him, Steve, and she may have had time to think about it more calmly now. He is the child's father, after all – however weird it feels for me to be even thinking such things about Josie!' she added.

'Cheer up,' Steve said, sliding his arm around her and giving her a squeeze. 'When she comes home, she'll probably be far too full of this new chap she's met.'

'I hope she won't. She's got too much to think about before she starts any romantic thoughts again.'

'I agree, but it doesn't have to stop us having romantic thoughts, does it?'

Charlie laughed, snuggling into his side. 'I don't see why it should!'

If anyone had told her how easy it would be to fall in love again, she wouldn't have believed them. She knew her feelings for Steve had been there for a long time now, steadily and guiltily growing even while she had been engaged to

Melvin, so perhaps she hadn't really been so much in love with him after all. Josie, too, would find love again one day . . . but not yet, Charlie thought. Please God, not yet.

'Are you looking forward to going home?' Freda asked, when they had begun the return journey to Braydon, the ever-reliable Ned assuring her he would be around the farm all day should her mother need anything.

'In one way, I am,' Josie said honestly. 'In another, I'm definitely not! I don't know what mood Dad will be in, and I have to face them all over again.'

'You've braved it once, and you'll do it again, girl. And if me and Mother have been a help, then I'm glad.'

'You have – more than you know,' Josie told her. 'If ever I feel the need to escape again, I'll know where to come, if you'll have me.'

'There's always room for you at the farm, Josie. And a certain young fellow wouldn't mind seeing you again, either. Young Walter took quite a shine to you.'

'I doubt that he'd be quite so keen if he knew the truth about me,' Josie said, her spirits plummeting. She wouldn't say she had exactly taken a shine to Walter, but she had to admit that she liked him.

'You don't know that.'

'Oh well, I'm sure he'll be taking some other girl to a Saturday night hop now he's got up the courage and discovered he hasn't got two left feet after all.'

Josie wasn't quite sure how she felt about that as the car took them back the way they had come, through the country lanes, fragrant with wild flowers and foliage in midsummer now, through the small hamlets and villages with their quaint thatched cottages and picturesque settings. Going back . . . It occurred to Josie that you could never really escape what had to be faced, and she didn't know why she had ever used that word. There was no escape from what lay ahead for her.

Afterwards, she wouldn't have said it was like the return of the prodigal daughter, though Ruth made a great fuss of her, and Charlie hugged her, and Milly asked cheekily if she had hayseeds growing out of her ears now. She had met her father's eyes and then he had given her a hug, and if she wasn't exactly forgiven, and knew she would probably never be, she felt a sense of reprieve wash over her.

Freda didn't stay very long. She wanted to get back to the farm before it got dark, even though everyone knew that wouldn't be until late. But Josie instinctively knew the real reason she couldn't bear to linger. For those few weeks there had been youth and lightness inside that farmhouse, despite the circumstances of Josie being there. Apart from the workmen there would be just the two women again now, one old and one middle-aged, and Freda was going to feel her loss. Josie flung her arms around her cousin when it was time for her to leave.

'I won't forget what you did for me, Freda,' she said, willing the tears not to fall. 'You never know, perhaps you and Ned will make a go of things one day.'

'What an idea!' Freda said, pretending to be shocked; then she grinned mischievously as Josie walked her out to the car. 'Any messages for Walter?'

'I only saw him a few hours ago, for goodness' sake, but you can tell him I enjoyed our dance. Now go, before I cry all over you. I'll write soon, Freda.'

'You be sure to do that. I'll be watching out for the postman, mind.'

She started up the car with its usual crunch, and Josie winced as she steered it haphazardly out of the hotel yard. She stood still for a moment or two before she turned to go back inside to her family. Freda had been gone all of a minute, and she was missing her already. But now she had to resume her real life, even if it seemed stranger to her now than the one she had lived on the farm. In a week or so the annual carnival would take place in the town, and she tried to feel excited about it, the way Clover had always done; but for the life of her, she couldn't. Looming ahead of her, too, was the next visit to the doctor that had already been arranged.

'Do I have to see him, Mum?' she asked Ruth. 'I don't feel sick any more, and it's going to happen whatever he says, isn't it?'

It wasn't meant to sound defensive, but Ruth took it that way.

'You'll do as we think fit in this, Josie, and there are arrangements to be made. Doctor Jacobs will be able to give us advice on that when we see him.'

Josie felt her heart begin. 'You mean he'll give us advice about sending me away until it's born and then having it taken away from me, don't you?'

'Darling, you know it's for the best.'

'Well, I know it's for the best for you and Dad and everybody else, of course. But what about me? What about what I want?'

Ruth looked at her in alarm. 'What *do* you want, Josie? You know it's a sin to try to interfere with nature, and I wouldn't hear of such a thing.'

For a moment Josie didn't understand what she meant, and then her face went white and she was totally shocked. When she'd first known the truth, she had screamed and ranted to be rid of the growth inside her as if it was an alien being. She had almost willed it to be gone from her body . . . but she knew she could never harm it personally. She would never allow any interference to induce its removal. It would be even more wicked than the way it had been conceived. It hadn't asked to be born, but it had a right to life. She felt choked as she answered her mother.

'Of course that's not what I mean, Mum, but I don't want to be sent away and then have it taken away from me, either. How would you feel if it had been me or Charlie or Milly? Could you bear to have been parted from any of us?'

'It's hardly the same, Josie.' Ruth's face was as red as Josie's was pale now.

'But it *is* the same. It's my baby, and if I want to look after it and care for it myself, I have to go away from my family. Is that what you mean?'

Of course it was. One look at her mother's face told her it would inflict too much shame on them all if she stayed. Any fanciful ideas that her mother might even agree to bring up the baby as her own flew right out of her mind. But she had to make one last try.

'You can't stop me doing what I want.'

Ruth spoke more sharply. 'I most certainly can. You may think you're an adult and that you should do the right thing

176

by your child. But Josie, admirable though it may seem to you, you forget that you're not of an age to make such decisions. You have to abide by what your father and I think best for everyone.'

Josie stared at her dumbly. She could see how difficult it was for her mother to say these things. It wasn't Ruth's way to discuss intimate matters, but presumably once she had been sent away to some awful place and the baby was born and handed over to someone else, Josie would be allowed back and life could resume as before. Except that it couldn't, not ever.

'I refuse to discuss it any more until we've seen the doctor,' Ruth went on briskly. 'He'll have some information for us and we can talk more then.'

But Josie had to talk to someone. The night before she was due to see the doctor she sat on Charlie's bed, as angry and confused as Milly ever was. But these were far from childish matters to discuss. Charlie let her pour it all out, and then sat with folded arms while Josie caught her breath.

'Well, you've had a couple of months to get used to the idea now, Josie, and no matter what Mum and Dad and Doctor Jacobs say, I also think that you must have your say in this. But if you really want to keep the baby, I don't see how you can stay here. You'd have to be separated from your family for a start, and you can't manage on your own.'

'I know Freda would have me. She said so, and I'm sure she'd help me take care of the baby too.' She really couldn't remember if Freda had actually said those words, but she hoped desperately that it would be true. Freda loved all small things, and she would love this baby too.

Charlie knew this was far too serious to smile about. All the same, she felt bound to say what she thought. 'I can't imagine you living permanently on a farm on the wilds of Exmoor, however much help Freda would give you! But Mum's right in one thing: you're too young to make this decision, Josie.'

'I'm not too young to have a baby, am I?'

The bedroom door suddenly flew open and Milly stood there in her nightgown, her eyes big and round, her mouth gaping open.

'Who's having a baby? I knew there was something funny going on, but nobody ever tells me anything, do they?'

Stunned, they both knew there was no possibility of hiding it from Milly now. They overlooked the fact that she must have been eavesdropping outside the door, even if she hadn't heard very much. Smothering their nerves, they explained it as simply and carefully as they could, considering the way emotions were flying high. Milly was alternately awed and excited to think she would be an auntie. And then she said the one thing that stopped her older sisters in their tracks.

'So is that why you went away, to get married?' she asked Josie. Then she frowned. 'Nobody told me, and I could have worn my bridesmaid dress after all.'

She ignored the fact that she hadn't particularly wanted to wear it at all, and clearly she hadn't worked out the timing, nor considered the fact that Josie wasn't wearing a wedding ring. Josie looked at her dumbly, her brief euphoria at Milly's childish excitement fading fast.

'Josie didn't get married, Milly love,' Charlie said at last.

'How can she be having a baby, then?' Milly said, frowning even more. 'You have to be married to have babies. We learned it at school. It has to have a father as well as a mother, doesn't it?'

'I did get married in a *sort* of way, Milly,' Josie said desperately, 'but then he died and I'll never see him again. I was very upset, which is why I went away to stay with Freda and Aunt Mary.'

It was yet more lies, but in Josie's mind it was the only thing she could do as Milly was concerned. At least it was true that she would never see Tony again. Her father had told her how he'd tried to trace him and what had happened.

'Gosh,' Milly said at last, clearly seeing Josie as the most tragic figure ever now. 'Was it that fairground chap who died?'

Josie nodded, her eyes lowered and her lips trembling.

Milly swallowed, seeing how distressed her sister was. 'I'm really sorry, Josie, for reading your diary and all that,' she mumbled. 'So when is the baby going to be here?'

The excitement was back in her eyes, and sensing how Josie was nearly ready to fall apart, Charlie took charge, speaking urgently.

178

'Listen to me, Milly. You can imagine how upset Josie is over all this, and how difficult it would be for us to have a baby in the hotel when we're always so busy. So Josie may decide to go and stay with Freda until after it's born.'

'She'll come back, though, won't she?' Milly said, not seeing any significance in this. 'I can help to look after it!'

'We'll see,' Josie said faintly, thinking that matters had been practically taken out of her hands now, no matter what her parents and the doctor thought. If this was the only way to keep Milly's innocence a little longer, then it had to be. She had always felt irritated with her younger sister, but now she felt such a need to protect her from the truth it was almost painful.

'Go to bed now, Milly. You should have been asleep hours ago, anyway,' Charlie ordered. 'And you're not to repeat any of this to anyone, especially not to Dorothy. We don't want people feeling sorry for Josie and making things worse. This is private family business, and it has to be *kept* private; and you're old enough now to be trusted. Do you understand what I'm saying?'

'Of course I do. I wish I could tell Dorothy, though.'

'Not even Dorothy,' Charlie said. 'It's important, Milly, and if I find out that other people know, I shall know who's betrayed a confidence and been disloyal to her family, won't I?'

Josie broke in shrilly. 'How do we know we can trust her?'

Charlie slid off the bed and went to a drawer in her dressing table. 'We'll make sure,' she said.

She grabbed Milly's hand and thrust it over the object she held.

'Milly, press your hand tightly to Clover's old Bible, and swear never to reveal anything you've heard in this room tonight, and that you will never betray any of your family's business. So help you God,' she added for good measure.

Trembling, Milly did as she was told. Then Charlie smiled and shook her hand as if she was a grown-up.

'Good girl. You're one of us now, Milly. The three musketeers who always help one another and never betray secrets,' she said, knowing the literary allusion would appeal to Milly's school snobbery.

She was right. There was an undeniable spark of pride in

Milly's eyes as she nodded. She almost ran out of the room, no doubt remembering other times when she had been disloyal to her family, and vowing silently never to do it again.

'Do you think she'll do as you say?' Josie asked in a strangled voice.

'What – with the fear of God in her? I should say so!' Charlie said. 'I didn't want to frighten her, but it seemed the only way. But we've got no choice now, Josie. We'll have to let Mum and Dad know what's happened. They won't be pleased that Milly's discovered the truth, but if the little sneak hadn't been eavesdropping she'd have been none the wiser. Not yet, anyway.'

'Not yet,' Josie said bitterly, 'but it can't be kept a secret for ever, can it? That's the one thing I can't do.'

'You handled it well, love, telling her you were sort of married. Seeing the kind of rough-and-ready bloke that Tony was, she'll probably think it was a kind of romantic gypsy wedding.'

'You don't think I added to my wickedness, then, for telling more lies?' Josie said, awash with misery again.

'I think if you don't stop covering yourself with sackcloth and ashes we'll all be weighed down with it. Let's go and face the music.'

Josie caught her sister's hand as Charlie got up from the bed.

'I do think the world of you, Charlie, and I don't deserve it after what I did.'

'I've already told you that you did me a favour, so I don't want to hear any more about it. Besides, now I've got Steve.'

She allowed a small smile to play around her mouth as she said his name, knowing it was true. There could be nothing worse than being married to the wrong man. For so long she had thought Melvin was the man she loved, but now she knew what love really meant.

Donald and Ruth were enjoying their late-night cocoa when the delegation entered the small sitting room. They relished these last private moments together after the bustle of the hotel day, and their daughters had always respected that. But they both sensed, from their set expressions and heightened cheeks, that Charlotte and Josie had something important to tell them.

'What is it?' Ruth asked quietly.

'Milly knows,' Josie said flatly.

Her father gave an expressive oath that made Ruth flinch, but before he could say anything, Charlie quickly told them all that had happened, and that swearing on Clover's Bible would ensure that the girl would respect their confidence.

'I hope you're right,' Donald snapped. 'This thing is going from bad to worse, just as I knew it would.'

'Donald, please,' his wife remonstrated, seeing the tortured expression on Josie's face. But Josie was feeling calmer now, and it was far too important to her to throw a tantrum the way the old Josie would have done.

'I've decided what I want to do.' She spoke up as steadily as she could. 'And before you *tell* me what to do, I have to do what's best for my baby. I know it was conceived in the worst possible way, and I'm bitterly sorry for the pain I've caused you. But it deserves a chance to life and to know that its mother loves it, even if I never want to see the father again.'

She finally choked, never having made such a speech before, and not at all sure how her father would receive it. Ruth was gripping his hand, and finally he spoke a fraction less aggressively.

'So how and where do you propose to bring up this child, may I ask?'

'Not here, Dad. I won't embarrass you any more than I have already.'

'Josie, dear, we only want what's best for you,' Ruth put in hastily.

'Then believe me when I say haven't thought about this on the spur of the moment. It's been on my mind for a while now – and before either of you says I'm still a child and can't possibly know my own mind, I've grown up quite a bit in these last couple of months.'

They couldn't mistake the quiet determination in her voice now, even though it quavered now and then.

'Go on, Josie,' Ruth said gently, already anticipating what was coming.

'I want to live with Freda and Aunt Mary on the farm. They'll take care of me, and the baby too. I don't want to be sent away to some cold place where nobody knows me and then face having my baby taken away from me. I grew up in a loving family, and I want that for my baby too. But I want your blessing as well. I couldn't bear to go away, knowing that you hated me for what I'd done.'

She finally dissolved in tears, but she had said it now, and she had never meant anything so deeply. She had always been a wayward daughter, and she knew she was paying the price for it. Then she heard her father's throat clearing, and she felt her mother's arm go around her.

'We don't hate you, girl,' Donald said gruffly. 'We can never condone what happened, but we don't hate you. You've given us something to think about, but it's late and we're all tired, so I suggest we all go to bed and talk about it again after you've been to see the doctor tomorrow.'

'All right,' she whispered. 'But whatever he says, my mind's made up.'

'Did I go too far?' she asked Charlie nervously, when they went upstairs. 'It just came tumbling out and I couldn't seem to stop it.'

'As a matter of fact, I was proud of you, especially when you said you'd grown up quite a bit in the past few months. I think that's true, Josie. You're not the same girl you were when you flounced about the place and generally annoyed people. Clover would be proud of you too,' she added.

Josie's eyes prickled with tears again. 'That's the best thing anyone could ever say to me, Charlie. And I think I can sleep tonight now, without being too worried about seeing Doctor Jacobs tomorrow. I was dreading it, but now that I know what I want, and that Freda will help me, it doesn't seem so awful any more.'

'We'll all help you in any way that we can,' Charlie assured her. 'And when all's said and done, having a baby in the family should be a happy occasion, shouldn't it? There's a lot to look forward to.'

For the first time that evening, Josie's face broke into a smile. 'Thank you for that. I don't feel so isolated any more.

All I have to do now is to make sure Freda knows what she's in for, and that she really did want me to stay there.'

There was no time like the present, and once Charlie had gone back to her own room, Josie began the letter. She told Freda everything that had happened on a night that had become one of momentous importance in Josie's mind now. They all seemed to have come so far – even Milly, sworn to secrecy on Clover's Bible, which she would never betray, and going to bed with such a spark of pleasure in her eyes at being one of the three Elkins musketeers.

She didn't intend to finish the letter tonight. There was still tomorrow to get through, and decisions had to be made before she asked Freda the most vital question of all. Her resolve faltered for a moment as she considered it. Could she and Aunt Mary really cope with a young girl and a baby living with them permanently on their remote farm, and would they really want to? And could Josie seriously cope with it herself?

Seventeen

Josie found an unexpected ally in her mother when they sat across the desk from Doctor Jacobs. Once he had given Josie a brief examination, asked some pertinent questions and told her that all seemed to be progressing normally, he produced some leaflets and the details of what he called a mother-and-baby home. He droned on about the facilities and that she would be looked after until after the birth, when she would be allowed home. Depending on how long her father was willing to pay for her keep, she could go as soon as she pleased, to get used to her surroundings and the staff. It sounded as cold and clinical as himself, and very much as if he was sure Donald would want to be rid of an awkward situation as soon as possible.

'What if I don't want to go to one of those places?' Josie burst out.

The doctor frowned. 'Well, the other alternative, of course, is if your family are willing to take you in and look after you and the child. You must be aware of the stigma attached to this idea, and I'm sorry to say it's rarely acceptable among professional families such as yours, Josie.'

'What do you mean – *take me in*? I already live at home!' she said, trying to ignore how insulted she felt by the rest of his words.

'I know you do, my dear, but your father has a reputation to uphold in the town, and so do you, and I'm sure your parents only want— '

'If I hear anyone else say they only want what's best for me, I shall probably go mad!' she said, starting to shake, because although she was in a fury she had never spoken to a doctor this way before. It was then that Ruth took a hand.

'Doctor Jacobs, I want to ask you about an alternative. Supposing Josie had distant relatives living away from here who would look after her and the child, and support them afterwards?'

'Are there such relatives?' Doctor Jacobs asked.

'There may be,' Ruth told him, giving nothing away, 'though I have to say they do live in a very sparse rural community.'

The doctor sat back, looking at them shrewdly. 'Then as the girl's doctor I feel it my duty to advise you that there are other things to consider as well as the support of well-meaning relatives. Is there a doctor in the vicinity, or at the very least a competent midwife? Should complications occur, which I don't anticipate, although such things can never be ruled out – is there a hospital nearby and the means of getting there in a hurry?'

'I don't know, but those are things we would naturally have to find out before anything was decided,' Ruth said, starting now to find his superior attitude as objectionable as Josie did.

'My dear Mrs Elkins,' he said, seeing the stiffness in her shoulders, 'I am merely warning you of any difficulties that could arise. If all seems well with these relatives, and they are willing to help, then it is up to you to make the choice. Josie is a healthy young woman, and I have no doubt she will have a healthy child.'

'Then we will make the necessary enquiries, Doctor Jacobs, and we will keep you informed, of course,' Ruth said.

'Please do, and I suggest you take these leaflets if you decide you wish me to proceed. If you eventually go ahead with your alternative arrangements, I will need to give you a letter for another doctor, together with Josie's medical notes. Now I wish you both good day.'

He ushered them out, clearly thinking they were behaving in a very foolish manner, and once they were outside in the street Josie let out her breath, feeling as if she had been holding it for ever.

'Mum, you were magnificent!' she gasped. 'I thought he was going to force me into one of those awful places there and then.'

'He's nothing but a pompous old goat,' Ruth said, using language that was totally unlike her. 'I must say he hasn't aged well over the years.'

Josie gaped in astonishment for a moment and then she burst out laughing. It seemed years since she had done such a thing, and then they were both laughing together, and several local matrons smiled back at them, commenting to each other that the middle Elkins girl seemed to be turning into a dutiful young woman after all.

Donald had been doing some hard thinking as well. By now the shock of what had happened was lessening, even to him. It was something that had to be faced, and in a way that would cause the least disruption. His girl had done wrong, and she knew it, but there was a new life beginning, and when he had finally drifted off to sleep last night he had found himself asking seriously what his mother, Clover, would have made of it all, and how she would have dealt with it.

He had almost imagined her standing indignantly at the foot of his bed, her sharp eyes flashing, her hands firmly on her hips in those outrageous and flamboyant clothes she liked to wear. He had almost heard her voice . . .

Are you telling me you could seriously think of abandoning your own daughter, Donald? She needs help, not condemn-ation. I'll agree it was a shock, but when all's said and done, the baby will be your grandchild. Are you prepared

to sacrifice it for the sake of your pride? Young Freda's got
more compassion in her little finger than you've got in your
whole body, but if she and Mary are going to look after
Josie, they'll need help on that meagre farm of theirs too.
Babies need cots and prams and clothes, and you're just the
one to provide it all.

He had awoken with a start, peering into the darkness. He
was almost afraid he really had conjured his mother up out
of the ether, and that he'd see her standing there, accusing
him. As if he'd been the one to do wrong, he'd thought indignantly, but gradually, her words, whether real or imagined,
began to seep into his brain and he couldn't get them out.
They were still there, nagging away at him, when Ruth and
Josie came home from the doctor's visit.

Josie went straight upstairs, leaving her mother to tell him
all that had happened, and finding it more difficult than she
had thought to finish her letter to Freda. She knew she was
virtually asking her cousin and aunt to take on the responsi-
bilities of parents, and she didn't know if it was fair. Aunt
Mary was getting old, and might not want a squalling baby
about the place. She was still dithering over what to write
when she heard a knock on her door. She called out to whoever
it was to come in, and Milly appeared.

'Why aren't you at school?' Josie said automatically.

'It's over for the day,' Milly said. 'Don't you know what
time it is?'

'I hadn't noticed. So what do you want, Milly?'

The girl came inside, closing the door behind her, looking
more uncertain than she usually did. She held out a card.

'I made this for you last night,' she said.

Josie took it without much enthusiasm and then stared. The
card said 'Congratulations' on the front, and inside was a
picture of a baby, obviously cut out from a magazine.

'I didn't put any words on it, 'cos I know I'm not meant
to say anything,' Milly said hastily, 'but I thought you might
like it.'

Josie felt her eyes prickle. 'Oh Lord, Milly, this is such a
responsibility for you, isn't it?' she said, only just now realizing it. 'I wish we'd never had to tell you, then you wouldn't
have had to swear to keep it secret.'

186

'I don't mind. I like secrets. Besides, I don't tell Dorothy *every*thing, and I'm not a kid any more! You will let me help when the baby comes, won't you?'

She was so eager and so innocent that it brought a lump to Josie's throat. All Milly saw was the excitement of having a new baby in the family. There was no stigma attached to it as far as she was concerned. If only everyone saw it like that.

'I don't know what's going to happen yet, Milly. I may stay with Freda for a while when it's born, and perhaps before it's born too.'

'Why can't you stay here?' Milly asked, puzzled.

Josie desperately didn't want to destroy her innocence, nor see the shock on her young face if she knew the sordid details. She said the first thing that came into her head.

'We think the country air will be best for the baby, and besides, everyone's so busy in the hotel it's not fair to Mum and Dad to land them with it.'

'But I'd never see it then!'

'Of course you would. I wouldn't stay away for ever, Milly, and I wouldn't want to, but we have to think what's best for everyone, don't we?'

'I suppose so,' Milly said uncertainly, clearly not seeing at all.

To Josie's relief they heard Ruth calling for Milly, and the awkward conversation was put to an end. Once she was alone, Josie tried to finish her letter to Freda and just couldn't find the words to say any more. It seemed that every time she spoke to a different person about her problem, her thoughts were in turmoil again, and poor Milly didn't deserve to have to grow up so suddenly. Pest though she had always been as far as Josie was concerned, she was still her kid sister, and she loved her. She screwed up what she had already written in her letter, and put the matter aside until she could think more clearly. She didn't have to decide on anything yet: the baby wouldn't be born until next March and it was only September. She felt her hand go to her stomach, wondering sadly if it had any idea how much trouble it was causing, and it wasn't even here yet.

*   *   *

187

Saturday was always turnaround day at the hotel. The guests who had been here for a few days or a week would be leaving in the morning, and any new ones arrived in the late afternoon. This gave the family time to change the bedding, organize the rooms and give them a thorough airing and cleaning, and prepare the menus for the following week. The three Elkins girls were all expected to pitch in with Ruth in these chores, and once breakfast was over, it began in earnest. It wasn't until mid-morning that they stopped for a welcome cup of tea before it was time to hang out the freshly-laundered sheets that had been simmering away in the wash boiler.

'Where's Dad?' Charlotte asked suddenly. 'I haven't seen him since the last of the guests left.'

'He's got a business meeting today,' Ruth told her. 'He probably won't be back until this evening.'

'Where's he gone – Timbuktu?' Josie said with a grin. Ruth didn't reply, busying herself at the stove, and Josie felt her heart begin to thud.

She didn't say anything until she could get her mother alone for a few moments while they hung out the sheets on the line, and then she spoke quietly. 'What's this business meeting of Dad's, Mum?'

'It's nothing that need concern you, dear.'

'Is that true?'

Ruth turned and looked at her. 'I'm not in the habit of telling fibs, Josie.'

'I think it does concern me if Dad's gone to find out one of these mother-and-baby homes the doctor was talking about,' she said shrilly. 'Please tell me that isn't where he's gone, Mum!'

'I promise you he hasn't, Josie, so calm down and don't get yourself in a state about it. It's just a business meeting to do with finances, and you know your father never likes to involve any of us in those matters.'

They all knew that only too well, remembering how humiliated Donald had felt when he had had to admit that they simply couldn't afford to rebuild the hotel after the old one had collapsed. And then the miracle had happened when they'd found Clover's old will and realized that they had been saved. The Retreat had gone for ever, but out of the ashes, literally, they had been able to build the aptly-named Phoenix. Josie conceded that it was the only time Donald had ever spoken to them about money matters, so she had to accept that what her mother said now was the truth.

'So now can we get on with the work and stop speculating?' Ruth said mildly. 'You need to think calm thoughts, my dear, difficult though that may seem. I won't say the worst is over for you, but you've faced it all so far and I'm sure you've got the strength of character to deal with the future, Josie.'

She turned to the washing line, struggling to contain the bedsheet in the breezy air, and Josie helped her in silence. Whatever financial discussions her father was having, at least they knew the hotel was more than solvent now, and there were no more worries on that score.

Josie would have been more surprised had she known in which direction her father was driving on that morning. He wasn't going to Bristol to deal with bankers and accountants, as might have been expected. Instead, he turned westwards, heading away from Braydon and out on to the open country roads and up into the hills in the direction of a small village called Gulliford on Exmoor.

It took several hours before he reached the place where his cousin Freda and Aunt Mary lived. Before he approached the sprawling farmhouse he stopped the car and gazed down at it and the surrounding moorland. The farm wasn't totally isolated. The village was nearby and from here Donald could see the top of the church and a few cottages. Apparently there was a village hall where occasional social activities took place. Was that enough to stop a young girl like Josie going mad with boredom? But she would be a more than a young girl soon. She would be a young mother, however impossible such a state still seemed to her father.

He stopped his meandering thoughts and drove down to the valley in which the farm stood. At least it was fairly sheltered and not open to the worst of the prevailing winds and wintry weather that could strike the top of the moors in winter.

A few chickens in the yard squawked and flew about at his car's arrival, but there seemed to be such a banging and hammering going on inside that no one seemed aware of his presence as he knocked on the farmhouse door. He was about to push it open and go inside, when he heard a voice calling his name from somewhere behind him.

'Donald, by all that's holy, what are you doing here? It's not Josie, is it? Don't tell me anything happened to the poor girl – or the babby.'

He turned around to see Freda coming towards him with a basket of eggs in her hand. She was dressed so comically that for a moment he gaped, wondering if he was seeing a younger incarnation of his own mother, Clover. But then he realized that the heavy, mannish boots, the trousers and the colourful knitted shawl around Freda's shoulders were sensible garb for a countrywoman, especially up here, where fashion was the least important concern in a woman's wardrobe.

'Here, let me help you with that,' he said, taking the basket of eggs from her hands, as if she hadn't been doing such tasks every day of her life. 'And there's nothing wrong with Josie, but it's her that I want to talk to you about.'

'Aye, I rather thought you might,' Freda said shrewdly. 'You'd best come inside then, and Mother will make us some tea. You must be starved, coming all this way, so you'll have a bite to eat with us too, and then we'll talk.'

Donald had never put her down as a woman in control, but up here he realized she was very much in her own domain, and he was the outsider. Presumably Josie had never felt like that, or she wouldn't have wanted to stay.

He greeted Aunt Mary and was told to sit down in the parlour while she made the tea and a dish of rabbit stew to keep out the cold, and he began to feel slightly light-headed. Mary had shown no surprise at seeing him here, unlike Freda. It was almost as if he'd been expected. It was the way Clover would have behaved, bossy and quick, and accepting. Mary was her sister, of course, with the same small bird-like features and inquisitive manner. If she lived to be a hundred, she'd never lose that, and Donald felt a pang of sadness that he'd never hear that same sharp voice from his own mother again. He cleared his throat.

'What's all the hammering going on?' he asked Freda.

'Didn't Josie tell you? We've had a wall knocked down and

a new indoor lav installed. It's for Mother's benefit really, so she don't have to go out in the cold at night, though she'd say she's perfectly capable of doing what she's always done. She's not getting any younger, though. It's taking a long time to do, since the lads have other work to do as well, but we're in no hurry. We're not going anywhere, and it's not like you towns-folk who want everything done in a minute,' she said agreeably.

'I remember Josie saying something about it now,' Donald said, although he'd truly forgotten. It hadn't seemed that impor-tant compared with everything else to do with Josie. Now, it did.

'Are you having a bath put in there as well?'

Freda laughed. 'Lord bless you, no. We might think about it one day, but we're not made of money, and we can keep ourselves clean without fancy bathrooms. It was nice to use them in your hotel, though,' she admitted.

'What if I paid for it to be installed?' Donald said.

Mary came back to the parlour with three mugs of tea on a tray and three bowls of steaming stew. She dumped the tray on the table unceremoniously.

'Now why would you want to do that, Donald Elkins? Do you think we need your charity?'

He knew he had to go carefully. They might not have much compared to what he and his family had, but they were proud women.

'It's hardly charity, Aunt Mary. Clover was your sister and when she died and left us all that money we never did anything for you, did we? I think she would have liked us to, so why not give us the chance to do something now to make your lives a bit more comfortable?'

'You never knew your grandfather, did you, Donald?' Mary said. 'He was an adventurer and he and Clover had a gadabout life. My Barney was nothing like that. He was steady and stay-at-home, but he provided well for me and Freda.'

'Well, don't you see that's just what I want to do for Josie?' he said, glad of the lead she had given him.

'And a proper bathroom bath would be nice for Josie when she comes to stay,' Freda stated.

'That's really what I've come to talk to you about,' Donald said at last.

'Thought so,' Mary said, taking a great slurp of tea.

'Josie's very fond of you both,' he said carefully, 'and I don't need to tell you about the bit of trouble she's in.'

'Some folk would say that having a babby is God's gift, not a bit of trouble, Donald,' Freda said sharply.

He gave a heavy sigh. He wasn't being his usual forthright self, but these two were making him nervous, and it wasn't a state he cared to be in. He took a deep breath, having just taken too large a spoonful of stew, and found himself spluttering and coughing while he steadied himself.

'Cards on the table now, lad,' Mary said sternly. 'What have you come here for? Don't go telling us it's just to install a bath – though if it's what Freda wants, I'll not say no to it.'

'All right. It's Josie, of course. I can't have her living at the hotel for the next months, for her sake and ours.' He ignored the sniff from Mary and plunged on. 'I won't have her sent away to some clinical place for the birth. Ruth insists that she wants to keep the child, and however hard-hearted you think I am, I couldn't see Josie heartbroken by having it taken away from her. She needs to be somewhere where she's loved.'

'I don't think you're as hard-hearted as you pretend to be, Donald,' Freda told him. 'And there's nowhere she's more loved, apart from her own home, than here. So of course she can come to us. She can live with us as long as she likes, and the babby too. It'll be a joy to have them both.'

'Mary?' Donald asked, startled by the sudden eager look in his cousin's eyes. She'd never had children, but it was plain to see that she would welcome this one.

'You heard what Freda said, lad. Whenever she wants to come, there's a home for her here.'

'Well then,' Donald said, clearing his throat, 'it has to be put on a proper financial footing. A baby needs a cot and a pram, which we will provide in due course. It also has to be fed and clothed. I shall send you some money every month. Initially this will be for Josie's keep, and when the baby comes I will increase it. Before you say anything, it's a father's duty, and I'll hear no arguments.'

Freda gave a large grin. 'I wasn't going to give you any,' she said. 'So finish your stew and then we'll show you the work that's being done.'

Donald wasn't sure who was in the bigger daze now, but it certainly didn't seem to be the two women, he realized. They accepted the state of things so much more naturally than he and Ruth had done, and it humbled him to know that his daughter would be well cared for among relatives who loved her, and that went a long way towards easing his conscience.

When they had finished the meal, Mary cleared away the crockery and said she would be having a nap, as she did most afternoons now. Freda and Donald went through to where the two workmen were pausing in their labour to have a sandwich and the flask of tea they brought from home.

'This is Walter and Perce.' Freda introduced them easily. 'And this is my cousin Donald, Josie's father.'

To Donald's surprise, the younger man jumped to his feet, wiping his hands on his overalls before offering to shake Donald's.

'It's good to meet you, sir, and I hope Josie's well. She's a lovely young lady,' he added without thinking and then blushed right up to his thatch of hair.

A bit nonplussed, Donald replied quickly. 'She's quite well, thank you, but we're here to talk business. My cousin wants to know if you can install a bath in here as well as the lavatory. Or perhaps you would need to hire some professional people to do it?' he added, not sure just how competent these two were.

The man called Perce laughed. 'Bless you, there'd be no need for that, sir. Me and Walter are general handymen, and there ain't much we can't do between us. We get called on for all kinds of jobs in the village and hereabouts.'

'I see. So do you think it's possible?'

'Course it is. If that what the missus here wants, we can do it right enough.'

Donald realized he wasn't the important one here. They deferred to Freda and Freda said it definitely was what she wanted. The men would sort out the details and costs and let her know as soon as possible. Which may take a week or two, as they were doing other jobs in between doing hers. It all seemed pretty haphazard to Donald, but if that was the way they worked, so be it.

'Just as long as it's installed by Christmas,' he said, tongue in cheek, at which Perce whistled between his teeth and said they would do their best.

Freda laughed at Donald's face once they had gone back to the parlour.

'Don't worry, that's just their way, and it'll get priority. I can tell you one young person who'll be pleased to see Josie again too,' she added.

Donald frowned. 'You mean the one called Walter? Is he the one Josie went to the village dance with?'

'He is, but before you make anything of it, they hardly know each other.'

'Well, I don't want to say anything against the boy and I'm sure he's perfectly respectable, but when Josie comes here, in the fullness of time he'll be perfectly aware of what's what, and he may not feel quite so inclined towards her. I'd rather they were kept well apart before any such complications occurred.'

'Good Lord, Donald, what a pompous old preacher you are. Walter's a lovely boy, and as he'll be working here for a while yet, it's not likely that he'll be kept in ignorance of the situation for very long. Especially as his auntie's the local midwife and layer-out, so I'd say it's up to the two of them to decide things for themselves, wouldn't you?'

He felt that odd sense of light-headedness again. She was his cousin and yet she might have been from a different country for all that he knew of her and the way of life of the people around her. And now there was this mention of Walter's auntie who was also the local midwife and layer-out . . . a strange combination if he ever heard one! He began to feel more than a pang that he was virtually shutting Josie out of their lives in sending her here. His only consolation was that he knew she wanted to come and he spoke more briskly.

'Well, I don't want Josie to disappear from us just yet. We have to let our own doctor know what's happening, and you and she must decide between you when she wants to come, and Ruth and I will bring her, of course. I'd like her to stay until after Christmas, but that may not be for the best.'

'I'd say not, if she's showing well by then,' Freda said dryly. 'Besides, the weather may not be too good up here at Christmas. You can never tell. Give it another month, Donald, and then let's decide. The end of October can be a pleasant time on the moor.'

They made their goodbyes, and as Donald was getting back in the car for the journey home, Walter called out to him, his face reddening again.

'Please remember me to Josie, Mr Elkins, and tell her I've not forgotten her.'

He was obliged to agree, aware that Freda was watching him. But on the long journey back to Braydon he felt uneasy. It was not so much at the thought of a nice young man like Walter taking a shine to his girl. Who could blame him for that? He had no idea if Josie felt the same way, and if Freda were to be believed, they hardly knew each other. But if they were thrown into close proximity in a small village for any length of time, who knew what might happen? Walter would discover soon enough that Josie wasn't the innocent that a seventeen year old ought to be, and when that happened, Donald's precious girl could be heading for another bitter rejection.

Eighteen

Once he had told Ruth all that that had occurred, Donald called Josie into the small sitting room. Her uninhibited response was to throw her arms around her father and hug him tight. Then she burst into tears.

'Oh Dad, you don't know what this means to me! I know I've been a horrible daughter, and I did ruin Charlie's wedding day, however happy she is with Steve now; but I know I did the most terrible thing, and I couldn't bear it if you had to hear people in the town whispering about me and feeling sorry for you and Mum for having such an awful daughter—'

'Slow down, for goodness' sake, or you'll expire long before this baby's even born!' he said with a throaty laugh.

She gave a great gulp. 'That's the first time I've heard you refer to it as a baby,' she said shakily, 'but it will be your grandchild too, Dad.'

'Have you been taking to Clover?' he said without thinking.

She stared at him. 'I do talk to her sometimes. I know she can't answer me, but it makes me feel better, and I know how daft that sounds.'

'It doesn't sound daft at all, my love. But we must think of the future now. Freda thinks the end of October would be a good time for you to move to the farm,' he said delicately.

'Yes,' she said, knowing she couldn't hide her condition much longer than that. 'Oh, I know I want to do this, but I will miss you all so much!'

'We'll miss you too. But Gulliford's not the end of the world – and by the way, I had a message for you.' He didn't really want to say it, but he had promised. 'Someone called Walter asked to be remembered to you.'

'Did he?' Josie said, her eyes sparkling for a moment, and then she shrugged. 'When I've been at the farm for a while it'll soon put a stop to any romantic notions he might have about me, won't it?'

'Even sooner,' Donald said, with a wry attempt at humour. 'His auntie's the local midwife and layer-outer. She sees 'em in and she sees 'em out.'

It was so unlike him to make such a joke that Josie wondered if she had heard him properly. Then she saw that his lips were twitching, and she began to laugh with him, while wondering just how soon Walter's auntie would have to be made aware of her condition when she moved to Gulliford. Not *too* soon, she hoped.

'So it's settled,' Charlotte told Steve Bailey. 'I'm glad for Josie. I never thought she'd want to go and live on a farm, but she and Freda hit it off so well that it's probably the best thing that could have happened.'

'For your parents too,' Steve said.

'Yes, and I can see their point of view, Steve. In their position it would have become very embarrassing for them, and it's not something you can hide, is it?'

'Well, I've never been in the family way myself, so I wouldn't really know,' he said, poker-faced.

She laughed, breaking the small tension between them. 'Well, neither have I, but you know what I mean!'

'Would you like to be one day, Charlie?' he asked, looking straight ahead as they strolled along the seafront on that Sunday evening. 'In the family way, I mean, and once you found a suitable husband, of course.'

Charlie felt her heartbeats quicken. They were walking out properly now, but they had never spoken about being together for always, nor about intimate things like marriage and children. Ever since her break-up with Melvin Philpott too much had been going on in the family with Josie to think seriously about herself. She was just happy to have Steve around as a sympathetic shoulder whenever she needed it.

'I never really thought about it,' she said slowly.

'Well, think about it now. I mean it, Charlie.' He drew her to a nearby bench and they sat down together. 'You must know how I feel about you, and how I've felt about you from the day we first met. You were out of bounds to me then, and I respected that. But you've got the rest of your life ahead of you, sweetheart, and so have I. I want a wife and children, and you're the one I want to share my life with. I know you'll say it's too soon and that we should wait awhile, and I'm prepared to do that if only you'll say the word.'

'What word is that?' she murmured idiotically, taken off guard at such an impassioned little speech.

He caught her hands in his, regardless of who might be watching on that late-summer evening. 'I think you know the word I want to hear.'

'Then it's – *yes*,' she said. 'Providing we wait until Josie's had her baby before you dare to ask my father, and land the family with another shock!'

'I can wait for ever now that you've said the word,' Steve said fervently.

Charlie laughed, her nerve-ends tingling. 'Well, I can't!' she said.

It wasn't hard to guess that Charlotte Elkins had found a new love who adored her. Before Josie left for Gulliford at the end

October, Charlie couldn't resist telling her sister everything, who said airily that it had been obvious for ages, and nobody was going to be surprised if they set the date.

'It won't be until after next March at the earliest. There's someone else to be added to the family before Steve. And no matter what's been said in the past, Josie, you should try to be happy about the baby and not resent it.'

She grimaced. 'I know, but I'm not looking forward to actually having it. I haven't said this to anyone else, Charlie, but I'm really scared. Well, terrified might be a better word for it! I find myself looking in prams when I go out and studying the size of babies' heads and I'm sure I can never do it.'

'You haven't got much choice, you goose, and women have been having babies for ever, so it can't be all that terrible, can it?'

She hoped she sounded more convincing than she felt, and she asked Josie how she felt about Walter's auntie being the midwife.

'I'd much rather it had been someone else! But at least Walter will find out what's what pretty soon, and then if he thinks I'm a bad girl and doesn't want anything more to do with me, I'll know that too.'

'Do you want to have anything more to do with him?'

Josie considered. 'I don't know. I don't want a boy at all right now. But Walter and Tony are as different as chalk and cheese. I know I could trust Walter, and he was more fun that I expected at the village hop. I don't suppose he'll want to go dancing with me when I'm as big as a house, though,' she said gloomily.

Charlie didn't know what to say to that. They were sitting on Josie's bed, as they had done so often in the past, and she had intended to cheer her up with some good news about herself. It didn't seem to have worked, and Josie's moods were as up and down as a yo-yo. She was about to go when Josie gave a sudden exclamation and pressed her hand to her gently-rounded belly.

'What's wrong?' Charlie asked.

'I don't know. A funny feeling. There it is again. It's almost like fingers fluttering inside me. It's like something moving. It's like – like something alive!'

Charlie laughed out loud, although her laughter was tinged with awe. 'It *is* alive! It's your baby. If you'd bothered to read those leaflets the doctor gave you, you'd know that just about now you could be feeling it move for the first time. Don't you know *anything*, Josie?'

Josie scowled.'Well, it's a bit creepy, knowing I've got something alive inside me, and that it's moving about! How long is this going to last?'

'Until it's born, I think. Ask the doctor about it, for goodness' sake. If you know what to expect, you won't be so scared.'

'I wouldn't guarantee it,' Josie muttered. 'Anyway, I'll be seeing him again to check that everything's all right. Not that I'd let him stop me leaving!'

'That's my girl,' Charlie said with a hug. 'Oh, I'm really going to miss you when you've gone, Josie.'

'You'll be all right. You've got Steve.'

When Josie had her last visit to the doctor, she requested more information about what happened to the female body in a pregnant state. She was given more leaflets, which were very clinical and didn't do much to allay her fears. She had felt the baby move on more than one occasion now, and it both alarmed her and made her feel protective, but now that she knew exactly what it was, she realized she had begun to think of it as a real person, however tiny. She wouldn't think about whether it would be a boy or a girl, but she desperately hoped it wouldn't be a boy. She wanted no miniature reminder of Tony Argetti.

The hotel clientele had dwindled by the end of October, and on a cold and sunny Saturday morning Donald, Ruth and Josie set out on the journey to Gulliford. Milly had begged to go with them, and at the last minute it was allowed. Charlie was manning the hotel reception in case any casual visitors arrived, and Steve had promised to look in from time to time.

It was a tearful parting from Charlie, and from the regulars at the hotel too. They rarely went outside except to take a short, bracing walk along the seafront occasionally, but as long-time friends now, they had been privileged to know why Josie was leaving. After the initial shock, the Misses Green had excitedly promised to knit as many little garments for the baby as Josie could wish for, and had promised to teach Milly to do the same. Josie's old employers at Hallam's Stores had been airily told she was going to help her cousin on her Exmoor farm, and that it would be a lark, and they had accepted it with their usual tolerance of the madcap Josie Elkins.

'Promise you'll write to me the way you used to write to Freda,' Charlie told her fiercely on that last morning. 'I'll want to know everything, especially about Walter whoever-he-is.'

Josie laughed shakily. 'I doubt that there'll be anything to tell, but I'll write often, I promise.'

They hugged each other tightly for a moment, and then Josie was bundled into the car before they disgraced themselves by undignified weeping. She wasn't being banished to the other side of the world, but right then it felt like it to both of them, knowing it was the first splintering of the family unit.

But the nearer they got to Gulliford, the more relaxed Josie became. This was going to be her salvation, and if her parents too were feeling the pang of parting, then they could all be glad that Milly had been included in the journey. She was allowed to mention the baby within the family, and her innocent chatter did much to relieve the tension in the rest of them.

'I'm going to start by knitting a vest for it,' she said excitedly. 'How big do you think it will be, Josie?'

'Not too big, I hope. About the size of your baby doll, I expect. If you can make it to fit her it will be about right. You've got plenty of time, anyway. It's months and months away yet.'

She often willed it to stay as far away as possible. She wasn't ready yet, and sometimes she had moments of sheer panic, wishing she could wake up one morning and find it was all a dream – or a hideous nightmare. And then she would feel that tiny kick in her stomach again, and she would experience a weird sense of guilt about being unkind to the baby, however foolish it seemed. It wasn't as if it could read her thoughts, was it!

'You've gone quiet, Josie,' her mother said, after a while.'Are you unwell?'

'I'm all right, Mum, just thinking.'

She was thinking, as she often did now, that this thing inside her that she had once so uncharitably called a growth was by now developing tiny hands and feet and a face with features that would probably resemble her own. And as the time went on, she knew she wasn't hating it any more. She wasn't yet ready to say she loved it, because it wasn't real enough for that. But she knew she had some feelings for it, even before it was born, or else why would she have said she wanted to keep it? She gave a small shudder, thinking that there were more things going on inside a person's mind than they ever dreamed of.

She felt Milly snuggle up to her in the back seat of the car, as if her small shudder had affected her young sister.

'I can't wait to see the baby,' Milly whispered.

'Neither can I,' she said, without thinking. She had to admit that she was becoming irresistibly curious now. The questions still remained. What would it be like, and would it look like *her* and nobody else . . .?

They were all tired by the time they arrived at the farm, and then it was all excited greetings and welcome mugs of tea and showing Milly the farm before hauling out Josie's things from the car and taking them up to her bedroom. They inspected the rudiments of the new bathroom, still far from finished, and with no workmen there today, which produced mixed feelings in Josie.

Mary had made them a meal to sustain the three who would be going back to Braydon and, when the time came, Ruth's eyes were moist as she hugged Josie. She looked at Freda over Josie's head.

'Look after her,' she said.

'You need have no fear of that, Ruth,' Freda replied. 'I've told her she must telephone you from the village once a week without fail. If you need to get in touch with us urgently for any reason, you can always leave a message at the post office, and they'll bring it to us.'

'It would be far better if you had a telephone here,' Donald said suddenly. 'I'll see if it can be done, and if so, I shall organize it.'

'Now, Donald,' Mary said warningly. 'I've told you what I think about you doing stuff for us.'

'It won't be for you. It'll be for Josie. Anyway, it may not be possible. You may be too remote to have it connected.'

'I daresay we're not. A farm farther up the valley has got one,' Mary said.

'Well then,' Donald said with a smile, knowing he had got his way.

It made him feel better, knowing he could do this. Josie had done wrong, but she was still his daughter. He would see about the telephone first thing on Monday, and he wished he had thought about it sooner. If they could speak to one another frequently they would hardly be out of touch at all.

Finally, Mary, Freda and Josie were alone at the farm, all of them aware that this was the start of a new life together to which they would all have to adapt, especially next spring, when there would be four of them. Mary cleared her throat and said she was off to her bed after all the excitement, and the other two felt a sense of relief.

'Now we can make plans,' Freda said. 'I've decided that you should have my bedroom, Josie and I'll have yours.'

'Oh no, I can't turn you out of your room! This is your home, Freda, and my room's a lot smaller than yours.'

'That's exactly my point. Where are you going to put a cot in your room? No, I've made up my mind. We'll leave things as they are until after Christmas, and then we'll get Walter and Perce to change the furniture around. By then you'll probably be too big to get in the small room yourself, let alone have a cot in there as well!'

Josie felt her eyes smart. 'I don't deserve you, Freda.'

The older woman flushed. 'Don't you know what a boost you're giving to our lives as well? We're two old women stagnating here, and now we'll have a new young life to look forward to, as well as your own lovely company.'

'Oh well, if you put it like that!' Josie said.

The farm routine wasn't so strange to her now, and Josie relished the comparative freedom of the outdoor life, away from the conformities of living and working at the hotel. Walter and Perce resumed their activities on the new bathroom on Monday, and there was no doubt that Walter was glad to see her again. She was cautious, though, not wanting to give him ideas, nor to get attached to him. The time would surely come when he would realize she wasn't all that she seemed.

It came sooner than she expected. Freda took her into the village the following week to introduce her to the local doctor and call on the midwife.

'Must we see her yet?' Josie said uneasily.

'Best to get things fixed up,' Freda said briskly. 'The sooner you and Walter can stop creeping around one another like sparring partners, the better.'

'It's got nothing to do with Walter!' But it had, of course. She didn't want to see disillusionment, or disgust, in his eyes. She liked him. It was nothing more than that – but she liked him.

She discovered that Freda could be just as firm as her father when it came to getting things 'fixed up', as she called it. They walked down to the village and into the doctor's surgery. He was nothing like Doctor Jacobs, Josie thought with relief. He was a genial old boy with white hair and a jolly manner, who told her she looked a fine and healthy specimen and that she could look forward to seeing a healthy Miss or Master Elkins when he arrived on the scene.

Next they called at a cottage with smoke curling lazily from a chimney and a welcome mat outside the front door. Freda walked straight inside when someone called out in answer to her knock, and they followed the voice to the kitchen, where they saw a plump woman up to her elbows in flour and pastry.

'Sit you down, both of you, while I finish this off for our Walter's supper, and then I'll make us a nice cup of tea. You'll be Josie, I daresay,' she said with a smile. 'Our Walter took quite a shine to you, and he's told me all about you.'

Not all of it, thought Josie . . .

Freda spoke quickly. 'This is Walter's Auntie Belle, Josie – Mrs Hayes. And our Josie's come to live with us now, Belle.'

Mrs Hayes beamed. 'And a right handsome girl you are too, Josie. You'll be good for those two up there; they need a bit of lively company.'

Josie felt herself blush. So this was the midwife and layer-out, as friendly a countrywoman as you could wish, but she wondered just how friendly she was going to be when she knew why Josie was really here – and how much she'd care for the fact that 'our Walter' had taken a shine to her.

The two older women carried on with their chit-chat until Mrs Hayes had deftly finished the pie and put it in the oven, and a while later they were sitting in the parlour with cups of tea and Belle's speciality shortbread biscuits.

'Now what can I really do for you?' she said at last. 'I don't often get visits from you, Freda, so I'm thinking it must be something to do with Josie here, or am I guessing wrongly and putting my foot right in it?'

'You're not guessing wrongly, Belle.'

'Ah. I did wonder. Even our Walter thought there was a bit of mystery about the lively young lady who'd come on a visit and then decided to come for good.'

'Did he?' Josie said stupidly. Oh God, could everybody tell? If Walter, with his simple country ways, could think there was a bit of a mystery about her, was she already branded?

'There's no need to take on, girl. You're not the first and you won't be the last. So when's it due?'

'March – I think, Mrs Hayes,' Josie mumbled.

Belle consulted a calendar and smiled. 'Good. I haven't got anyone else due in March, so that's no problem. And call me Belle. Everybody else does, except our Walter. Don't you worry, we'll have your babby safely delivered when the time comes, and if it's as pretty as you, it'll be a lucky child.'

'I wouldn't call it lucky,' she murmured without thinking.

'Well, you should. A babby is one of God's miracles. You may think it takes two to create it, but make no mistake, it's one of God's creations, first and foremost.'

'I suppose so,' Josie said, feeling more wretched than re-assured at knowing that this God-fearing woman must realize that the baby hadn't been planned, or wanted, and would never know its father . . .

She patted Josie's hand. 'Look, my dear, I'm not as daft as I'm cabbage-looking, so am I right in thinking that there's no daddy on the horizon?'

Josie nodded, her eyes lowered.

'Well, I'm not here to condemn, just to make sure that the babby comes out in one piece, and as long as it's got a mother to care for it, that's the most important thing. You must want to do that, or you wouldn't be here, would you?'

It was like a light at the end of a long tunnel. Of course she wanted to care for it, and love it, and watch it grow.

She gave Belle a tremulous smile. 'That's right.'

'Well, if you've just seen the doc, then I won't need to take a look at you now. I'll see you in a couple of months' time, but any time you want to drop in for a chat, or you're worried about anything, you just call in and see me. We don't stand on ceremony here, not like townie medics do,' she added, unable to resist the small barb.

Josie felt considerably better by the time they left the village, even though she knew it would be impossible now to keep the truth from 'our Walter'. It shouldn't be so important to care what he thought, but she knew it was. He was her friend, and the only one, apart from Freda and the few other young people she had met at the village hop, that she had in Gulliford.

'I think I should tell Walter myself,' she said as they neared the farm.

'I think that's very wise,' Freda said.

When it was time for him to pack up work for the day, she asked if he wanted to take a walk around the farm. He agreed with alacrity and a little surprise.

'I've got something to tell you,' she said nervously, 'and I'd rather you heard it from me than from your auntie.'

'What's my auntie got to do with it?' he asked.

'He took it better than I expected,' she told Freda later. 'I don't really know *what* I expected, but it was a fairly calm reaction. I think he must have had a sort of inkling, and he said it didn't have to stop us being friends, unless I wanted it to.'

'And do you want it to?' Freda said.

'No, of course not. I just thought he wouldn't want to be seen anywhere near me when I get fat and horrible.'

Freda laughed. 'You won't get fat and horrible – well, not horrible, anyway. You look blooming already, and don't forget that it happens gradually, not overnight. We'll all get used to it.'

'Oh Freda, you're such a tonic to me!' As always, her cousin could make her feel as though the world wasn't such a bad place to live in after all.

Freda refused to let her hide away and Josie soon became a familiar figure in the village. By then the new bathroom was completed and the promised telephone was installed so that she could speak to her family often. Her parents came for a day about a month later, and Charlie brought Steve to see the farm. And then Christmas was approaching and with it Josie felt a great longing to be at home with her own family – and she didn't know how to say so to the two women who had done so much for her. While she was telephoning home one evening a week before Christmas, her father asked to speak to Freda.

'I'll see if we can arrange it, Donald, but it can only be for a couple of days. Good as he is, I can't expect Ned to be in two places every day. I'll let you know tomorrow.'

She turned to Josie when the conversation had finished. 'Your father's invited us all there for Christmas. It depends on the weather, of course, but if you don't think the journey's too much for you in my old car, I'll go and see Ned in the morning.'

Her answer was to have Josie squeezing her tight.

'It's just what I hoped for,' she said tearfully. 'You know, Freda, I'm beginning to think there is a God after all, and that He doesn't think of me as a totally black sheep!'

Nineteen

Christmas Day was also Josie's eighteenth birthday so it would be a double celebration. By then, her figure was well rounded, back and front, and she eyed Freda's old jalopy with some trepidation, wondering how the jolting was going to affect the baby. But Belle had told her cheerfully that a baby was firmly fixed inside its mother and, short of an earthquake, it should come to no harm. Anyway, nothing was going to keep Josie away from spending Christmas with her family, even though there had been strong winds and showers in recent weeks, and on some parts of the moor there was a smattering of snow. Gulliford was usually lucky in that respect, nestling in a valley and sheltered from the worst of it.

On Christmas Eve Walter Hayes turned up at the farm with a small parcel. 'This is for you,' he told Josie, blushing furiously. 'I bought the wool and my auntie made it. It's to keep you warm, you not being so used to our weather.'

She opened it, all fingers and thumbs, and pulled out a bright red knitted scarf. For a moment she couldn't speak, not because she was embarrassed by the gift, but because it reminded her so much of the kind of thing that her grandmother Clover would have worn. Before she could stop herself, she had burst into tears.

Walter looked desperately at Freda. 'I didn't mean no harm, honest, and it don't mean I want anything in return. It's just a gift from a friend.'

Freda soothed him. 'Take no notice, Walter. Come and have some supper with us. It's a lovely thought, and Josie will thank you properly in a minute.'

'Why's she crying then?' he said under his breath, but Josie heard him, and gave him a wobbly smile.

'You should ask your auntie about that, Walter. She'll tell you that ladies in a certain condition often cry for no reason at all. This is a lovely gift and I love it!'

Impulsively she threw her arms about his neck and kissed his cheek, at which he grew even redder. He really was sweet, Josie thought, and not the country hick she had once thought he was.

'So now we've got that out of the way, let's eat this food before it gets cold,' Aunt Mary said.

Walter sat down and cleared his throat again. 'Ned says he's coming up here to help out while you're all away for a coupla days. I could help him, if you like. I've got no work for the next week unless somebody's pipes burst.'

'That would be good, Walter,' Freda said. 'Ned can only spare a bit of his time to see to the feeding and all, and we'd pay you, of course.'

He insisted that there was no need, but Freda said business was business. By the time he was ready to leave that evening,

207

they had all played several games of cards and drunk a little of Freda's home-made wine, and he dared to kiss Josie again. It was only a fleeting touch on the lips, but it was a good feeling to know she had a friend, even if he was never destined to become anything more. She couldn't think about anything like that yet. She just felt better, knowing him.

Christmas Day was a Saturday, and they arrived in Braydon without mishap before midday, well wrapped up in coats and scarves, with blankets around their knees for the journey in the draughty car, and Josie was glad to snuggle her nose and chin down into the red scarf Walter had brought her. Milly noticed it at once.

'It reminds me of something,' she said. 'Was it Gran's? Clover's, I mean.'

Josie laughed. 'I don't think she'd mind you calling her Gran now, love. No, it's a bit like one of hers, but it's not. It was a present.'

She felt herself going a shade less red than Walter, and caught Charlie's glance, knowing she'd have to tell her all. Not that there was anything to tell. Water was just a friend, and he didn't exactly make her heart beat faster – well, only sometimes, when he turned up unexpectedly. She ignored the thought and concentrated on opening presents from the family and the regulars, and exchanging them with the gifts they had brought from the farm, fresh eggs and a cooked chicken to put in the cold store for whenever they needed it.

They dined and drank well that Christmas. Steve Bailey was included in the festivities, making Josie more certain than ever that he and Charlie were destined for one another. Even Steve's dog, the boisterous Rex, was included in the day, and the odd bone tossed to his place in the hotel scullery.

The two older girls took a walk along the seafront on Boxing Day afternoon. It was cold and bracing, but the sea sparkled from the glint of a weak sun, and as they linked arms affectionately, it was suddenly so reminiscent of other days, when Milly would go running ahead of them, shouting to them to wait for her; or the sight of Clover ahead of them, buttoned up to the neck in one of her outrageously garish outfits – such lovely days that were never recognized until they were gone.

'What are you thinking?' Charlotte said.

'Oh, so many things. You, me, Milly, *all* of us – and especially Clover. What would she have thought of me, do you think?'

Charlie squeezed her arm, hearing the uncertainty in her voice. 'I think she'd have been proud of you. You made a mistake, but you've dealt with it in the best way possible. And I know one thing: she'd have been so excited about this baby, she wouldn't have been fit to live with!'

'I shall call it Clover, after her,' Josie said suddenly, having never had such a thought in her mind before.

'Let's hope it won't be a boy then,' Charlie said dryly.

'It won't be. I've decided,' Josie said.

They turned as they heard Milly's voice, and saw her hurtling along towards them. Involuntarily, they released each other's arms, and Milly came between them, holding on to them both. There was a brief, silent moment of unity while Milly got her breath back before she began chattering again.

It was like a symbol of the way they felt about one another, Josie thought. The three Elkins girls, together again. The three musketeers. Seeing Charlie's smile, she knew she felt it too.

All too soon the small holiday was over, and they were saying goodbye again. For Josie, it didn't feel so bad this time. She felt that her father had finally made his peace with her, and had promised that as soon as they heard the news about the baby they would see about ordering a pram. It was bad luck to do so until it was born, Ruth had told her. It wasn't bad luck to have the small pile of baby clothes the Misses Green had already knitted for her, though, and the tiny vest that was Milly's first effort too.

And in the back of the car was the small crib that had been Milly's. How they had saved it after the vicious storm that had wrecked their old hotel, heaven knew, but they had, and it was just the kind of family continuity that Clover would have adored. Josie knew that once she saw the crib beside her own bed at the farm, the baby would finally seem real.

In the next week or so, she and Freda were to exchange bedrooms, and all the furniture would be moved around. Walter and Perce had already promised to see to it in between jobs.

By now, Josie knew how important these two were to the small community, jacks-of-all-trades and no mistake. She felt that special glow again at knowing Walter would make every effort to fit in the jobs for Josie Elkins as soon as he could. She was special to him too, and she realized how much she enjoyed his uncomplicated company.

'Day-dreaming, Josie? Mother's already asleep in the back seat, so why don't you doze off too if you want to?' Freda said, intent on covering the miles back to Gulliford in the ancient car.

'I don't feel like sleeping. I feel, oh I don't know, more alive than I've felt for ages, somehow. I thought I'd be sad at leaving them all again, but I'm not. I feel as if I'm on the brink of a big adventure. Does that sound mad, when we're only going to Gulliford?' she said with a laugh.

'You *are* on the brink of a big adventure,' Freda told her, 'and now we've turned the corner after Christmas, you'll be counting the days until it happens.'

'It's still three months away,' Josie said, knowing what she meant, 'but I'm already impatient.'

'You always were, weren't you? Wanting everything tomorrow, or sooner if you could have it.'

Josie considered. 'So I was, but this is different. *I'm* different. I'm not exactly in my dotage, but I'm not a child any more, either. I think I'm finally ready to have this baby.'

'Well, that's good, because I don't see any way of sending it back!'

Josie laughed. It was odd how they could talk so freely in the confines of a car, even with Aunt Mary gently snoring in the back seat now. They were in a little, jolting world of their own, where no one could hear, and words were merely extensions of thoughts that were private and special.

'I'm *so* glad I came to live with you, Freda,' she said with a catch in her throat.

'If you say it many more times, I shall begin to believe you, Josie love,' Freda said affectionately.

January on the moor arrived with cold blustery winds and occasional downpours of slashing rain, along with the odd bright day. This was the year her baby would be born, Josie thought, and it was probably her imagination, but she was sure she felt the baby kick at that precise moment, as it did quite often now. She was no longer afraid of the feeling, knowing that it was a sure sign that the child was healthy and strong inside her. As far as its father was concerned, she found it amazingly easy to forget that he had ever existed.

She wouldn't be so wicked as to think of this as a virgin birth, because that would be blasphemous, but it was enough to know that Tony Argetti would play no part in either of their lives. Young as she was, she had discovered that there was more than one truth in being called an expectant mother. There was an expectancy of excitement in every day that passed, knowing that the important day was coming.

In what Aunt Mary called the bad month of January, the women at the farm stoked up the fire and huddled around it every evening, reading or knitting or playing cards or dominoes. On a particularly bad night, when the wind howled around the moor, Aunt Mary told Josie that this was the worst side of living in a remote area. It was lovely in the spring when the sun shone and new lambs were being born, and when the moor was coming alive with heather and all kinds of wild flowers, but right now it could be called hell on earth.

'I quite like it like this,' Josie said truthfully, surprising herself. 'It reminds me of a book I read. It was about Yorkshire folk, but they lived on the moors too. It was about a girl called Cathy.'

'I know the one,' Freda said. 'We've probably got a copy here somewhere, but heaven knows where. If you wanted to read it again I'm sure they've got one at the library behind the chemist's shop in the village.'

Josie liked the small library with its hotchpotch collection of books, and there were always people there who asked after her, and always the chance that she would bump into Walter somewhere in the village too. She also called in at his auntie's sometimes, just to say hello. She knew she was subtly and easily being drawn into the lives of these people. In any case, she would see Walter again soon. He and Perce had had to wait until the weather improved to change the bedrooms over while they were busily repairing roofs in the village, but now it was done. The diehards clung to their thatched roofs, but the newfangled cottages had their tiles being constantly blown off at the first sign of bad weather.

To Josie it was quaint to hear tiled roofs being called new-fangled, and it was endearing how so many village folk knuckled down to help one another in a way that wasn't so evident in a busy town, even one as small as Braydon. Here, everyone knew everyone else, and Josie had long been accepted now as Freda's cousin who was in the family way, and that was that.

Walter didn't only come to the farm to fix things. He went walking with her when the weather wasn't too bad, and she enjoyed tramping over the moors with him, feeling a bit like the Cathy in the book she had read. He invited her down to the village hall when there was a beetle drive or a games' evening going on, and such things didn't seem quaint and tame to her any more.

There was no doubt he had taken a shine to Josie now, even if she didn't give him any real encouragement – certainly not the kind of teasing encouragement she had once given Tony. She knew how wrong it would be to tease a boy like Walter, who wasn't sophisticated in any worldly sense, and besides, she didn't want to tease him. If anything should come of their friendship it would happen naturally, and there were more important things for Josie to think about than romantic entanglements.

The most serious thought of all was to wonder why any young man, not just Walter, would want to be saddled with a young girl and a child, especially one that wasn't his own. Such thoughts had a habit of tormenting Josie just when she thought she was coping well, and in her darkest moods she wondered if she was going to be labelled for ever as a woman who had had a baby without a wedding ring on her finger.

She spoke on the telephone frequently to Charlie. She felt close to Charlie now, in a way she never had before. She had done a terrible thing to Charlie, yet it had been the best thing too, and they both realized that. And in the end, it was Josie who was paying the price.

During the first weeks of February she had strange pains in her stomach and she was fearful that something was wrong. By now Belle had become a familiar ally, and she assured

Josie that this was nature's way of preparing her for the birth. They were just 'practice pains', Belle told her cheerfully, and nothing to worry about. Babies had their own way of letting the mother know that they were getting ready to be born. All the calmness Josie had talked herself into went out of the window at the midwife's words.

'Well, *I'm* not ready yet!' she said, in a momentary panic. 'There's still another month to go.'

Belle laughed. 'Bless you, my dear, it don't really matter if you're ready or not. When the babby wants to be born, it'll be born, and there's nothing you can do to stop it.'

'So this – this tightness I keep feeling – that's the sort of pain I can expect, is it?' she asked anxiously.

'Oh well, that sort of thing,' Belle said, telling her nothing. 'But you'll know what it is when the time comes, and you can call me on the telephone, no matter when it is. Babbies have a habit of arriving at awkward times, like the middle of the night, but that's no trouble to me. If the weather's too bad for me to cycle up to the farm, our Walter will bring me in his van.'

Josie wasn't at all sure she would want 'our Walter' in the parlour at the farm when she was yelling and hollering upstairs. Of course, she might not need to yell and holler at all, she thought desperately, and she might be terribly brave and smile through the pain – but remembering the size of other people's babies she had seen, she wouldn't like to bet on it.

'I'm sure it's nothing,' she told Charlie on the telephone that evening. 'But I've got an odd feeling now that I'm not going to last out another month. Belle got all technical this afternoon, telling me the head's engaged, whatever that means, and that I'm not likely to go full term. She makes it sound as if I'm back at school,' she added crossly, trying to take the nervousness out of her voice, and wishing for the briefest moment that that was exactly where she was.

'She sounds as if she knows what she's talking about,' Charlie said reassuringly. 'And you're lucky that she can come whenever you send for her.'

'But that's just the point. She told me she had no other cases booked for March, but she has another woman in the village due at the end of February. What if she's so busy with this other woman that she can't come and help me?' The panic was back in her voice now.

'Josie, for goodness' sake, calm down. There's no point in worrying over something that may not happen at all. In any case, the doctor would come if she was somewhere else, wouldn't he?'

'I suppose so, but I don't want him. I want Belle,' Josie said, as belligerent as ever.

'Then I'm sure she wouldn't dare to be anywhere else!' Charlie said.

But nothing more seemed to be happening and although the practice pains didn't go away, Josie was lulled into thinking Belle had probably just been trying to prepare her for what was going to happen. Then, after she had undressed for bed one evening, she pressed her hand over her belly, murmuring inanely to the baby to stop giving her such a hard time, and that if this was going to go on for much longer, she might change her mind about having it!

She was smoothing the blankets in the crib beside her bed, the way she always did, trying to imagine how they would look with a baby snug inside them, when she gave a great gasp and doubled up in a pain far stronger than the others.

She thought she was going to faint, and then she felt a rush of heat between her legs and for a horribly embarrassing moment she thought she had wet herself. Then she remembered what she had read about the process of giving birth. With no more thought of being relaxed and calm, she shrieked out for Freda to come quickly. Her cousin rushed into the bedroom, telling her to shush or she would wake Aunt Mary, and if it was only a spider on the ceiling, then Freda would deal with it . . .

'It's not a bloody spider,' Josie shrieked again, forgetting herself. 'It's the baby. I think it's coming *now* and it's too soon, Freda! What should I do?'

Seeing the telltale dampness on the floor, Freda quickly realized what had happened. She handed Josie a towel and told her to dry herself and to sit down on the bed and wait to see if she felt any more pains.

'You mean there's going to be more?' Josie squealed.

'Lord love us, Josie, babbies aren't born as quick as opening a tin. It may be some hours yet before it arrives. We'll wait a while longer and then if we think it's really happening, I'll telephone for Belle. Try to think about tomorrow, when you'll most likely be holding your babby in your arms. It'll be worth it all then,' she said encouragingly.

Her words were almost drowned out by another howl from Josie. She had planned on being brave and not yelling or hollering, but that had been before she felt as if her body was starting to be ripped apart down below.

'Perhaps I'd better send for Belle now,' Freda said quickly.

'Don't leave me!' Josie gasped, gripping her hand.

'It'll only be for a few minutes, my love. Belle won't know she's wanted unless I call her, so try to relax and I'll be back in a trice.'

'Supposing she won't be there?' Josie said, her lips starting to chatter with nerves. 'She may be with someone else who she can't leave.'

'Now, Josie, it's too much of a coincidence that two babbies will be born on the same night in one tiny village. Let go of my hand, there's a dear. The sooner I can make the call, the sooner she'll be here.'

Josie lay down, willing the pains not to start again until Belle got here, but they were already relentless and more frequent now. She bit her lips so hard to try to stop herself crying out that she felt blood in her mouth. The ludicrous thought ran through her mind that at least there were no near neighbours to hear, however much fuss she made. There were only the sheep and hens and the wild moorland ponies, who would take such things as giving birth in their stride and with no help from anyone out there on the moors in all kinds of weather. How brave they were, and how humble they made her feel.

Such humility didn't last long, and a fiercer pain than before made her yelp out loud. To her horror, a figure in a volumin- ous long white gown appeared in the doorway, and for one heart-stopping moment she thought she was seeing Clover, her beloved gran . . . but it couldn't be, and she couldn't bear the terrifying thought that this was Clover's ghost sent to get her for being a wicked girl . . .

'Is it your time then, my dear?' said Clover's sister, Mary.

Josie sobbed as her aunt came nearer to the bed. 'I thought you were Clover. I thought I was going to be punished for my wickedness.'

'Clover would never punish you, Josie love. She thought the world of you girls, and I daresay she's up there on a cloud now, as eager to see this babby safely born as we all are.'

'Are you?' Josie said, between sobs.

'Of course we are. Birthing's a miracle and a privilege, and it's not only you and Freda who's looking forward to it.'

Josie couldn't speak for a moment as another pain shot through her, but by now Mary was holding her hand tightly, and it didn't really matter who she was. Through the muddle of Josie's thoughts, she was Clover and Mary and a ministering angel all rolled into one.

Freda came upstairs and told them that Belle was on her way. Walter was bringing her in his van. The weather had turned dry and frosty, and it was too treacherous for a bicycle in the frosty night.

'I've been told to boil water and have plenty of towels ready,' Freda said. 'Belle said it's unlikely there's any urgency unless baby Elkins decides to come into the world in a hurry.'

Josie managed a weak smile. Baby Elkins. It suddenly had a name of sorts. And she was as eager to see it as anyone. If only she didn't have to go through this agony to do so! She gave another great yell as the pain began again, and felt Mary wiping her forehead with a damp cloth. Part of her didn't want her aunt there, nor her cousin. It would be so undignified and embarrassing when the time came to push the baby out. She wanted her mother . . . but she knew in her heart that although Ruth would have been calm and encouraging, she wouldn't have had the same kind of compassion and understanding that these two did. They had seen too many animal births in all kinds of weathers to be afraid of dealing with this one.

She yelled again, gripping Mary's hand until her aunt complained mildly that she'd have no fingers left if she didn't ease up a little.

'I don't reckon it's going to be too long now, though,' Mary remarked. 'The pains are coming thick and strong, aren't they?'

'Oh, you've noticed!' Josie said through gritted teeth.

She knew now that the pains she had been having all that

day weren't merely practice pains, but the real thing. A momentary tingling excitement swept through her, knowing that Freda was right, and soon now, she would be holding the baby in her arms. The feeling vanished as another pain took hold and took her breath away.

They heard the sound of an engine outside, followed by a quick rapping on the door. Freda flew downstairs to let Belle in, and told Walter to sit tight in the parlour unless he wanted to go home and come back later.

'I'll stay,' he said, his face unusually white as he heard Josie's hollering.

'It don't hurt any man to hear what's going on,' Belle said, puffing as she went upstairs. 'We know it's not his babby, but he'll be concerned for Josie all the same. So let's have a look at you, love.'

'Make it hurry up,' Josie said weakly.

'I think I can promise you that. From the looks of you I got here just in time. Did you boil the water, Freda?'

She pointed to a covered jug in the corner of the bedroom.

'Go and do it again, then dearie,' Belle said; 'we'll all be glad of a cup of tea once this is over, and a new mother is always parched after her labours.'

New mother: the words seemed to swirl around Josie's brain. She was about to be a mother . . . One last howl and she was told to push as hard as she could, and then she felt something slithering away from her and a rush of heat, and finally heard a thin squalling sound. She lay back, exhausted for a moment, before lifting her head weakly, to see Belle wrapping something in a towel and then laying it on Josie's chest.

'Say hello to your daughter, Josie,' she said softly.

Her arms closed around the baby. Only her face was visible from the mound of the towel, a perfectly-formed miniature of Josie, the dark hair clinging damply to her head, her eyes blinking open in the unfamiliar light.

'Oh, she's so beautiful,' Josie breathed.

'So she should be,' Belle said briskly. 'They say Monday's child is fair of face, and it's a bright and early Monday morning for the last day of February.'

'Oh Lordy, I hadn't realized the date,' Mary said suddenly.

'Why should you?' Josie said, still too awed at the sight of the baby's perfect features to take much notice of what was being said.

'Well, it was our Clover's birthday. You shouldn't have forgotten that, Josie, you being her granddaughter, especially since you said you were going to name the babby after her.'

'I *had* forgotten, but that makes it even more wonderful. It's a sign, isn't it, that Gran was watching over me and giving me her blessing?'

'Well, I daresay it is,' Belle said, too preoccupied with the final business of seeing to Josie and telling her to push down gently one more time. And then it was all over: what Belle called the tidying-up was done, and they could all relax.

'Now, how about that tea?' Belle said. 'I'm parched, if Josie isn't!'

Josie looked up. 'Oh, and what about poor Walter? He's been downstairs all this time, wondering what's going on. Would it be all right for him to see the baby – if he wants to, as a – as a sort of honorary uncle? Oh, and then you must telephone home, Freda, and let Mum and Dad and everyone know!'

She was quickly recovering her old bubbly self. The sparkle was back in her eyes and her joy at the baby's safe arrival was unmistakable.

Freda called Walter to come and see the baby, and he bounded up the stairs, two at a time. A short while later, they were all drinking tea, and something a little stronger, and Clover Elkins was sleeping peacefully in her brand new crib. Walter always found it hard to express his feelings in words, but anyone could see how he felt as he stammered his congratulations to Josie. She smiled into his eyes and told him that he was an honorary uncle now, and more than one person among them was guessing that one day, in the normal course of events, he might be even more.